Alvaraz

Angus Malcolm Ramsey

PublishAmerica
Baltimore

© 2010 by Angus Malcolm Ramsey.
All rights reserved. No part of this book may be reproduced, stored in a retrieval system or transmitted in any form or by any means without the prior written permission of the publishers, except by a reviewer who may quote brief passages in a review to be printed in a newspaper, magazine or journal.

First printing

This is a work of fiction. Names, characters, places, and incidents either are the product of the author's imagination or are used fictitiously. Any resemblance to actual persons, living or dead, events, or locales is entirely coincidental.

PublishAmerica has allowed this work to remain exactly as the author intended, verbatim, without editorial input.

ISBN: 978-1-4489-2076-1
PUBLISHED BY PUBLISHAMERICA, LLLP
www.publishamerica.com
Baltimore

Printed in the United States of America

Prologue—1570

The tectonic plates moved under the sea, dropping beneath the western edge of North America. They forced up the land, bending and stretching the ancient stone exposing the bright ores of gold and silver as a gift to whoever wanted to take it. The indigenous people found little value in the soft metals. They were too soft to use as weapons or tools, but to please their women they used them in their art and jewelry. The Spanish on the other hand were obsessed with these useless bright metals because it represented arbitrary wealth and power to whoever possessed it.

The Spanish arrived sailing their tiny ships around South America or marching from the Atlantic. They moved across the land, and with their superior arms mowing down the indigenous people, leaving a trail of mortal disease behind to finish their work.

It wasn't the intension of the Spanish to eliminate the indigenous people. They needed workers, who they could force to extract the precious metals from the stone. At the middle of the sixteenth century they found themselves in possession of uncontested massive wealth all buried in the land without workers to extract it. The indigenous people of Mexico, upon every encounter, disappeared dying of European disease or hiding far away in the mountains.

In order to bring in laborers, the governors of Western New Spain devised a plan. They recruited Master shipwright Alvaraz Consollese de La Fuenta through the Spanish Armada. He was to sail to the island of Puerto Rico, take a ship to Vera Crux, then travel across the land to the west coast where he would find a suitable location to build ships capable of carrying several hundred individuals to the west coast of New Spain.

Alvaraz was twenty-three years old, when he made his first voyage. He ended his apprenticeship at the age of eighteen, having worked with his father from the age of six. The family built large fishing xebecs rigged with lateen sails in the tradition of Mediterranean fishing and trading ships. Upon finishing his apprenticeship he moved to Cadiz on the west coast of Spain, where he worked with the Armada for four years building galleons. He was an unusual looking man, compared to the other workers. He wore a black wool cap in all but the warmest weather to mask the fact that he had wavy blond hair. You could find him shouting orders to the workers high on the scaffolds dressed in a light shirt and trousers always with his wool cap pulled down over his ears.

Captain Rodrego noticed him one day, as he surveyed the new galleon he was to sail to New Spain. Alvaraz, in exasperation, pulled his cap off as he shouted profanities at the workers trying to install the last carvel plank on the top of the hull with the grain of the wood curving in the opposite direction to the curve of the hull. Captain Rodrego stood transfixed as he gazed at this tall young man shaking his powerful fist at the workers, his stubborn jaw protruding in his anger. When his cap was removed his blond hair cascaded to his shoulders tempering his apparent anger and his workers smiled and joked as they turned the plank around.

"You must be the young ship builder I've heard about," Rodrego said while he thought how inappropriate it was to have such a strikingly handsome young man working in a shipyard,

Startled Alvaraz noticed Capitan Rodrego standing beside him. With a flushed look on his face he responded. "Yes Capitan, as you can see it's difficult to get good work out of these louts. Don't worry your ship will be ready on time. In three months we will have the deck completed, then your men can come in and do the final appointments. I expect it to be in the water ready for rigging by January. Sea trials and commissioning should be completed by June. I know you want to leave for New Spain in the summer, and I assure you, we will do our part."

Rodrego was impressed. He remembered talking with a commissioner about recruiting a ship builder for the west coast of New Spain. Watching and listening to this young man gave him an idea. Even if he weren't chosen, this young man would make an excellent ship's carpenter for his new Galleon.

"Do you expect to stay at this work your whole life?" asked Rodrego.

"This is what I do well," responded Alvaraz.

"Perhaps you would like to sail to the new lands and build ships there? I know the Colonial commission is looking for a ship builder to build ships on the west coast of New Spain. Would you be interested?"

"I have nothing holding me here," said Alvaraz as they climbed some scaffolding so they could get a better view of the construction. There were perhaps a hundred men toiling over different aspects of the ship. The smell of hot pitch and burning wood permeated the air.

As they gazed over the toiling men, Rodrego felt confident his ship would be ready to sail the following summer. He asked Alvaraz "Could I give your name to the Commission?"

"Yes, of course," said Alvaraz.

1595

Alvaraz remembered these words, as he sat in the shade looking over the wall of his veranda. The tall Palm trees, now some twenty-four years since they were planted, were heavy with green nuts. The air was always hot and damp, there were always midges around and he yearned for the day he could feel the cool air of a Spanish winter on his face. At last he was able to arrange a passage home with his wife Imelda. His six grown children would stay in Navidad. If all went well with Imelda's father in Spain he would send for his three daughters who were keen to see the old land. He was contented as he listened to the children playing on the street behind his house. Imelda had told him the one hundred and seventy individuals he brought over from the Islands of King Philip in 1570 were now almost five hundred. He used to know them all but could no longer keep up with the new families and the grand children of his people. He had all the workers he could use in the ship building business and his people were moving out into the land establishing ranches and fishing villages all along the coast. The land was being repopulated with people from the East. Each year galleons departed Manila with passengers for the new land. One ship carried almost a thousand new immigrants the previous year. He'd managed to build eight galleons and dozens of coastal trading ships since he had returned some twenty-five years earlier. In 1593 a law had been enacted to slow the trade between Manila and Acapulco. He had no new orders to build Galleons. He felt old and tired now as he reflected on his life.

Chapter 1

He had taken Capitan Rodrego up on his offer. The Colonial Commission agreed to return him home in five years after he got the shipyard up and running. His father expected him to return to marry, Maria, the daughter of a wealthy merchant. His perspective bride was thirteen when he left and would be eighteen; old enough to marry, upon his return. He liked the idea and sailed off that summer with Capitan Rodrego.

Alvaraz had never been to sea before. His easy acceptance of the job and the prospect of coming home were erased on the first day of their voyage. With little wind the galleon rolled and pitched in the Atlantic swell. He became very ill and with his seasickness came an anxiety he had never experienced before. The prospect of feeling so close to death for the entire voyage of up to two months destroyed any enthusiasm he had for the endeavor.

As Alvaraz clung to the rail of the ship wondering when his next episode of heaving would occur, Ismel, the first mate came up beside him, put his arm around him, and said, "Alvaraz, sailors talk of many Gods in the sea. They all agree when you first go to sea you must pay. I'm glad I'm on this journey with you because you're paying for a safe journey with your sickness for all of us."

"If I knew the suffering of sailors, I would never build these ships," responded Alvaraz.

"One more day and you will be overcome with hunger and thirst and a new part of your life will begin," Ismel commented with a smile on his face.

As the days passed the wind came up steadying the ship and as Ismel had predicted, Alvaraz became hungry and his enthusiasm returned. He also noticed some design flaws in the ship. It was far too top heavy causing it to roll. The hull could be wider giving it more stability, more carrying capacity and more comfort. With these thoughts Alvaraz sailed to the new land.

The journey to America was uneventful. They arrived in Puerto Rico in early June ahead of schedule. Rodrego was to sail the ship around South America through the newly discovered Straits of Magellan then ride the wind and currents down the west coast of South America and on to Acapulco. This would take up to six months. Alvaraz would find a ship to Vera Crux and then take the overland route to Acapulco to search for a suitable place to set up a shipyard.

Alvaraz stayed in the Governor of Puerto Rico's compound and waited for a ship to the mainland. He noticed the black slaves working the fields and building a larger fortress. He was told his biggest problem would be labor. He had two apprentices with him but would need a sizable work force to build galleons. The black slaves were strong, but he had his doubts about their ability to build ships, besides they were very expensive.

Time went by slowly, as he waited for the ship to take him and his apprentices to Vera Cruz. He explored the island learning the brief history. The indigenous people were largely gone due to disease and mistreatment from the newcomers leaving the land largely disserted. The English had attacked, taken over the island, and then due to a plague, left it again to the Spanish. It was a beautiful land filled with colorful birds, abundant fish and game, but Alvaraz missed his friends and family back in Spain and pined for the time to go by so he could return.

A ship arrived in late August heading for Vera Crux with a very nervous Captain. He wanted to get to Vera Crux before the storm season arrived and he was already late. Alvaraz and his two apprentices barely had time to load there basic equipment and step aboard when the Capitan ordered the anchor weighed so the ship could float with the tide through the harbor mouth to catch the afternoon breeze. In less than a week they approached Vera Crux followed by big winds, huge seas and the beginning of rain. After the Captain had set two anchors and secured his ship as well as he could he allowed a boat to be put over the side to take Alvaraz and the other passengers ashore. The long boat carrying them continually took waves over the side and was near sinking when it finally arrived at the primitive dock. Eight soaked, bedraggled passengers including Alvaraz and his apprentices were put ashore. They leaned into the wind as they walked up the muddy street where they encountered a group of people fleeing to the hills. They were told the storm would carry off all the buildings. If they were lucky they would escape with their lives by fleeing to a high valley the indigenous people used to hide from the terrible storms.

Alvaraz took one last look at the ship in the harbor, barely visible through the rain, straining against its anchors. In the torment surrounding them they hurried to catch up with the towns people. They spent the night in a clearing above the town, wet and hungry but thanked God they weren't at sea as the wind shrieked and the rain fell in torrents around them.

Juan, one of the apprentices to Alvaraz, wanted to return to the harbor to see if he could help the crew of the ship that had dropped them off. "I know we can help them Alvaraz, please let me go." Juan was a strong lad of twenty. He wasn't big but had a very large head of hair.

"Juan, you mustn't go. You would be carried off with your hair acting like a kite. If you did make it to the harbor you would only be in their way. They know what to do to save themselves and their ship. The wind is already dying. In the morning we will go down and help them."

Jose, the other apprentice, agreed with Alvaraz as they huddled beside the other refugees.

They awoke to the sound of a few birds singing as if they were thanking God for their survival. The sun was filtering through the low bush atop the nearby hill. There was a smell of ocean beach mixed with the scent of the sap of broken trees in the air. Already Jose was up digging through his tool chest looking for something to eat. "Have you any food?" asked Juan.

"I thought I left some bread in here, but I guess not. Shall we return to the town to see what we can find?"

"We must take our equipment with us. It will surely be stolen if we leave it here," said Alvaraz.

The pathway back to the town was clogged with wreckage from the storm.

As predicted the town had largely disappeared and when they looked out into the harbor they couldn't find a ship. The sea was the color of turquoise milk surrounded by white beaches swept clean by the hurricane force winds. Juan pointed out some spars sticking out of the water on the opposite beach, "Could that be the remains of our ship?" he asked. They all hung their heads in silent prayer for the Captain and crew they had grown to know on their way from Puerto Rico.

They did their best to help the returning townspeople find their possessions and prepare some temporary shelter. They rebuilt a fire pit, made a fire and boiled water. They found piles of shellfish newly excavated by the waves and piled up in heaps high up on the beach. They boiled the shells and feasted on their succulent contents. Later that day they found a half dozen survivors of the shipwreck trudging up the beach.

Juan recognized the men dragging themselves up the muddy track as some of the crew of the ship. He shouted, "Tell us what happened. Where are Capitan Ortago and the others?"

It was Diago, a slim dark and wiry sailor, leading the others, who responded. "We dragged our anchors. We were fine until then. I thought we would make it; a violent gust hit the ship and started to drag the anchors. There was no stopping us and very quickly we were exposed to the full force of the wind and waves. The seas were higher than the masts. The whole world was a mass of white foam. We couldn't breath. Just as a mountain of water was to crash I heard the Capitan shout, 'Every man for himself, save yourselves.' The ship lifted in that mighty wave higher and higher. Then suddenly there was nothing under us and the ship hit the sand bottom and exploded into matchsticks. The water was filled with debris, thank God we all found pieces of floating wood to cling to. I found myself barely able to breath, high up on that beach over there."

He pointed to a white beach miles across the creamy blue water. It was impossible to comprehend the violence of the storm on this quiet morning with the blue sky and gentle breeze.

Diago started to shake, his emotions causing him to move his arms around in frustration as he recounted his experience. "The six of us found a bit of shelter on the other side of the beach. This morning we searched for—but found no other survivors—not a trace of anyone—we only found a few pieces of wreckage." Diago slumped on a palm log half buried in the sand and openly cried. He lifted his head and blubbered, I don't know what happened to Captain Ortago or the others. Will God forgive me"? he pleaded.

Chapter 2

After some discussion they all decided to make the trek to the west coast. This was wonderful news for Alvaraz because, if he could convince them to stay, these Spanish men would make excellent supervisors for his shipbuilding.

Alvaraz stood on the boxes of equipment and addressed the men he had gathered. "If you men agree, we can organize a party to trek the 800 miles to Acapulco then from there we can begin our search for a suitable harbor to build ships."

The men looked at each other, then at Alvaraz. Diago lifted his hand and shouted, "We will build the ships."

The other men followed enthusiastically. Then they all began discussing how to get to Acapulco. Diago had been part way to Mixico so they asked him to lead. They would need horses and a cart if possible.

"There is a ranch, run by a Spanish family, two days walk from here," said Diago. "If we get there, I'm sure there will be food and horses, then we will be on our way."

Without hesitation they all agreed to follow Diago to the farm of the Spanish family. The landscape was devastated for a long distance inland causing the men to constantly climb over fallen trees and debris. They found little food and the streams were muddy and absent of edible fish. It was good they had the extra six men to help carry the two large trunks of equipment through the devastation.

On the third day, all of them near starvation, Diago pointed out a cleared field on the horizon and announced, "We will be there in only a few hours."

"How do you know these people?" asked Alvaraz.

"Twice we delivered farming equipment and some slaves to them. The name of the rancher is Philip. That is the only name I know. He likes to live with his wife and children in solitude. The indigenous people are mostly gone and the land goes on forever."

They arrived starving and thirsty. At first Philip was suspicious, but after Diago reminded him of the delivery of livestock and farming implements he warmed up and welcomed them to his ranch. They ate and drank then slept the rest of the day away. Diago had to be dragged away to his cot after drinking too much Madera wine.

Philip's ranch consisted of a Spanish designed central court with four nice houses built into the walls. There were five families living there with quarters for the slaves and a large building housing the families' horses. The family had grown wealthy ranching cattle on the high country then driving them into Mixico for sale.

"The Spanish only seem to want the gold and silver they mine, but they must eat. I do very well," said Philip.

"You must know the best way to Acapulco."

"I don't know the best way to Acapulco, but I do know the easiest way to Mixico. Mixico is on the way to Acapulco. Beyond there you can find people who know the way," responded Philip to Alvaraz's questions. "When will you leave?"

"We need horses, and a cart if there is one. If we broke up the cases of tools, I'm sure they could be comfortably carried on the backs of horses. What do you think?"

Philip leaned back in his chair and pensively responded, "It would be better if you didn't need the cart. It's rough country and you would go much faster if you were on horse back. I have a light cart if you want it, but we also have some fine horses. They are expensive, twenty gold Spanish doubloons each, but I hear they are twice that in Mixico. You could ride them to Mixico, sell them and come away with a profit."

Alvaraz thought nine horses would cost him one hundred and eighty doubloons, leaving him with only seventy to make the rest of the journey. Or he could buy five and a cart for a little over a hundred. He decided to risk it and buy a dozen and sell some in Mixico. "Can you give me a deal for a dozen?"

"What did you have in mind?" asked Philip.

"I want young strong horses and provisioning to Mixico. I'll give you one hundred and ninety doubloons."

There was a long pause. "We have forty young horses ready for market. Only ten are broken. I'll give you ten for two hundred if you will accompany two of my drovers and Chappe, their supervisor, with the horses and some cattle for sale in Mixico city. I assume your men can fire a gun and protect the herd from bandits."

"That doesn't sound like too good of a bargain for us," responded Alvaraz.

"True, but, if you're successful I want you to have five percent of the profits from the sale."

"How much would that be?"

"Depending on how many cattle we send, at least two hundred doubloons. There would also be a cart to carry your equipment and the provisioning for the journey."

"How long would this take?"

"Not longer than a month."

Having dealt with suppliers at boat yards Alvaraz had a lot of practice bargaining and so he made what he thought was a clever offer. "I'll do it for ten percent of the profits."

"Ten percent is high, but, I like you and know you will do a good job for us. Remember it's only the profits. A horse costs me twenty doubloons, so if you sell it for forty your part of the profit will be two, not four. Do you understand? It will take some time to sell the livestock so count on at least two weeks in Mixico."

Alvaraz met with his crew, explaining the complications of the deal and explained if all went well they would all own their own horse when they left Mixico city for Acapulco. If things didn't go well the horses would be owned by the Colonial Commission of Western New Spain. "Do you all agree to doing this job?"

There was some talk then Diago who seemed very ill asked, "We are sailors. What do we want with horses?"

When you get to Acapulco you can sell your horse for several hundred doubloons and be a wealthy man. You could buy a small ship and be the Captain. This is a great opportunity for you. It's important you realize these horses are not yours unless you work hard protecting and keeping together the livestock. Philip has given us an opportunity to make some money and we are doing him a service by delivering these animals safe to Mixico. If anyone of you fails to do your duty: we as a group will determine if you should get your reward. Do you all understand and are you willing to protect the livestock?"

Everyone except Diago smiled and gave their consent.

It took the better part of a week for the party to organize the herd. Everyday the numbers of animals to be herded grew. It seemed Philip was using this opportunity well. It would be a long time before he had nine extra men to move his cattle to market. He didn't realize how inept these sailors were at herding. Most of them were barely competent at riding a horse.

At the end of the week all was ready. The gate to the corral was opened before the sun made its appearance over the cloud-shrouded mountains in the distance. All the men were mounted except Diago who was up late partying and drinking too much wine the night before.

Alvaraz had already given up on Diago; he had known men who drank too much and decided to leave Diago behind.

"We must wait for Diago," pleaded Juan.

"There's nothing much you can do with men like that, just leave him and when he wakes he can decide if he wants to catch up to us. I will talk to him about loosing his share of the profits. Maybe he will control his drinking in the future, but now as far as I'm concerned he has already lost his share." Alvaraz said with a hard look on his face as he pulled the reins on his horse stopping its contented grazing.

Philip and two other of his men came along on the first day to instruct the men on how to contain the herd. It was a glorious day and except for the pain of sitting in the saddle all day Alvaraz found the work very satisfying. It wasn't long before his men found their stride and that night after herding the cattle into a canyon and setting up camp they discussed their progress.

"At this rate we will be in Mixico in two weeks," announced Pepe, Philip's head drover. Tomorrow we will follow the same pattern, four working each side of the herd, Alvaraz with Chappy leading and Fredrigo and I keeping the rear.

The next morning Philip, after giving final instructions to Pepe, departed with his two men back to his ranch.

"If you see Diago send him back to Vera Crux where he can find a ship. On board he doesn't have access to unlimited wine like he has at your ranch, Philip," said Alvaraz

"Don't worry about Diago, I can tame him like a horse, when you return you will see, he will be a good supervisor for me. Hasta la vista y vaya con Dios."

About a mile back Philip came upon Diago, who was, on foot, hurrying along the path in a desperate attempt to catch the group.

"My friend, you are late," Philip joked as he saw the state Diago was in. Always looking for Spanish men to supervise his ranch, he asked, "Why don't you come back with us?"

"How far ahead are the others?" asked Diago.

"Maybe eight miles. If you walk all day you should catch them, they aren't going too fast."

Philip seeing the desperation on Diago's face took pity on him. "I can give you some water and food. I don't know if you will be welcomed. You can come back with us and I can give you a job."

"I've let these people down and I don't intend to do it again," stated Diago with a determined sound to his voice.

"As you will."

That evening Diago caught up and begged the other men for forgiveness. "I am a fine artist and can record, in drawings, our journey," offered Diago.

"Of course you can return. However, if I catch you with a drop of wine on your lips you can go your own way without any profits. Is this understood?"

Diago agreed and made a solemn promise to all to abstain from drink.

The days went quickly and after a week the weariness and pain of riding slowly wore off. The young men became more competent especially his apprentice, Jose. Alvaraz wondered if he would desert his career as a boat builder for the glory of being a cowboy.

In the middle of the third week just as the sun was setting they came to the top of a plateau and looked down upon a large valley filled with tall green trees and abundant vegetation. The air was surprisingly cool. Alvaraz wondered if they weren't looking into the Garden of Eden, and he imagined, Adam with a snake tempting him with an apple, while Eve looked on. A city of strange looking building rose up in the middle of a lake. On the near edge of the lake one could make out a few buildings built in the style of Spanish architecture. To the north in the haze strange symmetrical hills could be seen in the far off valley.

Pepe pointed out the city, "We will drive the horses and cattle down this valley in the morning, then across that terraced hill, to the city beyond. We must stay here the night. There are some indigenous people who have developed a taste for beef. They are very good at stealing cattle from right under your nose. Tonight we all must stay awake and surround the herd and in the morning we will move them to the yard of Senor Markis in the Spanish town, then wait for the market."

Everything went as planned. The cattle and horses were delivered to the yard of Senor Markis without the loss of a single animal.

"This is a miracle," said Pepe. We always loose one or two and sometimes a dozen animals before we get here. You have earned your commission. Now, let's hope we get a good price. Then you can be on your way with more gold than you brought.

The word went out to the neighboring cities and towns proclaiming the arrival of hundreds of fat cattle and dozens of young horses. The market on the following Wednesday was filled with wealthy Spanish colonists, their pockets stuffed with un-minted gold and silver bulging in their purses. The sale went well with Alvaraz increasing his purse by a hundred equivalents of doubloons. He owned his own horse and he was able to give each of his men their horse and ten equivalents of doubloons. It was a happy time for all. The men partied, drinking to excess, except for Diago who remained stoically sober.

"You have passed the test, Diago, you may pass wine over your lips. I won't think less of you," said Alvaraz.

"The devil lives in the wine. My mother told me this when I was young after my father died of drink. My mother couldn't support me so I went to sea. I now know what she meant. If I drink I will die young leaving my children without support. God loves you, but he tests me. Help me, Alvaraz, keep the devil from me, please!" Diago begged with a tear in his eye.

Alvaras, seeing his need, embraced Diago holding him strongly and said, "You are a good man Diago and I will do all I can for you."

Chapter 3

The church was only half finished, but Father Fernando was having services among the scaffolds. He met the men at the cattle auction and immediately tried to recruit them to help build the church. For the remainder of the week Alvaraz and his men had found equipment to make their passage to Acapulco more comfortable and now on Sunday he and his men attended Father Fernando's half finished church for mass. A sizable donation was made to placate the Father's request for help and now, as the men knelt, Father Fernando included a special prayer for the party's safe journey to Acapulco.

With full packs, spirits cleansed and healthy bodies they rode off towards the west. They were told a new road had been built near a town called Colima. They were to travel north, following cart tracks and horse paths through the mountains. There were a few tribes of indigenous people that may bother them, but with nine men moving fast on horseback, it was unlikely they would even be seen let alone be bothered by them. Alvaraz also felt confident they would find other groups of travelers moving across the country.

On the second day they found themselves completely lost, wandering slowly north through thick bush finding many false paths up canyons where mountain goats seemed to laugh at them. That night they camped near a stream. With a large fire of coals, they sat watching the kid goat Juan had shot slowly cook on the improvised spit they had over the fire.

"We should travel more west. In the morning I will climb to the top of this mountain and find the easiest route" said Jose.

Falso, a young apprentice navigator from the ship, interrupted with, "I know which way north is, but I think we need the help of God. Perhaps we should pray."

They mumbled their consent to Falso as they sat feeling the heat from the fire radiating warmly on their faces. Falso led, with a prayer mariners used when at sea, asking God to help guide their ship.

When he finished his prayer Falso rose, his hand making the sign of the cross over his chest and looked beyond the light of the fire. His inhalation of breath startled the other men. There before him was a man standing staring at them. He was alone, dressed in skins with a crude wool cape and a hat made of some type of reed.

Falso stood still while the other men madly dashed for their guns. In the end he stood alone, transfixed, looking at the stranger across the fire. The man stoically stood without the slightest hint of emotion on his face. On closer inspection Falso knew he was harmless. He saw a man, the size of a young boy, whose face was heavily pockmarked. Alvaraz stood by Falso and instructed his men to scout around the camp for more strangers.

Falso raised his arms open handed in friendship and the small man responded in kind. Alvaraz and Falso indicated the small man should sit on a log the men had vacated. The man turned and walked away only to return a few minutes later with a large pack with a strap that went over his forhead. He took his pack off; putting it down in front of the log that he was instructed to sit on. He opened his pack took out a piece of pottery and placed it on the fire. He then made dough with water and yellow flour he brought from his bag and preceded to make thin pancakes on the now hot ceramic. The kid goat was ready to eat so the men sliced off some meat offering it to the little man. With a huge smile he lifted one of his pancakes accepting the meat, sprinkling some garnish on the meat then rolled it in the tortilla and handed it to Alvaraz. Alvaraz didn't know what to do with it so the little man held up another tortilla and the men put meat on it. The little man rolled it as before and proceeded to eat it from the end. Alvaraz tried it and exclaimed it was very good. Before long all the men were waiting for the next tortilla so they could enjoy the meat wrapped taco.

They stayed up late that night trying to communicate with the small man. Falso and Diago drew pictures of the sun indicating with the shadow where they wanted to go. The little man pointed to himself and indicated he was traveling a bit west of north and would guide them.

As they were preparing to sleep Falso said to Alvaraz, "It's as if God sent this tiny man to guide us. We are truly blessed."

None of the Spanish men stirred until the sun's light filtered through the trees. Alvaraz looked up in the morning light to see the small man, his face set, stroking the neck of a horse. The horses seemed to completely accept him and made no protests as he moved amongst them. Alvaraz realized they didn't have a name for him and decided they should call him "Gregorio" because he was so accommodating to everything he encountered. It was as if he weren't there only he made everyone's life better.

It wasn't long before a breakfast of bread and left over kid goat was behind them and they were all mounted except for Gregorio. Alvaraz tried to get him to put his pack on one of the horses that was carrying the boxes of tools, but Gregorio would have none of it as he hoisted his pack and adjusted the strap across his forhead.

He led them at a good clip down a path towards the valley bottom. Falso was a bit concerned but when he asked Alvaraz if they should turn back Alvaraz insisted they follow him down a rocky path beside the stream they had camped beside. They came to the bottom of the valley where they found a well established path paved in part with cobbles. They made good progress stopping at pleasant streams and grassy glens. At the end of the day Gregorio instructed Alvaraz to stop and went ahead on foot. He came back a few minutes later leading an old man. He was even smaller than Gregorio, dressed the same and having deep pock marks on his wise face. He looked at Alvaraz, his men and the horses then slowly spoke a sentence in Spanish. The men became quiet, even the horses seemed to restrain their whinnying.

"I am Toochima of Tlaxcala"

Alvaraz dismounted his horse and responded, "I am Alvaraz of Spain. Mucho Gusto."

"Mucho Gusto"

"Are you the father of this man we call Gregorio?"

Toochima looked at Gregorio, and with a broad smile said, "I don't know this man. He comes from far away in the west. He says his name is Vangatoon, but I like your name for him. Gregorio is a good name for him. He tells me you were lost in the mountains and he is leading you to Tzacapu where you can find a road to the sea. He saw your smoke and wondered who you were. He has never seen animals such as yours, and has only seen devils from a long way away. He says you have been very kind to him. When Vangatoon came, telling the story of seeing you, the young men of my village wanted to fight you and the old people wanted to hide. The chief ordered everyone but me to hide in the mountains."

"You speak so well, Toochima. Where did you learn Spanish?"

"My people were wiped out by the sickness. I was taken as a young boy to the mission at Acatlan. Do you know this place?"

"No, I have only been in New Spain for a little over a month. I know very little of this country. Is this a good place to make camp?" asked Alvaraz, "My men are tired."

"No, there is a better place further along where there is water."

They were led to an abandoned camp beside a cool spring. There was evidence of an old village with falling down stonewalls and buildings. They made themselves comfortable camping in the empty center of the old village. Beside the fire, Toochima explained about the food and drink of his people. He promised to show the Spanish the field of corn his people grew explaining about the different varieties and how the corn was ground and made into tortillas. He brought out peppers and tomatos to share in the evening meal. With full stomachs the men listened well into the night about the story of Toochima's people.

"My people lived in a valley near Acatlan for countless generations. We had a history man who remembered all our ancestors. He told of three and ten generations before the Aztecs came. Like most families our family were farmers. My grandfather's brother joined the Spanish man, Cortez, in his fight against Montezuma, the ruler of the Aztecs of Mixico. It was soon after the plague came and my family received word that my grandfather's brother had died of the plague. We escaped by living in the mountains. It was a hard life in the mountains and after a generation we heard the disease had gone and life was good without the Aztecs. So when I was a boy we returned to our lands. Within a year the plague hit again and all my people died. I barely survived and was taken to the mission, to be looked after by the monks of Acatlan. I ran away when I was twenty and now I live with these people who have never known the plague. I try to keep them safe by never allowing them to see the devil Spanish. I don't think you are the devil, but still you must stay away from my children and my family for I fear for them greatly."

With sadness Alvaraz responded with, "I am so sorry to hear of the death of your people, Toochima, and I respect your wishes. We will simply pass through your land and be gone in the morning. Thank you for your kindness and I will pray to God for you and your people's safety."

Unfortunately Gregario doesn't speak Spanish. He speaks Nahuatl and many dialects, but no Spanish. His people were also annihilated with the plague and he was one of the few survivors. The difference is, he wasn't taken in by a Spanish mission. Toochima translated what he said to Gregario who moved his head in understanding. Juan and Falso were also with the group. All day he and Falso had been riding beside Gregario using hand signals to communicate. Already they knew some words. Toochima stared at Falso when he heard him using some Nahuatl words to help translate what was said.

"I think your young friend speaks Nahuatl," interjected Toochima, "I don't think you will need my services as a translator for long."

Falso blushed and explained how he and Gregorio had talked of their families. He knew Gregorio had three wives and was going to see one of them in Tzacapu.

"This is what he told me too," explained Toochima in Spanish, "Gregario's third wife was taken to Tzacapu by her father. He is retuning to claim her back. You must help him when you get there."

We all have a duty to have as many children as we can. I have six wives, but only two of them have children. I have one new child and eight grown children."

Alvaraz who was listening asked, "How can we help Gregorio when we get to Tzacapu?"

"Gregorio didn't pay a dowry for his third wife. She ran away from the family to be with Gregorio, and then her father came and took her away. He has collected some pieces of iron and copper as payment. What he needs from you is protection. Sitting on your horses looking like Gods should be enough. Believe me if you go to the village the people there will be impressed."

Before the sun was fully up Toochima took the men on a tour of the nearby village. They found several large fields of corn, a field of tomatoes and several fields filled with beans and peppers of many different varieties. It was at this time Alvaraz realized this world was very different from Spain. He'd never seen corn plants, tomato plants, or pepper plants before. Toochima showed him a bush covered with long bean shaped pods. He picked one and opened it and ate the pulpy outer covering,

"These are called mou-chillies." He gave some to Alvaraz and his men who were pleased with the sweet pulpy flavor.

Alvaraz looked around and saw a Garden of Eden. He had never seen anything like this before. The birds made different sounds. They were colorful and didn't seem afraid of the gathered men. He looked at the strange trees and wondered about the quality of the wood. He would need forests of trees to build ships, but he knew nothing of these trees. He asked Toochima if he could cut the branch off a promising looking tree to take with him. He would dry it and test its hardness and resistance to rot. He asked Toochima about the trees that didn't rot, the ones that died and laid on the ground for decades with out rotting.

"I will show you some trees that fell before I came here and are still whole."

They walked into the forest away from the field. There on the ground was a massive log, its bark long gone.

"This tree fell at least three decades ago before I came," said Toochima.

Alvaraz sent his men to get some tools while he examined the log. With his knife he cut into the wood and found its white surface color was sun bleached, underneath the wood was the color of a rose. It was hard and firm. He would have his men cut a plank to see how flexible or brittle it was.

Toochima pointed out living trees of the same species. They were few and separated by long spans in the forest. Alvaraz and his apprentices examined the living trees memorizing the shape of the leaves and characteristics of the bark.

"This wood would make fine planking, but I fear it is too brittle to be used as keels or framing. When they got back to the tree they were pleased to see the men had cut a long notch in the wood to start the saw and now had a good length of plank sawn.

"You can stop there. Square the end and we will take this wood with us to test," said Alvaraz.

The day was half over when Alvaraz embraced his new friend and said good-by. Toochima, with his emotionless face, stood on the roadway and waved as the men trotted of led by Gregorio.

"You never know what they are thinking. They show no emotion of happiness or sadness on their face," complained Ernesto, the ship's carpenter, as he rode along beside Alvaraz.

Although the land was often mountainous, the paths Gregorio chose always seemed to be easy. Often the paths were paved. Falso, if he understood the words of Gregorio, explained the old paved roads were used in the past to transport royalty. Normal people weren't allowed on them. But since the demise of the Aztec Empire almos two generations earlier, anyone could use these special roads.

For the last few days Gregorio had consented to ride on Falso's horse, in front of Falso's saddle, holding on to the horse's mane.

"Gregorio tells me we will be in Tzacapu tomorrow," said Falso as he rode by Alvaraz.

After they stopped and rested Gregorio would often jog contentedly in front of the horses then he would ask Falso for a ride. His pack was securely tied with a box of tools on one of the two horses that had no riders. So he had little problem keeping up with the normal speed of the group.

"You can't tell what Gregorio is thinking by his face, you must look for the spark in his eyes. I think these people communicate their feelings by looking in each other's eyes," Falso said as he rode along beside Alvaraz.

"That's ridiculous, Falso, their eyes are black. I think I could see the fear on his face when we first met," contradicted Alvaraz.

"Gregorio says there are serpents here that can kill with a single bite. He has some medicine for it. He also told me of a huge cat the color of the morning sky, that could easily take down one of our horses."

"Are you saying there are lions here?"

"We saw a small cat run behind a rock. Gregorio says there are giant cats that eat people and large animals."

This sent a chill down Alvaraz's spine. He turned and stared at Falso. "Should we be prepared? Why isn't Gregorio frightened?"

"He is frightened. He says his God will protect him. Did you see his necklace. He has some teeth from this animal. He says with these in his necklace the cats won't bother him."

"Those things he wears around his neck are the teeth from this animal? They are the length of a finger. This animal must truly be huge. We must keep our guns ready."

The landscape changed as they approached Tzacapu. They left dry lands and rode beside a beautiful river, through vine-shrouded forests filled with the sound of squawking parrots. Again Alvaraz took a plank off a fallen tree. The wood from this tree was blond with a fair amount of pitch. Alvaraz decide it was very similar to the pine trees of his homeland.

Juan, asked, "Don't you think this wood would make good decks?"

While closely examining the wood Alvaraz responded, "This wood is very similar to the wood we would use at home as the planks on clinker boats. It could also be used as light frames on smaller vessels. We need a tree like an oak. I've seen nothing suitable so far."

They rode in silence, listening to the loud clamor of the jungle. Gregorio insisted Falso stop his horse and let him run ahead. It was getting late in the day and Alvaraz was thinking about making camp, but when he saw Gregorio sprint ahead he decided to follow for a while. The track led them up a narrow canyon of hard earth. When they came to the top they were astounded to see a green valley before them with an organized village surrounded with fields of crops. They were surprised to see a church steeple rising up above the trees on the far side of the village.

"Alvaraz crossed himself. His men followed his example and he said, "Could it be, that is a church?"

The air was still in the evening heat and a lazy cloud of smoke rose up beside the church. The village was deserted and silent. The men could feel the ghosts of past inhabitants swirling through the thick air.

"Gregorio stopped the men and ran ahead. He came back a few minutes later, beckoning them to follow. As they approached the church they saw the priest with a broad smile on his face with his two young indigenous helpers staring impassively at them.

"Welcome to Tzacapu," said the priest as he rung his hands in a kind of anticipation. He was dressed in white vestments, as if he were ready to start mass.

"The people of the village have all gone into hiding. In the past when a group of Spanish came they did much harm to the people and took the young men as slaves. I am Father Adao Francisco de Fuca. I am Portuguese."

Alvaraz recognized Adao's thick Portuguese tinted Spanish immediately. "I am Alvaraz Consollese de La Fuenta from Spain. We mean you no harm. We are passing through on our way to the west coast."

"You are going a long way out of your way if you are trying to get to the sea."

Alvaraz smiled and confessed, "We don't know where we are. We are trusting this little man you see before you. We call him Gregorio and met him along the way. He has been a great help to us and we understand he is here to claim his bride. We have no interest in slaves, only good directions to get to Acapulco."

"He is here to claim his bride you say. I wonder if he is the heathen whom we have heard stole the daughter of Teicoplan. I think I know her, she pines everyday for him and her father only has trouble with her." The priest walked around the horses taking a good look at the men and said, "What will you do when you get to Acapulco?"

"I am a ship builder. We are looking for a suitable place to build ships that can sail to India from the west coast of New Spain."

"I think I can trust you. I will send one of these boys to let the people know you mean no harm. In the mean time you are welcome to set up camp in the village square and use the well."

As they set up camp they noticed people peering around the corners, looking at the strangers. Gregorio immediately went to the people. They formed a group in front of the church. There was much loud talking, then they all burst out laughing as Gregorio put his hands in the air and performed some type of pantomime. Soon the whole square was filled with laughing people. Only the children seemed interested in the Spanish men.

"I think our little friend is an entertainer," said Diago as he watched the people copying Gregorio's pantomime. "You don't suppose he is telling the story of how he found us, do you?"

"Yes, I do think that is exactly what he's doing," said Alvaraz as he noticed the people around Gregorio smiling and taking sideways glances at him and his men.

By the time the camp was set up, a dozen women came to the square with plates of food and drink for the men. Father Adao ate with the men, then stayed late into the night telling his story. He had joined the Priesthood when he was a young man and like Alvaraz found himself on a ship to the new lands. A compliment of Portuguese sailors and builders had come by sea, landing on the east coast and trekking towards the west. He and six monks arrived in the valley some twenty years earlier. The people were friendly and the land fertile so they stayed, converting the people and building the church. The church was built from the stones of a heathen temple the men had passed earlier that day. The spire was made of wood and one day Father Adao hoped to get a bell to hang in the belfry at the top of the spire. It was a simple church, rectangular, with a gothic entrance. The six monks had departed six years earlier with the prospect of returning to their order and asking for the Pope's blessing so they could become priests.

"When I hear of strangers coming to Tzacapu I pray they are the returning monks who have now become priests. There are many villages like Tzacapu just waiting for a priest to save their souls. You probably haven't seen any people and think the land is empty, but you can find them hiding in the mountain valleys. They are all deathly afraid of Europeans. So many of the people died from the plague or found themselves enslaved. The Spanish found out it was useless to enslave these people. They refused to work and most of them die of western disease. If you allow them to live as they always have, they prosper in their own way."

Changing the subject Alvaraz asked, "Where did you get the wood to build the rafters and door frames for your church, Father Adao?"

"Of course, you are looking for wood to build your ships. We found the trees on a hill to the south of here along the river. I can take you there tomorrow. The making of the rafters took a long time. The monks shared the task of cutting them with axes and shaping them with our one adze. We have no saws."

"I see that, your monks did a fine job. Does the thatch leak when you have heavy rains?" asked Falso who was listening to the conversation.

"No, the thatch doesn't leak. The people did the roof and just last year they replaced it after ten years. It's the same thatch used in their homes." One thing I have noted lately; the people are traveling more and communicating with their neighbors. For years no strangers ever came to the Valley and now we have strangers quite often. Your little friend has come a long way to find his bride. Her father's family comes from here and he returned six months ago with his daughter. He doesn't mind if Gregorio takes her, but he wants a dowry."

"Gregorio has a dowry," interjected Falso.

"This is what I've heard. The problem is her father doesn't think it's enough," answered Father Adao.

"Do you know where Gregorio is?" asked Falso.

"Yes, he's visiting his cousin who lives on the opposite side of the village."

Alvaraz asked, "What do you think would be a suitable dowry for this girl, Father?"

"She has been in such a foul humor for the entire time she has been here. You would think her father would want to give her away." The men laughed and Father Adao continued. "The people here like iron to make spear points and tools with, and they like live stock; goats and wool dogs."

"It's possible we can help Gregorio by making up the difference with some iron we can spare."

The word got to Gregorio early in the morning and he arrived at the camp just after sun up. With Father Adao translating he displayed the iron he had collected. They were small bits of old nails and a piece of hinge, barely suitable for anything.

Alvaraz found a small carving knife and placed it in Gregorio's collection. "Do you think this will help?"

Gregorio broke into a smile, picked up the knife testing it for sharpness, said something, and then laughed. Father Adao translated, "he says he will get a lot of status plus his bride if he offers this. He also said, maybe he should just keep the knife and forget about his bride."

"We owe him for his service as a guide. This will be his payment," said Alvaraz.

Just as Alvaraz and his apprentices were about to leave for the forest to examine the wood, Gregorio appeared with his bride. She had a young pretty face without the disfiguring pockmarks. Without emotion she came up to Alvaraz, put her hand on his shoulder touching her small body to his. She looked up into his face and gently stroked his arm. Alvaraz stepped back embarrassed.

Father Adao smiled and said, "Gregorio is offering her to you in thanks. He doesn't expect you to keep her. I've seen this many times before."

"When are you going to teach these people about Christian law, Father?" asked Alvaraz as he looking at Gregorio. "Tell Gregorio it's not our custom and if I did take his bride before him, I would go to Hell or at least live in purgatory for eternity after I died."

"Its not that easy to teach them about our Lord. The only way I can get them to come to church is if I let them worship their Gods as well as ours. They don't think I know, but I do. I am working on it and I know, with time, God will assist me and all these people will be good Christians. I will tell Gregorio your God does not approve of it, but you thank him for his offer."

The wood they found in the forest was hard and the color of a dark red rose. It wasn't the oak Alvaraz was hoping for. That night he went to sleep disappointed, but dreamed a dream of Gregorio's bride. It was a warm dream of gentle kisses and naked embraces. In the morning Alvaraz woke to find a warm feeling of lust. A part of him resolved to not let an opportunity to have a women pass, but another part of him looked upon the dream as a kind of evil. Gregorio's bride was obviously a sorceress. She was working for the devil. He got on his knees and prayed for forgiveness. He would give his confession to Father Adao before he left Tzacapu.

The men stayed for two days in the village resting and enjoying the hospitality of the indigenous people. All the Spanish men assembled and said good-bye to Gregorio and his bride. They were both carrying bulging packs with bands across their foreheads. Diago hurriedly sketched the scene, as was his habit. He would add the details later.

Father Adao offered the services of one of his servers, a man who they would call Tan, to guide the men to the beginning of the road to Colima, a city not too far from the ocean. When they got to the sea they could find a boat to Acapulco.

Unfortunately, Diago's horse had gone lame and was left behind in the village to be cared for. This meant the tools carried on one of the horses would need to be redistributed amongst the men. In the end it was decided Diago, who was a small man, would ride double with the other men. Tan also rode double so the party moved quickly.

The path Tan led them on ran beside a series of very large shallow lakes, down river valleys, through enchanted jungles where water falls cascaded over ancient boulders. Alvaraz was enchanted. He soon realized he had a fondness for the land, the people and richness of life. It was the birds that enchanted him the most. It seemed every day they would come to a new terrain and he would see flocks of different birds. In one lake he saw thousands of pelicans, then in the next he would see an equal number of white herons and egrets, while the jungles were filled with many different parrots. Everything around him was new and exciting.

Chapter 4

Late on the second day they could see a tall mountain in the distance. It was black and obviously volcanic. Smoke was pouring form its summit.

"Tan, what mountain is that?" asked Falso, who was riding double with him.

"It is Tlaklan. This is a place where the best spear points come from. It is also near the village your people put there called Colima. We should camp up ahead, then tomorrow I will show you how to get across that river. On the other side is a road built by your people going to the sea and inland to the village of Guadalajara. You won't have any trouble finding your way from there."

They camped by the river and that evening Alvaraz and some of his men examined the crossing. It consisted of a suspension bridge hanging between a narrowing in the canyon.

"There is no way we can get the horses across that bridge. Even if it didn't break with the weight of a horse, the horses would refuse to cross," stated Jose.

The water was low and, if they found a way down, they could swim the animals across.

"Tan, do you know of a path to the river where we can take the horses?"

Tan stared at the river, and said, "I don't know the best path but there are many paths down on this side. If we go back there is a place where the water travels slowly over gravel."

It was decided half the men and equipment would travel across the bridge and the horses would be led back by Jose and the other men.

All day the men worked at getting the horses down the embankment to the river. The horses protested the descent but, once in the river they didn't seem to want to leave and it was equally difficult convincing them it was a good idea to ascend the opposite embankment. The men who had crossed on the bridge found a very narrow path to the river. They carried all the rope they had and each animal was almost dragged up the steep side of the riverbank. By the end of the day they camped on the side nearest Colima. They found themselves, covered with cuts and burses, exhausted but all in one piece.

The next morning Tan pointed them in the direction of the road to Colima and said good-bye, then walked over the suspension bridge to Tzacapu. About a mile down the river they were all horrified to find a path across the river with a gentle descent on both sides.

"We wouldn't even had to slow down if we'd come this way," said Jose. It looks as if people have been driving herds of animals across here."

With a scowl Alvaraz said, "Next time we must explore more before we put ourselves through that torture."

They made it to Colima by noon. It was the first Spanish town they'd seen since leaving Mixico. There was a fresh breeze blowing through the town with the scent of flowers coming from the fertile valley. The sun was warm in the cool breeze adding to Alvaraz's excitement, and his men rode down the cobbled street to the church. By the time they arrived, the town square was crowded with Spanish colonists and an assortment of indigenous people. Alvaraz and his men went straight to the priest who was waiting in front of the church.

"Welcome to Colima. I am Father Ernesto of the order of San Bernadine."

Alvaraz got off his horse and introduced himself and his men to Father Ernesto.

"We are on our way to Acapulco where we hope to build ships for the Council of New Spain."

Father Ernesto was happy to see these men and before long he arranged for them to stay with families in the town.

Alvaraz and his men were invited to a party the following evening at the home of the Mayor of Colima; Cortés de Buenaventura. The large courtyard and surrounding buildings could have been in Spain. The next evening the men and dignitaries were welcomed with enough food and drink to feed twice their number. It was a good evening filled with much talk of the coming new developments of New Spain.

"We didn't expect you so soon. It was only a year ago we put out the request for a ship builder," commented the Mayor.

Alvaraz told the assembled group how he was recruited and his subsequent journey across the Atlantic and his luck at finding the castaways after the sinking of their ship in the hurricane. When he told of his trip across the continent, there was much laughter.

"You should have gone to Panama, it's only six days on a good road across the narrow neck of New Spain, then take a coastal ship to Acapulco," said one of the Colonists. "You can save months and you wouldn't have to endanger yourselves with the savages. All my livestock as well as my stable of a dozen fine Spanish horses came through that way."

Another man commented about his wife and daughter who had died of the night vapors when in Panama. "You are all here whole and healthy. I think it's a far better way than losing half your men to the night vapors."

"But, Julio, you came through during the rainy season. You should have come with me in the dry."

"Enough," said the Mayor, "you are here, you are healthy, and you have some fine horses and equipment to start work. You have done an admirable job so far, Senors. I have sent a message to the port at the Bay of Salagwa on the coast. I would like you to rest here, and when you are ready continue your journey. The farms and the villages all along the coast are suffering because we don't have enough workers. We are told there are thousands of strong people who live in our island colony to the west, founded by King Philip. Many have sailed the route so that isn't a problem. The problem is we don't have enough ships to carry the workers. You know, ships have been built in the Bay of Salagwa twenty-five years ago. These were the ships used to carry the soldiers who conquered the Islands of King Philip. So shipbuilding is possible."

"I'm sure we can build suitable ships for this work," said Alvaraz. "You may have noticed the wood we carry. These are samples of wood grown along the way, which we are testing for suitability in shipbuilding. We need large groves of pine for pitch and planking. So far we haven't found anything suitable for knees and keels. Do you know is there are any forests of oak?" asked Alvaraz.

"You should talk to Miguel Sanchez, He is the man who supplies us with lumber to build our houses." The Mayor stood and shouted across the courtyard asking Miguel to join the conversation. He was an older man, unusually slim, dressed in clothing that was at one time in style, but now was old and tattered. Alvaraz's two apprentices followed him to the table where they sat.

"Miguel, our young friend needs your help," stated the Mayor.

"Yes, I know what you are asking. I've been talking to your apprentices, Jose, Juan and the ship's carpenter about your problem and I think I have an answer. You are looking for a hard wood like oak to build the frame of your ships, yes?"

Alvaraz smiled at his men, "Yes, that is precisely what we have been discussing here."

"There is a tree that grows prolifically along the coast know as Manzanillo. It is not too hard and not too brittle. It reminds me of oak, but the color is like walnut. I have some samples here I can show you in the morning. They used this wood when they built the fleet in Salagwa. I understand it worked very well. I must tell you there is one problem with the wood. The sap is poisonous and a small amount will kill a man very quickly. It is necessary to fell the trees and leave them for a period of time to dry up the sap before they can be used."

"How long does it take to dry up the sap?" asked Alvaraz.

"It is best to leave them for one year," responded Miguel.

The next day Alvaraz saw the samples Miguel had. He took the six-foot length and bent it. It proved flexible, not showing the slightest cracking. It seemed just hard enough to hold fasteners. Alvaraz was pleased and eager to see a living tree. He hoped it would grow like an oak with natural bends that could be used as frames in the curve of a ship's hull and knees to join the deck to the hull.

With only two day's rest the men were eager to head for the coast. Miguel couldn't accompany them but instructed them to see his head man in Salagwa, who would take Alvaraz into the forest to see the Manzanillo trees.

In two days, on the good road, they descended towards the sea. The air became hot and humid and a lush green jungle spread out before them.

"I can smell the sea," exclaimed Falso as he rode up the final hill.

There in the distance a glimmer of blue could be seen through the trees.

They all stopped and gazed at the view of lush forests allowing this tiny vista of sparkling ocean in the distance.

They rode through a dry patch, then they saw a long arch of beach and smoke trailing from some houses built behind the natural burm. As they approached the village some young boys ran towards them. There were perhaps a dozen native children with one European child, all running beside the men, speaking in a language Alvaraz couldn't understand.

"Do any of you speak Spanish?" he asked.

The young European answered. He was perhaps ten years old with sandy brown hair. "We all speak Spanish," he exclaimed.

"Where are your parents?" asked Alvaraz.

"My mother is home, and my father and brothers are fishing. They will come home soon," said the young boy in difficult Spanish, Alvaraz identified as coming from northwest Spain.

At the end of the beach, nestled in the hook of the bay, they could see boats lined up on the beach and two small sailing boats anchored in the bay. Alvaraz and his men made quite a spectacle as they rode proudly on their healthy young horses down the beach. It wasn't long before the men were having problems controlling their horses. They gave up and let the horses run in the surf. All the men were filled with excitement and expectation as they let their horses gallop into the sea, breaking waves almost tumbling them. They found themselves wet to mid thigh stomping up towards the beached boats, the gaggle of children running excitedly behind. Alvaraz dismounted and took in the sun, the blue sky and the smell of the sea. Again he thought this must be like the Garden of Eden. Silently he prayed; 'thank you, God, for bringing us to this beautiful place safely after so many trials.'

On closer inspection they found more buildings and some deteriorating scaffolding obviously used in the past for shipbuilding.

"What do you think of this Jose?" asked Alvaraz.

"It's a place that was used to build a ship or maybe more than one. The measure of the ship would be seventy feet in length with a beam of twenty."

"Very good, Jose, these are my thoughts also. And I wonder if there is any left over planks. I would like to see what they used for planking."

Some of the men, with Juan in charge, unloaded the boxes of tools. Juan, in anticipation of his master, found a hammer and chisel and was walking up towards the structure when he heard a loud gravely voice behind him say, "Ahr! What ya dooin Laddy!"

He turned to find an old skeletal man standing dressed in rags, his runny eyes deep in their sockets, looking out at him.

In the politest way he could, Jose approached the old man, put his hammer and chisel in one hand trying to hide them behind his leg, and said, "Sir, we have come from Spain to build ships. My name is Jose Mendoza Narvaez of Grenada." He held out his hand. The old man took it and introduced himself formally as Alejandro Gonzales of New Spain.

"Mucho Gusto, We have come at the request of the Council of New Spain."

The old man mumbled something about the council being a pack of fools who wished nothing more than to destroy this Garden of Eden.

"It's interesting, Sir, that you talk of the Garden of Eden. My master is always comparing this place to a Garden of Eden."

"Who is your master?"

"He is Alvaraz. I am his apprentice." Jose pointed to the group of men standing beside the old scaffolds.

The old man walked out on the sand in his bare feet, cursed and returned to his shack to fetch his crude sandals and large straw hat. As he left his shack for the second time he stopped and replied to someone inside his shack with a mixture of Nahuatl and Spanish, "I must go and meet these men."

The old man proved nimble enough. Jose almost had to run to keep up. "I heard the council was looking for a ship builder. They think I'm too old," he mumbled as he strode towards the assembled men.

Jose introduced Alejandro to the Alvaraz and the men.

"So, you have come here to build ships in the Garden of Eden. It's good to meet you. I am a ship builder, originally from Spain. I've built many ships. The two anchored in the bay I built. There are at least twenty still working the coast from Panama to California."

Alvaraz took a deep bow and said, "Sir, it is a great honor to meet you. We need all the help we can get. Could we commission you to consult with us."

"How will you pay me?"

"If you are as you say, and if it proves profitable, I can offer you one gold doubloon per month. Is this satisfactory?"

Alejandro had never been paid so much before. So with suppressed joy he put his hand to his chin as if thinking about it and said, "I agree."

The men set up camp beside the old boat works and that night they were treated to fresh, fried fish served with peppers and melted goat cheese rolled in tortillas. Alejandro's wife and two daughters cooked and served the fish bought from the fisherman who made their homes a short distance down the beach. Alvaraz noticed the Bask fisherman and Alejandro were both living and having children with women from the country, unlike the men of Colima who only had Spanish wives. They learned there was a Spanish colony in the next bay at Tlacotla.

"It's a steamy place in the wet season so not too many live there. They prefer Colima. I think some of the people will be returning soon. There is a tree cutter named Miguel Sanchez who should be down now."

"I met this man, when I was in Colima. I understand he does a good job of cutting trees. He showed me some wood from the Manzanello tree that looks promising for frames and keels. Do you know of this wood? I would like to see the trees."

The old man smiled at Alvaraz's request. "The wood you talk of is the best wood I've seen. It's just hard enough. It won't crack, doesn't change much when it's wet or dry. It makes the best pegs for fasteners and doesn't seem to rot. The problem with the wood is the sap poisons the skin, causing boils and can kill a man. I've seen this. You must fell the trees and let them lie in the forest for at least a year, preferably two. I laugh when you say you haven't seen the trees. If you rode in on the road from Colima you must have ridden through forests of them. You can find the best trees in a bay a day's sail to the north of here called Navidad."

"Could you show me some trees tomorrow? I am looking for the shape of the tree. Do they grow with curved limbs like the shape of a ship?"

"Yes, tomorrow we can see some. You will be well pleased. These trees grow for the pleasure of the ship builder."

"What about planking? What wood do you use for planking?"

"We use the wood of the mangle tree. It is easy to come by and Miguel can have it delivered to the site." responded Alejandro.

"We want to build galleons."

The old man looked at Alvaraz and said, "You will need men for that. We don't have enough labor to even build small ships. Where do you think you will get the labor?" he asked Alvarez.

Alvaraz took a look at Alejandro as the weight of the problem sunk in. In his mind he struggled against the problem. He was here to build ships to bring in labor and he couldn't bring in labor because he didn't have any ships. "Is there no where I can go to get labour? What would you do Alejandro?"

"Look at me Alvaraz; I am fifty seven years old. When we came I was twenty. At first we had three hundred strong young Spaniards. They sailed to Manila and then back to Spain. If I am lucky I can find 10 men, half of them will be lazy and if you're lucky you can get two honest hour's work out of them a day. If you had a ship, you could go across the sea and bring in people from the islands of King Philip. But you need men to build the ship."

Alvaraz lay in bed that night with frustrated anger. He had everything but the men to build ships. With his eight men and the men Alejandro could recruit he could perhaps build a ship worthy of sailing to distant lands, in five years, but he was to go home to his bride in five years. This was surely an impossible task.

Early in the morning, as he gazed sleeplessly at the stars, a plan came into his mind. The lumber for framing the ships needed a year to season and dry out the poison. He would start Miguel cutting trees immediately. Next he would convince the council to allow Capitan Rodrego to delay his planned trip to Spain for six months. In six months he could make one trip to the Islands of King Philip to acquire a hundred strong men knowledgeable in shipbuilding. If all went well, Rodrego should be arriving in Acapulco in two months putting them into December. It could be possible to arrive here on this very beach with a shipbuilding crew the following June.

That morning, at first light, Alvaraz found Alejandro wandering around their camp. His men were asleep and he wanted someone to talk to so he quietly got up and wandered down the beach. After hearing his plans, Alejandro gave him a lot of encouragement.

"I know some of the men on the council who will listen to me. I think I can help you in convincing the council to delay the shipment of treasure for six months. The first thing they should consider is, if they leave in December, they will be in Tierra de Fuego in the middle of the southern winter storms. So it would be wise for them to delay that trip until the following September. I like your plan and I hope you will like my plan for today."

"What is your plan for today?" Alvaraz asked with a smile of curiosity.

"I want to take you to Navidad on my ship, the Nina. She is the one anchored the furthest off. The wind is fair from the south. We should be there before nightfall," Alejandro shyly said. "I found Navidad when we were building ships here. I couldn't convince the ship builders to move but when you see it, I know you will agree. There is a large lagoon with a deep entrance. The water behind the beach is still and deep. As you can see here we must move the hull a great distance into the sea to float it in the shallow water. Then, fight the waves when launching the hull and after that constantly fight the rolling of the ship in the swell as we fit her out."

"I have six able bodied seamen here. I think they would enjoy some time on the sea. Myself I'm not so sure. I have the curse of seasickness, and sometimes get sick for days, but maybe I am cured. I didn't get too sick when we sailed from Puerto Rico. Yes, this is a good idea."

The tide carried them around the hook of the bay out into the wind and off they went. Alejandro sat back like a king as he directed the men. He smiled at Alvaraz and said, "With your men, life is good. I feel young when I see Nina sail so well. We will be there hours before the sun sets."

After five hours of being at sea with a swell and some wind waves tossing the forty foot sailing ship around Alvaraz and his men all reported they seemed to be cured from the evils of sea sickness. Feeling the freedom Alvaraz pulled of his cap and let the wind blow through his blond hair. Then he removed his shirt exposing his pale back to the sun. The other men followed and soon they were all running around the decks throwing buckets of water over each other like children.

The rocky outcropping frightened the men as they approached the entrance to the lagoon. They could see breaking waves over hidden rocks, but Alejandro assured them there was no danger. He took the helm and guided Nina through a channel at the end of a sandy bar. Wisps of smoke could be seen coming from behind the sand as they glided with the tide past the entrance. Within minutes they were anchored in flat calm water away from the rolling sea.

"This is truly an exceptional place," stated Alvaraz as he listened to the boom of the surf on the outside beach. "Do you know the depth of the channel?"

"Yes, it's a minimum of two fathoms at low tide, and almost three when the tide is in."

Jose excitedly said, "We could float a galleon in here easily."

A boat left the sandy beach and came to them, the native man paddling, shouting a welcome to Alejandro in his native Nahuatl.

The men listened as they conversed and at last Alejandro reported to the men, "this is my friend, Tolok. He welcomes you all, and invites us for a feast of fish on the beach." Alejandro addressed Alvaraz with the news. "Tolok speaks some Spanish. If we have time before it gets dark we can get him to take us to the groves of Manzanello trees growing on the other side of the lagoon."

As it turned out there was no time to see the Manzanello trees. Tolok's family prepared a feast of fish, fresh vegetables, and tortillas. The afternoon wore into evening, night and then talking until well after the moon had risen. Alvaraz couldn't help planning a shipyard. That afternoon the group of them walked along the beach identifying sites for a saw pit, a place to store and cure lumber, a perfect piece of beach to build the dry-dock where the framing and planking would take place and they marveled at the ease of launching the hull into deep, still water. Alejandro wanted to make a deal with Tolok, but Alvaraz was reluctant.

"I must talk to the council before any of these details can be made. I love this place and when I go to Acapulco I will insist on using this place to build the ships. But, as you know, I am only the servant of the council."

They spent the whole of the next day paddling with Tolok around the lagoon. Alvaraz noticed they were riding a strong tidal flow into the lagoon. This current must be why the channel is clear, he thought. The lagoon was large and filled with many different types of birds diving for the plentiful fish that could be seen in the murky water.

"In the wet season the water runs out in a great torrent carving the channel and making these deep bays," said Alejandro.

All along the beach they noticed tall trees, limbs outstretched making a perfect place for a multitude of birds. The noise of the birds made it difficult for Alejandro to talk. "These are the trees I've been talking about. This grove stretches for miles inland, enough to build hundreds of galleons."

Alvaraz, Jose and Juan found a downed tree and began cutting into the bark. "Just a minute," said Alejandro. He took a piece of bark, inspecting it for the poisonous sap. "This is OK, the sap is totally dried up."

The wood, as promised, had a variety of curves. Some of the taller, straight ones would work well for keels and all the scraps could be used to make pins and fasteners.

"This is fantastic. It's as if God made this place to build ships," Alvaraz said with reverence. "When can we go to Acapulco? I would like to talk to the council as soon as possible."

They left the following day making slow progress, in light winds, down the wave swept coast, passing long stretches of beach and a few rocky patches. They anchored the first night in Alejandro's bay. The families were keeping their horses well watered and fed and the young boys reported that they had taken them riding bareback in the surf. Alvaraz wrote a letter to Miguel explaining his plan and asked a young man to deliver it to Colima.

The next day they left the bay again. As they drifted with the tide and the light winds out to sea. Alejandro's native wife and family waving forlornly from the beach, Every day they left early with the wind blowing from the land, and then spent the better part of the day slowly sculling south. In the afternoon the wind would blow onto the land and they would find themselves sailing quickly through the choppy waves. They usually found places to anchor, where a few indigenous people made tiny fishing villages on the shore. After ten days they finally sailed into the large Bay of Acapulco. The air was hot, steamy and still; far too hot for Alvaraz. When he was in Navidad he had a man shear his hair and give it to the native women and now he wore a large brimmed hat, made of straw, fastened around his chin. He was glad of his new cool and shady look, because without it the heat it would be insufferable. As they approached the anchorage a boat came from the shore with a Spaniard asking what was their business.

"We have traveled from Spain at the request of the Council of New Spain. We are ship builders," responded Alvaraz.

"Thank God you are alive," said the man, "We received a message that you were on your way over two weeks ago, and thought you must have been killed."

Without delay they were taken to a newly built edifice overlooking the shore. They were greeted by an older man who took them to the council chambers where they were given refreshments and asked to wait for the Governor who was doing his toilet.

Within the hour a man dressed in proper court apparel, with shoulders puffed, wearing caprices, all properly buttoned up, in the armor of the court. He appeared with two similarly dressed accomplices. They stopped and stood at the top of the stairway leading down into the sunken interior courtyard. The Governor with his long bony nose looked down at the simple ship builders, standing with his mates as if he were judging some felons in court.

The man next to him announced, "Don Syllvester Castille de Aragon, Governor of Western New Spain."

"I received word you were coming." The governor said with a haughty air. "We expected you earlier." He was a short statured older man, gray hair, angular face, standing erect pacing on the landing above the men like a cock overlooking a hen house. Addressing one of his followers, he said "We must do something about this tardiness." Then turning to the men, he said. "You are here to build ships and ships you will build. We need two large galleons to carry treasure to Spain by next May. I believe you sailed with Captain Rodrego to Puerto Rico and know his ship the Lydia. She is fully armed and will accompany the two ships you will build. In May you will begin building ships to sail to the west to the new lands named after our esteemed King Philip. Is this all perfectly clear?"

Alvaraz was incredulous. How could this man be so ignorant of what it took to build a ship? He could hear Alejandro snorting, just barely restraining his laughter. With a sudden outburst, Alejandro broke the silence of the chambers with a burst of laughter. Then he said, in a very loud voice, "you must be jesting your eminence. Even if we had a thousand men building these ships in Cadiz, Spain we couldn't get two fully rigged galleons ready for next May. You must, also, consider the timing of the voyage around Tierra del Fuego with the treasure. The ships shouldn't leave until September at the earliest to avoid the storms on the passage to Spain."

"Are you Alvaraz?" the governor asked. The man beside him turned him aside and whispered something to him. The governor's color changed with his anger and he instructed one of the guards. "Get that man out of my court!"

Alejandro was escorted out at the end of a spear point by two guards dressed in leather armor and tri-cornered hats.

Leaning on the balustrade, his anger just under control, the governor asked, "Which one of you is Alvaraz Consollese de La Fuenta?"

Alvaraz stepped forward and bowed, "I am Alvaraz, Your Honor."

"When you are in this court, you are expected to take off your hat," said the man beside the governor.

Alvaraz took off his hat exposing his closely cropped blond hair and his men followed exposing their unkempt black hair. The governor smiled at the young man and his unlikely hair. "So you are the young boat builder I've been sent. What do you have to say for yourself?"

"I am Alvaraz, and yes, I have been asked to come to this new land and build ships. The man you just threw out of the court was very generous in sharing his knowledge of the area. He has aided me greatly in finding the materials and a proper site for building the ships you require. I hope you can forgive him for his out burst."

"It's of little importance," stated the governor, "now go on."

"I have briefly surveyed possible shipbuilding sites. The best site I have found is at Navidad. Everything I require to build the ships you require is close at hand and there is a deep still water bay with an excellent deep channel to the sea. I have two apprentices and six knowledgeable men including a ship's carpenter to supervise the work." Knowing labor would be a problem Alvaraz decided to drive the point home and remove the responsibility of completion dates by demanding a hundred strong men to do the work. "I have come to collect the hundred strong men to do the work that is required."

The governor turned to his advisor and asked him about the availability of workers. After a brief talk the governor's assistant responded with, "we will make the men available to you. Please make yourselves comfortable in the town. The governor would like another meeting with you tomorrow at two in the afternoon. We will expect only you. Your men will not be required." With that the men were dismissed.

As they walked out Jose smiled and said, "You are a clever man, master. Now if they can't find the labor they will have no choice but to go with your plan of sailing to the new land of King Philip to get the workers."

"So, you saw through my plan, did you? We will see if he can come up with the workers. It's possible they have thousands of men for us to chose from that can do this work. I think you know I must be home in Spain to marry my betrothed in five years. I don't want to be delayed here. I hope you can help me work to this end. I have a contract saying I can't leave until I have established a shipyard capable of working without me. Would you like to take over after I go?"

"No, I yearn to return to Spain. Jose will have completed his apprenticeship by then. We must convince him to stay."

Alejandro was waiting for them at the gates to the house. "You see what you are up against, don't you? These people are ignorant fools; they haven't the slightest idea about anything and will destroy this land. What was decided?"

"Nothing," responded Alvaraz, "He wants to meet with me again tomorrow afternoon. When I signed up for this work, I asked the council in Spain about many things. Where I could find the materials, where I could find a good site to build ships and where I would get the labor I needed. The council told me I would need to find the materials and the site in the new land. The council of Western New Spain would supply the labor including the supervisors. I have lessened their burden by supplying the supervisors. Tomorrow if you are correct, and there is no labor available, we will try to manipulate them into suggesting we take a trip to the land of King Philip to acquire the labour. Does the governor know you?"

"No, I don't know the governor, but I do know his henchmen, Felix, the big man he conferred with just before he threw me out. He has been here for as long as I have. He never listened to me before and considers me a trouble maker."

"Dealing with people like this can be a bit tricky. You can't tell them anything. If you need something make it their responsibility, and if you have a plan you must make it their idea. I talk as if I can change things. Tomorrow we will see if my wit can meet my mouth."

Chapter 5

Acapulco was beautiful with its craggy outcrops and stark hills protecting the harbor from the fierce summer storms, but as they stood looking down at the still sea the heat, the humidity and little breeze made for a place of little energy. They wandered through the town stopping frequently to answer questions from the merchants and workers that lived there. They made their way to a fort called Fort San Diago and talked to the few soldiers and workers building a higher thicker wall. When Alvaraz asked about the availability of workers the supervisor laughed and said, "I'm so short of hard working men that I have to put these soldiers to work. I could use a hundred more men myself. I don't know where you think you're going to get a hundred strong young men to build your ships," he said with a laugh.

When Alvaraz attended the court, the next day, he was shown into a private room where the governor sat behind a large elevated desk attended to by his two advisors. They were polite, in an arrogant way, as they invited him to sit in a low wooden chair in front of the desk, the three of them staring down upon him.

"You were requested by our previous administration. They told us you would build the ships we require and now we have information to the contrary. For some reason the previous administration didn't consider the paradox of needing workers to build ships so they could bring in the labor from afar. What comes first the horse or the cart?" The governor chuckled at his small joke then looked sternly at Alvaraz. "With out bringing things to a complete standstill, we don't have the one hundred men you require to build your ships. I am requesting you scour the countryside for the men you require."

Alvaraz sat pensively for a long moment then said, "I crossed the new land from east to west and found the land empty except for a few people who were old and sick. I heard of some tribes that are still well, hiding in the mountains. Perhaps if you could lend me a dozen soldiers to find them and rout them out we could find sufficient workers."

"This is out of the question; everyday we get reports of more pirates sailing this coast. Just the other day I received word, Dutch pirates are on their way as we speak. No, you must do this on your own," responded the governor.

"Are there any ships due in to Acapulco that may have workers on board from Manila? I have been told, there is an abundance of strong men there, wanting to come."

"We have two ships due in the next month. One a small packet from Manila probably stuffed with indentured labor, but they are all spoken for, the other ship the Lydia from Spain with only sailors aboard."

"I know the Lydia. She was built in our yard under my supervision just over a year ago. She is capable of carrying several hundred indentured workers," said Alvaraz.

With an interested look the governor looked up and said, "You built the Lydia?"

"Yes and I sailed with her from Spain—as I think you know."

Brows furrowed the governor looked at Alvaraz and asked, "How long do you think that ship would take to sail to Manila and back?"

"I understand it would take six months, I have been told there are fair winds all the way there, and a fast route to the north on the way back."

"We need that ship here in eight months to carry treasure safely to Spain. The weather is best around Terra del Fuego in December through February, so she would be laying at anchor here waiting for six months. When Rodrego arrives I will discuss this with him and if he says, he can do it, I want you to travel with him to pick the men you require. When you return I expect you to build a ship ready to sail one year from the day you return. Is this possible?"

Alvaraz couldn't believe his ears. Could it be this easy he thought, he then responded suppressing his glee. "If I was at my shipyard in Cadiz, I could guarantee you a ship, but I think you can understand there are so many variables as to promise you anything at this point. If you will give me permission I will instruct my men to construct the scaffolding and framing loft while I am away. I also need your permission to cut the trees down so they can season for a year before we start construction. All of these activities will cost money and therefore I would like you to set up some accounts to various people who will work for us. The first one is Miguel Sanchez. He is a wood cutter from Colima who I hope can fell and harvest the lumber we need for framing."

"We already have an account with Mr. Sanchez," reported the governors assistant. "He supplies wood for the construction of our buildings here, Your Honor."

With a contented smile the governor closed the meeting with, "I like what I see in you, Senor Consollese. It seems things could work out well. We will await the Lydia and expect her to sail, post haste, to Manila upon her arrival. In the mean time I would like to meet with you on a regular basis."

Alvaraz bowed and left the room with an excited feeling in his stomach.

Chapter 6

The shipbuilding crew was busy for the next month, all going their own way, preparing the foundation for the shipyard in Navidad. Alejandro was surprised no one questioned the location and wondered what magic Alvaraz had with the governor. Without effort he managed to convince the governor to follow his plan exactly with no argument.

Three weeks after the meeting Falso came running up the dirt track with exciting news. A ship had been sited off the coast some 20 miles to the South of Acapulco with the appearance of the Lydia. The soldiers at the Fort worked feverishly to complete the armaments in case the ship was a pirate ship and the entire town was in a tumult of excitement.

She was the Lydia and as she approached the bay three long boats crewed with soldiers and some of the shipbuilding crew set out with lines ready to tow the ship into port. Alvaraz stood in the stern sheets of the fastest long boat smiling and waving his hat as they approached the ship. When Captain Rodrego saw Alvaraz, his face contorted into a smile of joy. He lifted his hands and head in the air as if thanking God for this happy reunion. Then he motioned the man standing beside him to give him the speaking trumpet.

"Alvaraz, my friend, I can't tell you how happy I am to see you. We received word you had been sunk in a hurricane when you were on your way from Puerto Rico. How is it you are here?" he asked with emotion causing tears to come to his eyes.

Alvaraz tried to shout back his greeting, but his voice didn't carry above the exclamations and shouting around him. When they came up beside, offering their lines, Rodrego and Ismel greeted them and insisted Alvaraz come aboard. When aboard Rodrego embraced Alvaraz and the three of them conversed on the high aft deck. It was an emotional time for Alvaraz. He didn't know he was missing and didn't know how much Ismel and

Rodrego cared for him. Alvaraz quickly told his story as the ship crept into the harbor towed by the straining men at the oars.

When Alvaraz told Rodrego about the plan to sail for Manila, he was at first perplexed then after a minute he burst out with. "Alvaraz, we will sail together again on the ship you built. It will be my great honor to take you to Manila."

They were deep in conversation, filling each other in on their adventures when Ismel interrupted them. "The governor's launch is here sir. They have orders to take you to the governor forth with."

"Before you go, I should tell you about the governor," said Alvaraz.

"You'll have to tell me later. I know these governors and it's best to get on their good side to start with. God has blessed us both. When I get to the chapel I will say a prayer of thanks."

Rodrego left orders with Ismel to secure the ship and post a watch after they were properly anchored. With that he was off, leaving Alvarez to think about the perils of dealing with Governor Sylvester if you didn't know the man.

Jose came on deck and the two of them returned to their long boat for the trip to the shore. Alvaraz had the men row around the Lydia so he could see her condition and was well pleased with what he saw. She was huge, with nice lines. He stood in the stern sheets of the long boat in deep thought. He could build a better ship if he reduced the height of the fore and aft decks, increased her beam and the depth of her keel she would sail better and be more stable.

"Diago, bring me pen and paper," asked Alvaraz.

Jose looked around with a wondering look in his face and asked, "What ever for master?"

As Diago brought forth his pallet box and a selection of pencils, he said, "I have no pens here master only my carbons. Do you want me to draw the ship?"

"I would be pleased if you would. This is a good idea. You see I want to modify the design. I think we can make a faster stronger and more stable ship."

Diago drew a quick sketch of the ship as it stood, then Alvaraz asked him to draw another with a lower fore and aft deck.

"Captain Alvaraz. We are perishing in the heat. Could you find us some parasols or can we return to the town where there is some shade?" asked Juan.

Alvaraz was so focused on his work he hadn't noticed the time going by. "Of course, I didn't realize the time."

With one last look at the Lydia, now surrounded with all manner of vessels, he instructed the men to row to shore where already there was a large crowd of partiers to greet them on the shore. They were told there would be a fiesta in the square to celebrate the arrival of the Lydia. It was a scene Alvaraz had seen many times in Cadiz. A ship would arrive and dozens of merchants he had never seen before would appear, their rosy cheeked faces speaking excitedly to their neighbors about the rich cargo they were expecting from the ship.

Alvaraz and Diago returned to their rooms to continue the redesigning of the ship while the rest of the shipbuilding crew enjoyed the party going on in the town square. Alvaraz brought out his drawings and design specifications of a typical galleon then he and Diago proceeded to redraw them. They worked well into the night and finally with the morning sky glowing in the east they fell into a sleep.

Chapter 7

The following week Alvaraz, Rodrego, the governor and his advisors discussed plans for the trip to Manila. Every one agreed it was feasible and a good idea. The Lydia would be put to good use and still the orders from Spain, to send the treasure, could be fulfilled. The town's people, with the help of the purser of the ship and his crew, busied themselves with the work of provisioning the ship for the three month journey to Manila. Alvaraz' s men were sent out to begin the process of building a shipyard, in Navidad, to accommodate Alvaraz's new design and others were sent to Colima to work out the details of felling the Manzanillo trees with Miguel Sanchez. One of the cargo holds on the Lydia contained nothing but equipment to build and fit out many fully rigged galleons. There were many long saws made of the finest Toledo steel, along with augers, fasteners, hundreds of barrels of pitch, rolls of fine linen caulking, miles of fine hemp cordage of varying sizes and tons of bar and flat stock steel to be used by blacksmiths who would make the fittings for the ships.

"Rodrego, instead of unloading the materials here we should sail to Navidad and unload them there," suggested Alvaraz one evening as they ate at a small inn with the officers of the ship and some merchants from the town.

"We have room in our ware house here," said a merchant with bulging cheeks and braided thick hair that hung down the front of his clean white shirt. "It wouldn't be a problem and you could move it to Navidad at your leisure."

"Thank you for the offer," said Alvaraz. "The Lydia needs some work, her bottom needs to be careened of barnacles and I understand there are some minor leaks needing caulking, and you mentioned the rudder thumps when you bring her round. There is a possibility she needs new pintles and gudgeons. I would like to try doing this work in the lagoon at Navidad before we leave. We may not get another chance until we arrive at Manilla. The

Acapulco shipyard is far too small and with this big surf it would be dangerous to beach her here."

Rodrego started to speak, but stopped when they heard shouting on the street. They all turned to listen and stood when they heard the news. A heavily armed ship had been sighted to the south. Rodrego instructed his officers, "gather the men and prepare for sea immediately. Philippe before you go, what is the state of the tide?"

"It should start to ebb on the hour," he responded.

As the officers left the restaurant Rodrego yelled, "Prepare the ship for battle."

"What's happening?" asked Alvaraz as they ran out onto the narrow street.

"We received reports of a Dutch 'man of war' following us up the coast. I've been waiting for her. If we're lucky we can surprise her and put an end to her threat."

It was pitch black as they made their way down the road to the dock. The other two long boats were gone, only the small four man boat waited impatiently for Rodrego. Alvaraz followed him into the boat without thinking. As the four sailors rowed furiously through surf, taking a breaking wave over the bow soaking everyone in the boat, Alvaraz realize the peril he had put himself in. He would be on a ship at war with cannon balls falling all around him. He could easily be dead in a few hours. He gulped and felt his bowels loosen. He needed a toilet, but kept his council and waited for the small boat to bump on the hull of the Lydia. Within minutes they had all scrambled up the boarding ladder and the boat had been hoisted. Rodrego shouted orders to the men in the sheets to unfurl the topsails then watched as they filled. Alvaraz scampered onto the aft deck to do his business then returned to stand beside Rodrego and his officers as the Lydia slowly moved out to sea, powered by a light off shore wind and the tide.

The plan was for the Lydia to stand off shore and shell the intruder while the shore battery shelled her with the new cannons the Lydia had delivered. They hove-to a mile or so off the beach and waited. It wasn't until the early morning that the lookout shouted there was a silhouette of a ship covering the carpet of stars to the South. Rodrego scampered up the ratlines to the look out and agreed it was a ship slowly moving down the coast making for

Acapulco. He gave orders to take the ship in closer and ready all the cannons on the starboard side. They crept in towards the shore and patiently waited.

It was impossible to tell if the ship was friend or foe until daylight but as it turned out before the sun rose the other ship started firing onto the shore. Immediately the shore battery started firing. Rodrego, hoping they wouldn't be hit by friendly fire, ordered the men at the cannons to fire a simultaneous first round then fire with the roll of the ship. The glow in the east gave enough light to see the intruder unfurl all her sails, using the light off shore breeze to carry her out to sea. It was obvious she had been surprised and was now running, trying to save herself. Suddenly her port cannons opened up followed by the crash of splintering wood as a ball struck the outer planking of the Lydia.

"Fire, you swabs," screamed Rodrego, thinking he must practice the men at firing the cannons. They were hopelessly slow.

The attacking ship had been hit, as evidenced by smoke coming from amidships, but was moving with good speed out of range of the shore batteries. Alvaraz could see long boats ahead of the ship towing her in the light breeze.

"Do you see her long boats towing her?" shouted Alvaraz over the roar of the cannons.

"That's how she's getting away, damn," shouted Rodrego. "She must be heavily manned," he said as he looked around to see whom he could put in the long boats to help with the chase. Another ball hit the planking on the fore deck leaving a deep furrow in the wood, then rose just enough, to hit a man square as he ran down the deck. All that remained of the sailor was a red mist moving across the deck mixed with the smoke and stink of cordite in the still air. The Lydia was inching along under full sail in the diminishing morning breeze. The other ship was towed out of range and her cannons became silent.

"Take half the gun crew and put them in the boats to tow," ordered Rodrego.

The battle was over but the chase was on. The light breeze carried the ships slowly down the coast. Rodrego, Ismel and Alvaraz observed the men straining against their oars in the long boats. They had been rowing now for two hours.

"We aren't getting any closer," remarked Ismel.

"We need a wind, Damn!" Rodrego slapped his hand on the rail. "We are further out to sea than that Dutch pirate. When will the damn wind come?"

Alvaraz felt a light breeze from the north on his cheek. "I can feel it coming from the north. We should bring the braces around to catch the north wind."

Rodrego saw a tiny zephyr stir the still water and shouted. "Bring the braces around to port and look lively."

With in minutes the Lydia was moving slowly towards the shore and the opposing ship.

"With this wind we should be able to lob a broadside into her. I'll get the gun crews ready to starboard if you please, Captain," said Ismel as he rushed away to his gun crews.

The wind built and it wasn't long before the sails started to move the Lydia. "Get the boats aboard," shouted Rodrego.

The wind moved over the water like a fan, moving towards the shore catching up with the pirate ship, who chose the tack taking her out to sea. There was no doubt their courses would intersect well within range of their guns.

It seemed an eternity as the two ships came together. "Steady. Hold your fire until I give the command," shouted Rodrego.

Ismel could be seen running from gun to gun adjusting them for the range that the lookout cried down.

Alvaraz saw a flash on the other ship and shouted, "They've fired, Sir."

Rodrego who was timing the role of the ship, shouted, "fire."

As the guns roared the sea in front of the Lydia rose up, when the balls from the other ship hit the water, causing the sea to become a white seething mass. The distant sound of a crash was evidence the other ship was hit from the Lydia's broadside. The smoke drifted away from the pirate ship showing her mizzenmast still standing with the aft castle deck almost removed and splintered planks standing at odd angles. The smoke from the Lydia's cannons obscured Alvaraz's view for a minute, then blew away, revealing red flashes on the other ship meaning the cannons were firing. A ball could be heard shrieking through the air landing with a crash at the root of the main mast. The Lydia shuddered, followed by the scream of a man who stood watching blood spurt from his severed arm. A seaman beside him moved to help, not realizing his abdomen had been bisected by a large splinter. He looked down, his face a mask of despair, to see his bowels spill onto the deck. He stumbled for a few seconds, blood from the man he was attempting to help, spraying his face, then fell into the slimy mess below him on the deck.

The officers standing beside Rodrego looked to him for orders. For a second he looked stunned. Then pulling himself together, "have some men move the bodies and inspect the mast." Between the noise of the guns firing he addressed the other officer with, "I need a damage report. Go and report as fast as you can."

"I'll go with you," shouted Alvaraz as he left Rodrego alone on the aft deck. The noise of the cannon diminished as the ships sailed out of range of each other.

Within minutes the second officer came back with news. "We lost three seamen. Two are below being treated for their injuries. A ball penetrated the hull aft, went through your cabin, made a hell of a mess, then went through the opposite side of the hull. The deck has been splintered forward. The good news from Alvaraz is, no frames have been broken. The main mast only has half its girth at the root, but it's still strong and can be repaired in place according to the ship's carpenter."

Rodrego turned towards the fleeing ship, thought for a second, then gave the orders, "Wear around the ship, make fast, all sails in pursuit." The wind had increased blowing the smoke and stink of battle away, leaving the smell of a fresh northerly wind. The ship turned, heeling on the other tack. Alvaraz sprinted up the stairs to the aft deck and said breathlessly. "Captain, we are lucky. The ship is intact with a little superficial damage easily repaired."

"Thanks Alvaraz. It seems we may be able to sink this pirate yet. We'll see if the Lydia has it in her to climb above her in this wind. What do you think?"

"She's a good ship. It seems your sailors know to keep her speed up rather than stalling her by going too close, but I see our opponents have the same idea. I want to redesign the next ship. I think I can make a ship that will go faster and be more stable."

"And how would you do that, Alvaraz?"

"I would increase her beam, and lower the decks moving the weight lower."

"I like the idea," said Rodrego. "But if you are building ships for the crown you must build to their specifications."

"That's where I'll need your help. Can you help me change the minds governing the designs of Armada ships?"

"We should write a letter to my friend Jean Borton. He's the head of the academy designing new Armada ships. If we ask him for permission to build a new ship to transport workers, then you can build what ever you want, to suit the purpose, provided it's within budget."

"You would do this for me?"

"Of course. I like your idea and I trust you."

They sailed all day and night chasing the pirates, but on the second night the other ship disappeared leaving them alone on the sea.

In the early morning light of the second morning Rodrego stood with Alvaraz on the aft deck speculating on where the other ship had gone. "I don't think she'll bother us again. We gave her a nasty hit aft. I wonder if the officers were killed and now she is running short of officers?" speculated Rodrego.

"I think the reason she got away is because the hull of the Lydia is encrusted with barnacles," stated Ismel. "We must beach her and do a good job of careening the hull."

Alvaraz looked up and said, if I'm not mistaken we have been going north. The place where I want the shipyard should be east of us as we have traveled a good distance north. I think I can find it if you want to sail towards the coast. I haven't seen a better place on the coast to do this work. We were planning to go there anyway."

Chapter 8

They turned the ship to head east and waited for the coast to appear. A day and a night passed. There was much speculation about the pirate ship and where she had gone. They knew she flew a Dutch flag, she was slightly smaller and not as well armed as the Lydia. Alvaraz was positive her hull was built after the design of an East Indiamen trading ship and they were all confident they wouldn't see her again on this coast. She was probably headed for the Indies by circling the globe.

"This has been an excellent lesson for us. Ismel, you must practice the gun crews. once everyday for an hour. Have the men practice with light charge and no ball. We must be able to reload in less than a minute. Before we get to Navidad I want a battery of cannons on the beach pointing out to sea, to protect the Lydia, before we lay her out, helpless on the sand," ordered Rodrego. They were approaching the shore and Rodrego asked Alvaraz, "Are you sure this is the entrance to this lagoon?"

"We are very close to the correct latitude, this must be it," responded Alvaraz.

The next morning they sailed into a large, well-protected bay and anchored. Rodrego was impressed. They did find a small lagoon but it was very unlike the one Alvaraz remembered. There were a few crude huts on the beach. A boat was sent ashore with Alvaraz in command. They encountered an old man and women with a few children. None of them spoke Spanish. The few words of Nahuatl Alvaraz spoke brought forth a flurry of words Alvaraz didn't understand. When he spoke the word Navidad the old man understood and with sign language indicated he would guide them there in their long boat. Alvaraz allowed the old man aboard. They rowed to the Lydia and told Rodrego their plan. "Take the long boat and find your Navidad, Alvaraz. We'll stay here and wait." The navigator, Philippe, who wanted to chart the coast accompanied Alvaraz. Immediately they found a long promontory of rocks, far out to sea, just below the surface at the end of the first cape.

Philippe drew a crude chart of the area commenting, "If we hit one of these rocks the Lydia would be sunk in minutes. It's good we've come first in our launch."

They carefully made their way down the coast using the mast and sail found in the boat. The wind picked up from the north and within an hour they were in the next bay. Philippe insisted they examine the bay as a potential anchorage, and found it would be perfect, with a good depth, sand bottom and well protected form the north swell and wind. They sailed across the bay and there was the entrance to Navidad. Again Philippe took out his instruments and made a rough chart of the area.

As they stood off the entrance a canoe came charging out with Tolok in the bow.

"You there, Alvaraz, you've returned," Tolok shouted in his crude Spanish.

Alvaraz wished he had Alejandro, because there was a lot lost in the translation as he tried to inform Tolok he would return with a truly large ship on the morrow. The old man from the next bay who was Alvaraz's guide talked incessantly with Tolok. Finally Alvaraz and his crew were allowed to leave. The wind had died and the men were anxious to row back to the Lydia. Tolok seemingly returned to his village, but as the men pulled away from the shore; Tolok's tiny canoe powered by two men could be seen chasing them. Within an hour Tolok was beside them. It seemed impossible, but the canoe was beating them, and when it came to going around the cape the canoe made for a passage nearest the land. Alvaraz suggested they follow the canoe, because it would save them many miles of rowing. When they arrived tired and sore at the Lydia; Tolok's canoe could be seen floating aft tied with a long line to the Lydia, and there on deck was Tolok conversing with Rodrego.

It was an easy sail to Navidad. They carefully brought the Lydia through the channel and anchored her fore and aft at the head of the lagoon. That afternoon they found more than one spots to beach her and Rodrego, several times, complimented Alvaraz on his wise choice of sites to build ships. The cannons were unloaded and prepared to fire from the highest point of the beach at any ship approaching from the sea. It took a day to unload the hold containing the ship building supplies which were first stacked high up on the beach, then secured with canvas tarps. The following midnight they towed the Lydia to the beach behind the sand point and waited for the tide to run out. For the next week the sound of saws, hammers, and shouting men could be heard in the bay, mixed with the smell of burning wood and boiling pitch. A shelter was built around the supplies to protect them until a permanent shelter could be built.

"We are provisioned, our water casks have been filled, the bottom is clean, the rudder is repaired, the ship is ready and I've sent word to Acapulco informing them we will set sail for Manila from here the day after the Sabbath," Rodrego stood talking in the hot sun overlooking Alvaraz who was using a long tape to measure the dimensions of his proposed ship building dry-dock.

"I wish I didn't have to go," said Alvaraz, "There is so much to do here, but then I must recruit the men I need. The Sabbath is the day after tomorrow. I'll be ready."

The Lydia was re-floated at high tide on Saturday morning. Then carefully she was towed through the entrance of the lagoon and anchored in the unnamed bay to the north. That evening a coastal cutter from Acapulco arrived with a letter from the governor. The governor wanted to thank Rodrego for his assistance in chasing off the Dutch pirate. He also indicated the colonies needed as many workers as he could bring back. He offered Rodrego a bonus of two gold doubloons per head for each person he could bring back to New Spain alive.

After reading the letter Alvaraz asked, "how many additional people can you carry, do you think?"

"I barely have room for the hundred you requested. It's the additional food and water we require. I'll have the ship's carpenter see if he can add additional quarters for more people. As it is they will be living in the cargo hold. I don't know where we can put more provisions. We must sail north to 30 degrees then west. It's a very long and cold trip."

The Lydia sailed as planned on the day after the Sabbath. The ships priest Father Emilio said a mass, and then requested every member of the crew give a confession to cleanse their souls before they left.. The anchor was lifted and the Lydia was towed with the weak tide out to deep water. Jose arrived in Navidad with the coastal cutter from Acapulco and he and several of Alvaraz's crew helped tow the Lydia out of the anchorage. Alvaraz gave them final instructions and assigned Jose as the person in charge until he returned. There was little wind and by evening the Lydia could be seen rolling in the swell a mile off the shore. The light offshore wind finally carried her out and within a week she was sailing at a good clip down the trade winds towards Manila.

Chapter 9

Six weeks passed with life aboard the ship becoming a routine. The health of the crew became a concern for Rodrego. They needed fresh produce and water. He'd seen men slowly wither; their teeth would fall out as their bones stood out on their ever-thinning frames. It would be impossible to get any work out of them soon. So on the first Sunday of the seventh week, when they saw low lying islands, they anchored in the lee of an atoll and sent a boat ashore. Healthy looking people could be seen standing defiantly on the shore shaking their spears. Soon a large flotilla of outrigger canoes appeared. They could see a man, colorfully decorated with feathers, in the lead canoe.

"Load and fire the forward cannon over their heads," ordered Rodrego.

The cannon was fired with the shot bisecting a tree in the village behind the canoes. There was a moment of panic amongst the canoes then they turned and fled. The Spanish sailors followed in their long boats and found the village deserted except for two old toothless women who evidently couldn't be moved. The men found strange branchless trees with fronds and nuts growing on their crown. One of the officers identified the trees as those growing prolifically in the land of King Philip and demonstrated how to drink the milk from the nuts and then scoop out the flesh. Before long several trees had been felled and the nuts gathered to be taken back to the ship.

The following day a group of unarmed men appeared beside the village. Rodrego and his crew treated them well and more followed. No words were spoken, but the officers and crew of the Lydia couldn't help but think they were looked up to as Gods. When one of the crew indicated they were looking for fresh water, he was immediately shown a well. The same happened when they asked for meat. They were given three living, fat wild pigs, trussed on carrying poles. The ship's blacksmith brought some iron and showed the natives how to heat the metal and make tools. They left some axes and knives as payment. Within three days the tanks were full of sweet water and the hold was brimming with vegetables and fruit from the island.

Overnight the health of the crew improved and with their health their randyness. On the third day some women appeared dressed in nothing more than grass skirts.

"It's the devil himself come to temp the men" said the priest who had just finished blessing one of the old women. Rodrego, the Priest and Alvaraz looked on.

The women were young and nubile, their skin the color of almonds with black hair cascading over unblemished faces so sweet and expectant. Their near naked bodies had the shape of sirens with naked bosoms standing erect capped with dark nipples. Alvaraz could feel himself becoming aroused and knew by the stare of Rodrego and the priest that he wasn't alone.

"This is going to cause some problems," said Rodrego fingering his pistol. He turned and shouted to Ismel, "Have the men return to the ship and prepare to sail."

Ismel was about to give the order when the forest beyond the village erupted with shouting. The sergeant at arms and two of his men pushed two sailors towards Rodrego followed by two wailing young women.

"We caught these two coupling with the natives, Sir."

Ismel, in a loud voice, gave the order, "Everyone back to the beach for transport to the ship—on the double!"

Two guards stood on either side of the chief. They defiantly held spears sharpened and decorated with colorful feathers pointed at the sky. The chief looked on in dismay as if wondering why these Gods were turning down his gift of young women. Rodrego raised his hand towards the chief and advanced. He had a gift of a bag of colorful beads. Rodrego saw this island as an excellent re-provisioning stop for future voyages and wanted to leave on good terms with the chief. He made a sign by holding his hands before him with the bag of beads. . The Chief who was standing with his men took the bag, put his hand in the bag and drew it out some beads. He showed them to his fellow islanders, then looked at Rodrego quizzically.

"These are beads to adorn your cloths with." Rodrego explained. He looked around, found a young woman and pointed, "The young women will like these," he said dumbly.

The chief called the woman over and showed her the beads. She fondled them looking with intensity then smiled and said something to the chief. The chief made a low bow followed by his men as the woman stepped back. Rodrego bowed, stepped back, turned and was about to leave when the two guards moved in front of him baring his way. Rodrego who was the only westerner left in the village felt a pang of fear run through him. He reached down and fingered his blunderbuss. He turned to find the chief talking to one of the women. She ran quickly to a hut near by and returned with a necklace decorated with an intricate pattern of tiny colorful seashells. The chief held it up and placed it over Rodrigo's head. Again Rodrego bowed as he accepted the gift. This time when he turned to leave, the chief and a crowd escorted him from the village.

When Rodrego got to the beach he found a large group of islanders gathered around the last long boat with only Alvaraz and four sailors. The two women who had been caught having sex with the sailors in the forest were there wailing in agony, along with some strong young men who obviously wanted to accompany them on their trip.

The chief indicated he wanted Rodrego to take the four islanders with them on their journey. A flood of ideas crossed Rodrego's mind. He would take the four of them and keep the women in his cabin. He then remembered the trouble he had when he was a young man sailing off Portugal. He took some women on his coastal trading ship and for a week the crew did nothing but bicker and fight over the women. He nearly lost his ship.

"No, we can't take your people," said Rodrego. He pushed his way to the ships boat assisting the men with the launch into the surf. In exasperation he shouted, "God! I wish someone could talk to these people. Tell them we must go." No one said a word.

They were escorted to the Lydia by a flotilla of canoes. By the time they arrived and climbed up the ladder, islanders were climbing the rigging around the bowsprit.

"Repel these people!" ordered Rodrego.

Ismel, who was standing on the aft deck, repeated the order. "Shall we prepare a gun to scare them off?" he shouted the question at Rodrego.

"Yes, prepare a gun."

By this time a dozen islanders were trying to crawl onto the deck. "Push them over the side and get that boat aboard." Rodrego tested the wind. It was good they hadn't entered the lagoon. Out on the ocean they could escape.

Before he had the anchor up he ordered, "Set the fore sails, bring the helm to lee and look lively on the anchor windless."

The ship slowly turned as the anchor was hauled aboard. It would be a perfect escape "Set the main sail," Rodrego ordered. As it fell towards the deck and was sheeted in, the Lydia heeled and moved proudly out into deep water with all manner of canoes and swimming natives following. Within an hour all the followers except a large outrigger had fallen behind presumably returning to their island.

"I want every inch of this ship searched for stowaways," Rodrego ordered his officers, "And look lively."

They found two stowaways hiding in the hold of the ship. They were young men, perhaps twelve years old. They both appeared to be sick with fear when they were presented to the Captain and his officers.

"We could use some new crew," said Ismel.

"Could you use these children in your boat building?" Rodrego asked Alvaraz.

"I wouldn't choose them if I had older experienced men that could speak Spanish."

"It's settled then, these boys will only take up space and eat and drink our stores. Run the ship up into the wind and hail that canoe."

The two young men dove into the water without the slightest hesitation when the out-rigger came near.

Chapter 10

The warm breeze cooled Alvaraz as he stood at the rail, wearing his white shirt; his re-grown golden hair, bleached even lighter in the sun, blowing out behind his head. He felt good and asked, "How long before we make Manila?"

Rodrego was also feeling good. He'd been moody and a bit testy. Now with the weight of near capture lifted from him, his mood changed. The wind and weather was perfect for making a fast passage. With a smile he responded. "I've never sailed here before. We're on the correct latitude to land on an outer island where we should encounter the first Spanish settlement. I suspect it will be just a few weeks more. I'm convinced the Island was a gift from God. The men were getting sick and now look at them. I was so afraid the islanders were going to swarm the ship and murder us all. And here we are free, sailing well, on these winds that seem never to end."

Alvaraz looked at Captain Rodrego; his beard was getting gray, his hair showed white around the temples, his eyes seemed even more sunken in their sockets, but there was a new sparkle in his eyes. Leaning on the aft rail looking back, "It's been a long time since we've seen land. That island was magical. On my travels I keep encountering places I think of as the Garden of Eden. The old ship builder, Alejandro, said the same thing about Navidad. The strange trees, plentiful fruit, and oh, those young girls made it all so beautiful. I'm afraid if we stayed any longer, I wouldn't have been able to restrain myself. I would have taken one of those young women." He suddenly realized what he was saying and blushed, then tried to justify what he said by asking, "I'm sure this is a place of God. But then I ask myself, how could God create such a beautiful place and yet make it so full of sin and temptation."

"I must punish the men who were caught having sex with those natives. I need your help as well as the priest and my officers. Could you gather them up and also send me the sergeant at arms?" asked Rodrego.

Alvaraz sent the sergeant at arms, the priest and the officers to the aft deck as requested. Captain Rodrego was leaning on the rail deep in thought. He turned when he saw the men coming and asked, "Sergeant at arms, what have you done with the men who were caught coupling with the natives?"

"One's in the brig. We suspect the other is hiding on the ship. We haven't seen him. One of the men said he saw him slip over the side just as we got underway. He wasn't sure it wasn't a native so he forgot about it until we started asking."

Rodrigo's eyebrows went up, "So you think he's disserted. This is even worse than I thought. I need to come up with a punishment and I need help from all of you."

The priest said, "When we catch men sodomizing each other we give them six lashes for a first offence. This is a similar offence, fornication."

"Find the other man, and if we can't, we'll try the one we have in the morning and give the punishment of six lashes," said Rodrego.

Rodrego hated punishing the men he told Alvaraz. He knew the hardship they were going through and he also knew the consequences of a lack of punishment. Discipline was an absolute necessity on a ship. However as a young man he'd seen good ships ruined because there was too much punishment and also ships ruined because there wasn't enough. In the morning the offenders would be brought forth, a council of officers, the ships priest and Alvaraz would decide the punishment. Then the sergeant at arms would administer the punishment. To soften the action and to unify the crew, he would ask the ship's priest, Father Emilio, to take the offender's confession, and then talk to the men about their responsibility to God and their chances of a good after life. With these thoughts he retired to his cabin, telling Alvaraz, he felt extremely tired and immediately fell into a deep sleep.

Alvaraz was standing on the aft deck when the Cook awakened the Captain with a knock on his door. "Captain, I have your dinner. Would you like me to serve you in your cabin?" he asked.

In a groggy voice Rodrego responded, "Yes, and if you please request Alvaraz and Ismel share my dinner. I want to discuss some problems with them."

"They've eaten, but I'll ask them anyway."

The men met and discussed the dilemma they all shared.

"Alvaraz, you told me, you could barely restrain yourself when you saw the naked women on the island and I think there wasn't a man amongst us who, if answering honestly, wouldn't say the same. We will run into this again, I know we will. The question I have for you is, how can we maintain order?"

Ismel answered, "We must punish the offenders, and put the fear into the men. It's either that or we lose the ship. By the way we searched the ship again looking for Carlos, the other offender, and he was nowhere to be seen."

Rodrego explained his plan for the morning. Ismel agreed and asked that he be allowed to speak to the men after threatening them with twice the punishment and explaining the need for the punishment. "We must make it very clear, this activity will not be tolerated to ensure the safety of the ship. I also want to develop a strategy to keep the islanders off the ship."

They left the cabin together and found the wind had increased and the night sky was obscured with clouds. By the time the gray light of dawn appeared the seas had grown with a howling wind from the west. The ship could no longer be steered on a westerly course. Only two sails flew, to keep the ships bow to the waves, the rest were furled. The incredible motion caused any unsecured items to crash across the deck and be washed overboard by the huge seas. The sailors spent most of the night re-fastening the ship's boats and a number of cannons that had come loose. The planned trial for the morning was forgotten. All the crew could do was hold on and pray the storm would abate.

As Alvaraz watched from the raised after deck, a wave swept across the main deck taking with it two sailors who could be seen thrashing in the sea to port. He couldn't hear the other sailors on deck, because the wind snatched their voices away, but he watched proudly as they ran to the lee side and hauled the men in by their tethers. Alvaraz was struggling down the ladder to assist when he realized he didn't have a tether on. He could see a huge wave rear up and fall towards the deck. He shouted as loud as he could, "Look out there's an even bigger wave coming. Hold on!"

He saw the sailor look up and quickly tie the tethers to a cleat. He pulled himself to the ladder and held on as the green water flooded around him and the ship lurched and heeled as if a giant hand was playing with it. As the water receded, he could see the railing was gone where the sailors had been. The tethers were still tied to the cleat. He looked to windward, decided he had enough time then went as fast as he could to the tethers. He pulled as hard as he could and before long he had one of the men sputtering on deck. They both hauled on the other lines and retrieved the other three. The un-tethered crew had clung to his unconscious mate when the second wave came.

"Give me a hand with this fellow, shouted Alvaraz dragging the unconscious man towards the companionway amid ships. They managed to get below and close the hatch before the next giant wave swept across the deck. Rodrego ordered two additional men to the steering ore to assist with steering, then ordered the crew to stay below.

"We can't afford to lose any sailors," shouted Rodrego, "There's nothing more we can do on deck. This can't last forever; I'm convinced it's not a hurricane. We can wait this out. Come to my cabin and we can have a glass of Madera."

Rodrego's cabin door was stuck shut, when they tried to open it. The Lydia was bending and straining in the seas, but when she came upright for a minute they were able to open the door. The cabin was a wet mess inside with bedding, instruments, charts and clothes piled up on the cabin sole to port. They both sniffed the air simultaneously and Alvaraz said, "it smells like shit in here. Do you have a chamber pot?"

"No, What's that?" asked Rodrego pointing.

There was a young boy huddled in the corner trying to conceal himself with a blanket. Unable to comprehend what he was seeing Rodrego stepped back taking Alvaraz back through the door then closing it.

"I think we have a stowaway from the Island. He must have stowed away in your cabin and hid there," commented Alvaraz.

"Lets find the sergeant at arms. We'll put him in the brig and deal with him later."

The sun came out in the after noon, the wind and waves didn't diminish but clocked around to the south allowing the ship to return to a westerly course. It was much more comfortable with the waves and wind following the ship. The wind slowed down and the waves gradually diminished the following morning. The ship fell back into her routine.

Alvaraz found out he had rescued the sailor who would stand trial for fornication. At noon the court met; the charges were read and the offending sailor was asked to plead. Without hesitation he responded.

"I'm guilty, Captain, and I plead for your mercy."

As planned, the punishment was enacted; followed by confession, a sermon from the priest, and a talk from Ismel.

When the young native boy was brought forward, Rodrego addressed the crew, "Can we train this young lad to be a good sailor? That's the question I have for you. If you agree we will keep him, if not, we will drop him off the next time we make land fall."

Many of the crew wanted to teach him, so he was turned over to the midshipman who would co-ordinate his training.

Chapter 11

The lookout was doubled the next week because low-lying islands were often seen with the potential of unknown reefs in the area. At one point the lookouts reported the ship was sailing through an area of coral heads. Ismel and Rodrego became concerned enough to anchor the Lydia at night only sailing when the sun was high enough to see the deadly coral. It was a frustrating time but, without any charts, this was the only way. On the third day they thought they were free and in deep water, but just at nightfall the ship lurched followed by a resounding cracking noise. They had hit a gigantic coral head. Immediately Alvaraz scrambled below to inspect the damage. There was a tiny leak coming from the curve of the bilge on the port side of the ship. The ship's carpenter rushed up to tell Rodrego, "there is only superficial damage, some caulking has been knocked out and Alvaraz is re-caulking the leaking joint as we speak."

His heart in his mouth Rodrego ordered the ships boat launched to sound the surrounding area. Amazingly the sea had no bottom around the offending coral head. The ship's boats were reloaded on the Lydia that evening as the sun set. They had drifted to the west in the northeast winds and were well away from the menacing coral. They couldn't find bottom to anchor so Rodrego decided to let the ship drift until morning.

The young navigator, Philippe, who was responsible for making charts, stayed in the antechamber of the Captain's cabin that night and discussed the size of the reef they were in. The only measurement they knew for sure was a crude measurement of latitude; they got by using an astrolabe, taken from the elevation of the North Star. They knew they were north of their intended landfall. In the morning they would steer the ship to the southwest keeping a good eye on their latitude. The preferred landfall in the land of King Philip would be San Pedro Bay on the east coast of a large island called Letye. They should be able to find a pilot there to guide them the rest of the way to Manila. No one on the ship had sailed this area before. The only way they could insure that they make San Pedreo Bay safely was to go slow and post many lookouts. The next day the lookouts reported no bottom or land in sight so Rodrego set all sail to the southwest.

"The young native boy is learning some Spanish," reported Ismel, "He's always looking at the water. Sometimes we think he is trying to tell us there is land near by. Before we entered the reef he told us there was land ahead. We don't know how he knows but now he tells us there is no land around. He's a good sailor and the men are treating him well."

"This is a good thing. Maybe he will replace Carlos. Do you think Carlos survived on the island?" asked Rodrego not expecting a reply.

The days went by quickly as the Lydia, her cream colored sails filled with the warm trade winds, her tan streamers floating with the wind before the ship as it moved across the water. On the fifth day after they left the reef Ismel came to Rodrego's cabin to report "Nino is telling us there is land to the northwest."

"Who is Nino?" asked Rodrego.

"It's the name the men have given the young native boy sir."

"Have the lookouts seen anything?"

"No, all they see is a long strait horizon with the occasional cloud."

"Keep a sharp lookout," was all Rodrego could think to say.

On the following morning, sure enough the lookout called down to let them know there were clouds on the horizon that could be hiding some land. That afternoon they all saw it. It was definitely land, marked by faded green hills delineating the horizon. Nino pointed at some birds then indicated he could smell the land. Sure enough they all sniffed and agreed there was the smell of land in the wind.

"Do you think he knows there is land by smelling the air?" asked the young cartographer.

"We must teach him more Spanish. I think he has a lot to teach us," said Ismel.

The Lydia was moving well, rolling down the swells, caused by the dependable northeast trade winds. There was a shout from the crow's nest.

"We see a sail on the horizon. The ship is hull down, so we can't make out her colors."

There was a lot of excitement, but Rodrego remained calm, giving orders to ready the guns and adjust the course to intercept the unknown ship. Within the hour it was obvious the ship was a coastal lugger, with a Spanish flag flying proudly. Alvaraz, who knew the design intimately, identified her, as one used in the fishing trade in the Mediterranean.

"She's probably a coastal trader." remarked Alvaraz.

As they watched, the other ship changed course heading directly towards them on a tight reach. In less than an hour Rodrego gave the order for the Lydia to heave-to. The other ship, her Spanish flag flapping proudly in the brisk wind, came up along side dropping her sails as she passed. The crew of both ships lined the rails, shouting greetings and questions. Both ships drifted while a contingent of crew from the smaller vessel boarded the long boat they were towing and rowed to the Lydia.

"Welcome aboard," shouted Rodrego as the Captain of the other ship was saluted as he came up the boarding ladder.

His name was Capitan Don Ramondo de Cordoba. No one had expected Rodrego or any ship from New Spain. The two Captains filled each other in on what they knew of as current events. Ramondo's coastal lugger was one of the ships assigned to the duty of charting the islands. They were on their way to an archipelago in the South. The islands of King Phillip were being charted from the outer most islands then the inner islands would follow. Rodrego was happy to hear the route to Manila through the islands was partially charted and Ramondo would lend him a pilot to transit the narrow channel leading from San Padro Bay between the large islands of Leyete and Samar.

"You will find many tribal people there. It's best to avoid them. Keep your guns primed and ready with shot. These people can be aggressive. Your pilot Gugo speaks some of the dialects from this part of the land. He speaks enough Spanish to communicate with you but he has a mischievous nature. My advice is to not go ashore at all and don't let Gugo go either. He's probably too afraid of most of the people here to even speak with them. Here are my best charts." He laid them out and instructed Rodrego and Philippe on their use.

"Make a copy of this and return it to the Naval base in Manila. Please feel free to add to it if you want to help in the charting."

Ramondo was very enthusiastic about the project to bring people to New Spain from the islands of King Phillip.

"Manila is full of strong young men who build ships. You won't have any problems recruiting them. Many of them are trained in the shipbuilding trade. My ship Ninette was build in Manila in the yard of Campandaro. I will give you a note of introduction to the owner. His name is Timotemo."

Alvaraz didn't recognize the wood Ninette was made from and asked, "Where did the wood come from to build your ship? Is it durable as well as having that beautiful color?"

"It's wood from the local forests and is used in boat building every where here. It's a type of mahogany," responded Ramondo.

Chapter 12

The meeting only lasted for a few hours. Alvaraz, Rodrego and his crew watched, as the other ship made sail, moving toward the south. There was an excitement in the air with the anticipation of making landfall. Alvaraz felt particularly good. He had consumed many glasses of Maderia wine and as he absently stared out at the land, he thought, I will suffer for the wine so I might as well enjoy this feeling of elation. He leaned on the rail drinking in the beauty while the fresh breeze cooled his cheek. Details of palm forest could be seen as they sailed around the point into San Padro Bay. It was strange to feel the Lydia settle into the calm waters, out of the swell that had rolled the ship for months on the Pacific.

Two sailors on the foredeck carefully sounded the depths in the dark. They anchored deep in the bay coming to rest near the beginning of the channel. All along the shore they could see the fires of villages and smell their cooking fires.

With only a red flame from the morning sun lighting the clouds a contingent of canoes could be seen paddling from the far off shore towards the Lydia. To the men's unaccustomed noses the air had a heavy scent of old cooking fires, rotting humus, and the scent of frangipani flowers. The sight of a dozen canoes, with warriors brightly decorated with colorful bird feathers brandishing long deadly looking spears, filled Alvaraz with a mixture of fear and excitement. He nervously pulled his blunderbuss from its holster and examined the shot and firing mechanism. Behind him he could hear Ismel ordering the gun crews to prepare the cannons with shot and carefully position them to fire from all quadrants if necessary. Rodrego was speaking to Gugo with the help of his officers.

"We need you to translate. Do you understand?"

Gugo with a big smile responded by saying, "you have many guns. You should kill all these people. They don't know how to talk."

Rodrego looked him in the eyes and said, "You will talk to these people."

Looking pale in the morning light, his anxiety was plain to see as he fidgeted, his head turning from side to side at the assembled officers. "They don't like my people and will kill me when they see me. I don't talk to these people."

The lead canoe came up and stopped, facing the Lydia. A man spoke in a loud voice from the center of the canoe.

"What are they saying?" asked Rodrego. "Answer them."

Gugo looked helpless and said nothing. Finally the young officers pushed him up to the rail and he spoke in a language that sounded to Alvaraz like a monkey chattering.

The man in the lead canoe shouted at one of the other canoes and it came forward. They pulled a young paddler from his seat and stood him on the rail of the canoe. He immediately started to talk very fast to Gugo. Before he could say much the man beside him silenced him with a blow to his head.

Alvaraz moved closer to hear Gugo's translation. "He is slave and they kill him. They kill all his family." Gugo said with a satisfied smile on his face.

The young man spoke with his captors then said something Gugo translated as; "they want to trade for metal. They have fruits and fish for trade."

Rodrego talked to his officers and then gave Gugo instructions. "Tell them we want to trade. Tell them if we find any of their people on our ship we will, without hesitation, kill them. We will launch a boat and all trading will happen away from the Lydia. If there is any aggression towards our boat crew, we will open fire with our cannons and kill all of them. Tell them we will show them what will happen to them if they don't follow these rules. We will fire one of our cannons to show them."

Gugo translated to the boy who translated to the chief. After this Rodrego repeated the part about the practice gunfire and confirmed the islanders understood.

"Ismel have them fire the forward cannon close to the canoes, but don't hurt any of them.

The sound of the cannon, the smoke and the sea rising up as the shot struck the surface paralyzed the islanders and for a full minute after the shot there was absolute silence.

"Find some metal and beads and lower the aft long boat," ordered Rodrego.

The trading went as planned with no problems. Gugo smiled proudly and marched about like it was his idea. Fresh fruit vegetables and even a pair of squealing pigs were exchanged for a number of knife blades and a few bags of shiny beads.

While the trading was going on Alvaraz stood at the rail talking with Nino. In his primitive Spanish he told Alvaraz he knew some of the words of the Chief. Alvaraz thought this unlikely as Nino came from an Island a good thousand miles to the east, but then he thought maybe Nino's people were related to these people.

Rodrego sent a boat to explore the channel they were to transit that was reported to lead to an inland sea. With the heat of midday the islanders returned to their villages and the ships boat returned with good news. The channel was wide and deep with a tidal current running east with the flood tide.

"The tide will be lowest early in the morning. We should sail at first light and I will show you the way through the chanel to the inner sea." Gugo explained to Rodrego, "When we get to the inland sea we should sail all the next day through the night and the following day. If you would like we can anchor in a bay not far from Manila where I have family."

Before the sun rose on the second day, the sounds of shouted orders could be heard across the water. The anchor was hauled up, as the topsails were set. The Lydia slowly moved, seemingly towards the beach. Two long boats fully manned towed her towards the channel accompanied by canoes filled with islanders shouting and cheering excitedly. Within hours they were well on their way. The channel proved wide enough to set more sail, the long boats were hauled aboard, and the Lydia lost the flotilla of canoes. Gugo repeatedly told Rodrego to be careful of the people who lived on the other side of the Island. He heard they were very fierce, could move like ghosts, and liked to eat the brains of strong men. Sure enough, as the Lydia made the final turn pushed with the remnants of the trade winds into the inland sea, a new flotilla of canoes appeared paddling strongly towards the Lydia. The crew took up arms and stood guard along the railings of the ship with the anticipation of problems.

When the canoes were near enough to see details of their occupants Alvaraz became very apprehensive. The natives were brandishing spears decorated with the traditional colorful bird feathers as well as being crowned with human skulls.

"We need to teach these people some respect," commented Rodrego to Alvaraz and his officers. "Fire shot to land between us," he ordered Ismel.

The order was given; the loud crack of the cannon followed by the sea rising between the Lydia and the canoes had no effect. The canoes came at them at an increased rate.

"Fire into the lead canoe," ordered Rodrego coldly.

This time with the crack of the cannon at close range, the lead canoe vanished into a mass of flesh and wood flying into the air, leaving a red haze drifting over the sea. The two canoes immediately behind were both sinking spewing their contents of injured men and belongings into the sea. The dozen or so canoes following, paddled in confused circles dragging the injured and dead into their boats. There was no more aggression and the Lydia sailed into the evening with a steady breeze form the east.

The charts given Rodrego from Ramondo showed open water for two days sailing. So after posting double watches with men doing constant soundings Rodrego retired to his cabin. Alvaraz was invited with the other officers for their customary evening glass of Madeira wine after the meal, but they all knew to give Rodrego time to complete his log.

Alvaraz walked towards Ismel, the gunnery officer and the navigator who were talking excitedly with some of the crew as they watching a large fish swimming beside the ship. As Alvaraz approached, the gunnery officer shouted, "Alvaraz look at this fish, it's not a dolphin or a whale, its tail is erect not flat."

The fish was swimming in step close to the Lydia. "It looks like a large shark," said Alvaraz as he watched its huge dorsal fin and tail fin slicing through the water and its whale sized spotted brown body rise and sink in the waves beside the Lydia.

"What does this mean? Do you think it will attack us? Should we prepare a gun to shoot it?" The gunnery officer asked Ismel.

As quickly as it had appeared it disappeared into the sea and Ismel commented, "I don't think there is any need to prepare a gun. What a strange apparition. I wonder what it means. Could it be a message from God…or the Devil?"

As Alvaraz stood in the waist of the ship with the other men, watching the sea, he realized this land was so full of people and strange animals. New Spain has many strange animals but was empty of people. Here in the islands of King Philip the people come out in the hundreds to greet or attack them. But in New Spain the few people are diseased and flee the minute they see us. 'Where is God in this?' he thought. Were the islands of King Philip the true Garden of Eden contaminated with the evil the devil brought after Adam was tempted by the apple? Could it be God punished the people of New Spain because of their evil and gave the land to the Spanish to cleanse and make pure in the eyes of God. If he now brought people from the land of King Philip to New Spain would he be contaminating the purity of New Spain?

"Captain Rodrego is inviting us for a glass of wine." It was Ismel stirring Alvaraz from his thoughts.

On the morning of the second day, Gugo pointed to a bay on and informed Rodrego this was a good anchorage. "This is where my family lives. The people are good and friendly," he said. Rodrego prepared the Lydia to repel boarders then sailed the ship towards the bay. As usual, a flotilla of canoes came out. Some of the canoes had sails, made of canvas, making the canoes go even faster, in the evening breeze. This time Gugo didn't need to be asked to speak. He was on the rail shouting at the approaching canoes before they were within earshot.

"This is my family," he informed Rodrego in between shouting to the approaching canoes.

"Inform your family, we will not tolerate any one trying to board the ship. If anyone tries we will shoot to kill," ordered Rodrego.

Gugo couldn't believe his ears, "These are my people, they won't hurt anyone," he said with a disappointed look on his face.

"Do as I say or you'll be thrown overboard," shouted Rodrego. He then turned to Ismel and ordered the cannons loaded with shot to protect all quadrants.

As the lead canoe came along side Gogo relayed the orders he had been given, then said something that made the crew of the first canoe burst out laughing. Gugo talked for a few minutes then told Rodrego, "The people will be good, they don't want to trade, they have metal and beads, but they do want us to attend a feast today."

The Lydia was brought to the head of the bay where the water was smooth and clear, the shadow of the ship could be seen sixty feet down on the sandy bottom. The sun rose in the sky defining the palms waving in the breeze along the shore, the blue sky meeting the green land then the turquoise sea visibly supporting the bulk of the Lydia as she sat suspended between sky and sea. Alvaraz again was entranced and he thanked God for showing him these wonders. In the background he heard Rodrego giving orders to lower a long boat. He would be going ashore with a dozen crew and his navigator. Alvaraz hurried to the boat deck hoping he would be invited.

Rodrego welcomed him with, "Of course you should come. If all is well we will split the crew, one half to go ashore on leave and the other to guard the ship. I like this place."

It was difficult for the oarsman to row because the canoes insisted on paddling so close to the long boat. When they got to the shore a dozen strong men pulled the long boat up the beach before any of the crew could disembark. They were immediately escorted to a large hut on the beach, lead by Gugo, who was talking excitedly to the people around him. "We are going to the Chief's house," he said to Rodrego.

The hut was large and airy with a grove of palms shading it. There was a fence made of woven palm thatch surrounding the hut with mature blooming hibiscus and plumeria scenting the air.

"Only Rodrego should go to see the chief, we must all wait here in the courtyard," said Gugo with an unusual serious look on his face.

They were shown to a palapa shelter where there were chairs and crude tables. Young topless women brought them drinks in cups made of coconut shells, and platters of dried fish and fruit. Alvaraz diverted his eyes, pretending he was studying the beautiful shells used as plates on the platters.

The day progressed well. Alvaraz stayed with Rodrego and the navigator while the men were taken to a stream to bathe. The chief appeared to be very old, and on his left sat his queen, a very heavy lady, her hair piled on her head and adorned with colorful beads and shells. Alvaraz was pleased to see her breasts were covered with a necklace of carved abalone and beads. The chief had a translator who spoke better Spanish than Gugo. The Chief asked Alvaraz if he wanted to take any of the men from his village to New Spain and did he want any of the women. The Chief explained that he had many mouths to feed and the land wasn't large enough to hold them all. He then confirmed they were all welcome at the feast that was already in progress at the center of the village.

Alvaraz was dismissed and shown into the village square where he met the other crew. They were in good spirits after bathing in a stream behind the village. Alvaraz asked Gugo if he could bath there too.

Gugo was slightly intoxicated after drinking tubo, a wine made from the sap of the palm tree. He looked quizzically at Alvaraz then seemed to make up his mind about something.

"I like your golden hair," he smiled, then laughed heartily and shouted at a man he introduced as his brother.

"You want to bath, yes of course, the path is over there," he said as his brother looked at his hair and then seemingly studied his body.

"My brother will take you to the place to bath," he said between laughing.

The brother returned a short time later to guide him to the bathing pool. He led Alvaraz up a path between large stones where a clear stream ran. They got to a place where sparkling water ran into a large pool with golden sand lining the bottom. The brother indicated this was the place and left.

It was a very quiet place, the air was warm and the only sounds were the water running, the warm breeze blowing through the nearby palms and a few insect and bird calls. He was alone. In his modesty he walked back down the path to confirm he was alone then disrobed folding his clothes neatly on a stone by the bank and fell into the pure water. He felt erotic and decided to touch himself, then remembered the priest's warning about sin. He came out of the water and sat warming himself in the sun when he heard very faint footsteps behind him. He turned and saw her. She wore flowered leis over her chest, but he could see one of her breasts standing firmly. She held in her hands a sponge, a brush and something that appeared to be soap. Without hesitation she came to him and began to wash his naked body. Her small hands worked diligently, gently massaging and cleaning his head, his ears, his neck, then under his arms and his back. Not a word was spoken. He watched and listened to her smile and gently laugh when he squirmed. She worked her way down to his waist and rubbed his belly finding his erect member. She gaily laughed and reaching in around his waist putting her head on his shoulder and smiled invitingly as she rubbed her breasts on his shoulder.

    He was in shock. Never had he been so aroused. His seemed ready to burst. She gently pulled him into a standing position. He didn't resist and stood, trying to ignore his rock hard organ sticking out in front of him. He knew if she touched it, it would explode, but instead she removed her grass skirt and lay on the mossy rock beside him. She spread her legs and with her fingers reached down and parted her labia. He could see the pink flesh of her vagina, overflowing with glistening mucus, framed by her thick black bush. Without hesitation he quickly knelt between her legs his heart seemingly in his throat, and she guided his throbbing phallus into her vagina. He could feel himself being engulfed, his seed pumping out of his penis as his thighs madly pumped. His mind clouded, with a mist studded with bursting stars of pleasure as he lay on her soft nakedness.

    He came out of his haze slowly recognizing the sin he had committed. He felt her arms around him and her legs pulling his pelvis into her squirming vulva. He forced himself to disengage against his desire to stay in this position forever. She didn't resist and let him go. He looked for his clothes. His confusion was evident as he grabbed them from the rock then carried them into the water so he could wash himself. He put them back then looked at her again. She seemed to be bent over crying. He put his clothes back on the rock and went to her. He lifted her head; there were tears in her eyes. She stood, and held him, her naked breasts pressing on his chest. His limp penis became erect and a wave of lust past through him. They kissed as she pushed his erect member between her legs. A few minutes later she sat down on the mossy stone and took his penis into her mouth looking up to him with her legs open to him. She took his erection out of her mouth and lay before him. He followed her and again lay with her. This time they rocked gently for some time. He could feel his orgasm was close but his thrusting didn't seem to bring it closer. He could feel her body stiffen and move with renewed strength under him. She was making sounds like a hurt animal. She started to gasp with her pubis pushing against him. Her vagina tightened around his organ and they simultaneously clung to each other, their bodies one in a crystal haze of bursting white light as their orgasms flooded their minds with pleasure. This time he didn't disengage immediately but lay with her as she rocked on his still erect penis bringing herself to a series of orgasms.

They stayed at the bathing pool for a long time. Alvaraz had never been so close to anyone. He looked at her; she didn't have an attractive face. He wondered if she were here at the request of the Devil, but he couldn't believe all this pleasure came from the Devil and if it did, he would surely worship Satin. He abruptly decided this was God's Garden of Eden and all that had transpired was the work of God in his everlasting light.

He was deep in these thoughts when she left without him knowing. He stood to find her but she was nowhere to be found. He was alone. Could this have all been a dream? As he walked back to the village he resolved to tell no one. If Rodrego found out about it, he would surely have to punish Alvaraz as he had the other crewmember for fornication.

"Alvaraz, we've been looking for you, you've missed the party and the palm wine," said Philippe, Alvaraz's cabin mate and the navigator of the ship, his voice slightly slurred with the liquor.

"I was bathing in the stream and got lost after I followed it up the hill."

"The last boat is leaving to exchange the crew, do you want to come," Phil asked.

"Yes I should go back."

They walked to the beach together, Phil chattering about all the wonders he had seen and Alvaraz silently trying to resolve the contradictions in his life. On the one hand he felt proud and wanted to tell Phil or anyone about the wonders he had experience; his feeling of contentment and satiation, he was no longer a virgin. At the age of twenty-four he had been with a women; he was close to hysteria with excitement; on the other hand there was a deep loathing, a fear and he wanted to see the priest to confess his sins.

The ship seemed deserted except for the crew left behind to guard the Lydia. Rodrego was still with the chief. The priest had found a native man who was teaching the people about God and was still ashore. Alvaraz suddenly felt lonely and wanted to go back to the beach, but resolved to stay on the ship. He paced back and forth speaking to the crew and the gunnery officer. Everyone aboard had returned from shore so Alvaraz listened to their stories, while staying silent. It seemed the other men had gone to a pool much further down stream than he. There were four bathing pools, one for men, one for women, one for couples, and the highest was for bathing royalty or the Chiefs and their families. Time went by slowly; he could hear and smell the feast long after the sun set. He watched Venus follow the sun towards the horizon and the moonrise dulling the clarity of the stars then from the beach he saw the boats returning. Most of the men came aboard drunk from palm wine with cheery faces and sunburned cheeks. Rodrego ascended the boarding ladder with the priest who was excitedly telling him about a baptism he performed that afternoon on a dozen willing natives.

"Good evening Alvaraz," said Rodrego, "did you have a good day?"

"Yes, I enjoyed the hospitality of the natives this morning and had a good bath. What about you?" said Alvaraz with a grin like the Cheshire cat on his lips.

"I spent too much time with the chief. He and his wife took me to the royal bath. They were both carried on a litter while I walked. I must say it was lovely, but they insisted I swim naked. I did strip down to my drawers, but there is a limit. Later I inspected the canoes and watercraft. The Chief has a large out rigger canoe over forty feet long under a palm mat. I wish you were there to see how they build these large ocean-going out rigger canoes. They are lashed and pined with cordage made from the fibers of the palm trees; the sails are made from the woven leaves. They use these trees for everything. We must bring back nuts to New Spain. They tell me they are easy to grow, but the wood is useless as it rots very quickly."

"You like her!" shouted Gugo, interrupting Rodrego, coming up behind Alvaraz and slapping him on the back.

"She like him," said Gugo drunkenly. Then he wandered off with some of the other drunken sailors.

Alvaraz turned bright scarlet in the lamplight, but Rodrego paid no attention to Gugo and continued "Gugo has agreed to pilot us the rest of the way to Manila. The Chief says he's their best pilot. Gugo told us how Nino tells where the land is. He studies the pattern of the waves and can see the reflection of the land moving through the normal waves for hundreds of miles. I'm glad Nino didn't go ashore; Gugo said if he did, because he can't talk to the people, they would kill him or enslave him. I hope these men are sober in the morning. We will sail with first light."

With that Alvaraz was left standing on the deck, the smell of burning lamp oil from the ship's lights mixed with the scent of humus and frangipani moving in the warm breeze from the shore. Rodrego retired to his cabin, undoubtedly to record his day in his log and Alvaraz stood staring at the shore with his warm memories of the day.

Alvaraz dreamed that night of frangipani scented beaches and the touch of the young maiden he had encountered at the bath. His mind was slowly turning to resist the teachings of the priest. His world was expanding and his understanding of religion was being pushed aside by the touch and smell of the tropics. The pleasure and truth he was experiencing was eclipsing anything from his childhood. In his dreams he drank in his new knowledge and proudly displayed his erect cock to the maiden he knew would accept and love him as God had made him. The creaking of the capstan raising the anchor crept into his paradise. He awoke, leaping from his berth, his dream of diving into the warm green ocean and swimming to the shore, to share his happiness with the islanders, instantly faded from his mind as he faced the gray dawn light and the earnest crew on deck.

Chapter 13

Before the sun was fully up, the Lydia had found the swell of the China Sea in the light trade winds coming from the beach. She worked her way out into deep water making enough room to clear the next point.

Morning prayer came with the priest giving a sermon about the power of God and how the people of the village were being purified through baptism from their evil ways. Alvaraz didn't have much to do and because he couldn't talk to anyone of his anxiety he walked around the upper deck in deep thought.

"You seem troubled," said Ismel with a quizzical smile, "I've been watching you pacing up and down all morning. I don't know what it is but you seem changed, Alvaraz"

"I guess I just want to get to Manila. It's so close now. I've been thinking of how to choose the men we should take back. The chief of the last village wanted me to take people from his village. I will be taking these people from their families, probably never to return."

"May be you should talk to the priest," said Ismel.

"Good idea. Have you seen him lately?"

"I think he's on the foredeck at his confessional."

This would be a good excuse, to give his confession, without suspicion, thought Alvaraz.

The priest was on the foredeck being taught to tie a Monkey's fist by some crewmembers

"I had the same problem, Father. Think of it as the ears of a rabbit, then always go under his nose like this," Alvaraz instructed, trying to help the priest remember how to tie the complicated knot.

"You look troubled Alvaraz, is there something I can do?" asked Father Emilio.

"There is Father. I would like to do confession," Alvaraz said with a resigned trepidation in his voice, not being able to keep eye contact with the priest. The instant he said these words he felt better.

"I've already done confessions, son," he looked at the sailors around him and asked to be excused, "come."

They walked the short distance to where the priest traditionally took confession. It was between the bulwarks and the bits holding the bowsprit. It was protected from the wind and usually shaded by a sail. The priest sat on one side of the bowsprit facing the sea, the confessor on the other side.

"Let us pray," said the priest. They both got on their knees, the priest praying to receive this man's confession and Alvaraz silently uttering the same words.

"I have sinned, Father. I have been with a woman and committed fornication with her," he stated expecting to be struck down as he spoke.

"Are these all your sins," asked the priest after several moments of silence.

"I have thought carnal thoughts and ask forgiveness."

"May the Lord hear your prayer and forgive your sins," Prayed the priest. "Six Hail Marys and five minutes of prayer each morning to ask forgiveness."

Alvaraz couldn't believe his ears; he was expecting a hundred Hail Marys and series of self-flagellations. He had been given worse for the sin of envy.

They prayed together as the ship gently rose to the swell. When they were through Alvaraz asked the priest. "Why was my penance so light?"

"My son, I am only the instrument between you and God. It was not I who took your confession. It was between you and God. Go now, go and live for God."

With renewed spirit Alvaraz smiled and chatted with the men on his way to his cabin to do his penance. He ran into Gugo as he entered the companionway.

"You like her?" asked Gugo.

"What do you know about this?" asked Alvaraz.

"I like your blue hair and blond eyes, my brother say you strong in your chest; make good paddler."

Angrily Alvaraz asked, not bothering to correct Gugo's somewhat amusing Spanish, "What does this have to do with anything."

"The girl my brother's oldest daughter. She don't have man. She want baby. You make strong baby."

Alvaraz was horrified as the implications sank in. "You mean this was all staged. What if she does have a baby by me? Who will look after it? I can't go back as the father."

"I father, my brother father, he have many mothers, many aunties. He grow strong and big. He be shipbuilder like you." Gugo said while pointing to Alvaraz.

"How do you know it will be a boy? How do you even know she will have a baby?" Alvaraz responded angrily in a quiet voice looking around to see if anyone was listening.

Somewhat put out, Gugo responded, "She have baby, maybe she have girl baby. That girl baby have many babies, the first boy baby be strong like you, he be shipbuilder like you," he said trying to appease Alvaraz.

"Don't tell anyone about this, understand, or I'll break every bone in your body."

"Don't worry boss, you strong man, I don't tell anybody," said Gugo sheepishly.

Alvaraz worriedly ran down the steps, he found no one listening, then carried on to his cabin to do his penance.

Chapter 14

The morning of the second day they could see the masts of many ships on the other side of the final outcropping of land as they entered the bay of Manila. The wind died so the boats were put out to tow the Lydia to the anchorage. Manila was a bustling port with many large colonial buildings lining the shore with a half dozen ships of different nationalities anchored in the bay. As they approached, a longboat hailed them with instructions from the Port Captain, word from the Governor's office and an invitation to have an audience with the governor when they were settled. Instead of posting a full guard of half the crew to repel boarders, Rodrego ordered a two man twenty-four hour watch be set allowing the crew to go ashore on leave. Before they got to the beach, the entire town knew of the ship from New Spain and why she was here. A crowd of strong native men asked, as they were mounting the steps to the road above the harbor, in broken Spanish, how they could sign up to go to New Spain. Alvaraz was astonished and pleased with the enthusiasm, but told the men he would arrange interviews; then asked the purser to take the names of the men. He would contact them after he had spoken to the representatives of the Governor.

Rodrego, Philippe, and Alvaraz proceeded to the office of the Port Captain to clear their ship in and get permission for their crew to come ashore. While they were there Alvaraz asked where he could find the office of Timotemo, of the yard of Campandaro.

"He won't be at his yard today, but I think he would be pleased to see you at his house. It's not far—take the street beside the church. His house is at the top of the hill at the end of the road," answered the clerk to his enquiry.

Just as they left the building Alvaraz heard something he hadn't heard for a long time; the sound of a shorn horse pulling a carriage with iron wheels down a cobbled street. It approached them and stopped beside them. A man dressed in a light shirt and pantaloons stepped out. He was young, with the bearing of an older nobleman, his chin up, eyes staring straight ahead in a formal way. He greeted the men with a slight bow sweeping his feathered hat before him and said, "Antonio Saavedra at your service."

From the perspective of a passerby the scene would have been comical. An elegant young noble, exiting from his beautiful carriage, bowing to three scraggly sailors on the street. Each sailor in turn addressed Antonio, mustering as much bluster as they could in the circumstances, while introducing themselves.

Rodrego asked, "and who is this beautiful maid riding with you?"

Antonio stood beside the door to his carriage and introduced his new bride. "This is Antoinette Maria Saavedra's de la Courcey of the house of Timon."

She elegantly held her hand out the door as the three sailors took it in turn, introduced themselves, bowed, and stepped back.

"We heard you were new arrivals, it's a pleasant day, so we made an outing of it and by chance, have found you. You must understand there isn't a lot to do here and we wondered if we could have the honor of your company for the evening meal."

"We would be honored, I'm sure," said Rodrego looking at his men for any protests.

"We should first send a signal to the ship, telling them they are free to land the crew for their shore leave," said Philippe.

"Of course. Could I offer you the services of my carriage?"

"If there's room, yes, we'd love to ride in a carriage.

They all crowded into the carriage. Antoinette smiled, obviously enjoying all the burley men around her. After sending the boat crew back to the ship with news of shore leave Antonio and Antoinette took the sailors up a hill to a large house snugly built into a courtyard with a large patio in front with a view of the harbor.

They were shown to a guest area where servants brought them water and soap to wash and shave themselves. Alvaraz was first to finish his ablutions. His hair was freshly washed and it hung stylishly to his shoulders. He wore a new white shirt and imagined himself to be quite handsome as he sat on a stairway leading down from the patio. A forest of ferns and young palms surrounded him. The warm breeze was scented with the flowers on the hill. Alvaraz had a strong feeling of familiarity with this place. There was something here he knew. He looked across the garden into what appeared to be a neighbor's garden and saw her. She was staring at him. When she realized he had noticed her, she immediately turned her head, avoiding his stare. She was tall with long delicate fingers, her black hair combed above the flower resting on her ear. Her skin was light with just a touch of chocolate, the shape of her body and upturned breasts clearly visible through the yellow sari she wore. He only saw her for a fleeting minute then she was gone. Alvaraz was positive he had seen her before.

Antonio was the grandson of Saavedra, one of the first explorers to occupy Manila some forty years earlier. Presently he and his bride were on an extended honeymoon sailing half way around the world in an Indiamen ship to arrive at his grandfather's estate in Manila. He sat spell bound as Alvaraz told of his journey through New Spain.

The main course consisted of three dishes; fish, beef, and chicken. They were all prepared in ways the sailors had never tasted before. The fish wasn't cooked with heat but, as Antoinette explained, cooked in vinegar with spices.

"This is a land where there is no shortage of spices. We have two farms where we grow nothing but spices for Europe. One farm is along the beach to the north, and the other is in the mountains to the east. We are experimenting with teas. You might have seen the tea bushes in the garden. We also grow palms for palm wine and the flesh of the coconut can be dried and shipped." She explained proudly.

"Everything here is different, the fruits, the trees, the animals and birds; we've never seen anything like them in Spain. God has truly blessed this land with his bounty," added Antonio.

"Speaking of your garden," remarked Alvaraz, "This afternoon I wandered through it, and must say I was impressed. It is well done and the views of the harbor are extraordinary. I felt like I was in a part of Heaven itself. I wanted to ask you about something I saw. There was a young woman, dressed in silk, who was gazing at me. When I returned her gaze, she immediately disappeared like a fleeting bird. Who was this young woman?"

"Oh, you must have seen Gemelda. She is the daughter of our neighbor,

Timotemo Singh. He is closely associated with the Raj of Timor. They are a powerful family who assisted the Spanish in bringing order to this land. These people are Moslems and in so many ways don't respect the true calling of Christianity. You should stay away from her." instructed Antonio.

In defense Alvaraz said, "I knew many Moors in Spain and some of my finest shipbuilders were Moslems. The teachings of their Allah are similar to the teachings of our Lord. What I didn't like was their need to stop everything and pray at the most inappropriate times."

They all laughed as Alvaraz described a Moor running out from beneath a plank leaving it suspended by struggling Christians. "They are good at math and sums if you need to calculate the volume of a ship."

The lively talk went on well into the night. The men were invited to take the guest rooms and a runner was sent to the Lydia's launch to inform the officer on watch of their unplanned absence.

When Alvaraz awoke he found a message telling him Timotemo was awaiting him at his convenience for a late breakfast at his house next door to Antonio and Antoinette's place. The clerk at the Port Captain's office had sent him a message telling him of Alvaraz's request to see him. He dressed and accepted the offer of a servant barber to shave him and trim his hair. The image he saw in the mirror was of a young powerful man; square jawed, striking blue eyes all accented nicely on his well-tanned face. He wished the barber had simply cut off his hair. It looked so out of place. He supposed he was the only person on this land with blond hair. He wished there was a way for him to color it.

Timotemo's house was equally nice, but built more in the Moorish style with a pillared entrance way. A servant, dressed in the Indian style, wearing gold earrings and a plain sari, greeted him. She was old and had a black wart on the side of her nose, but she smiled and pleasantly invited him in, speaking Spanish with the typical Moorish accent.

"Please come in, my master wants you to think of this house as your house."

Alvaraz was shown to a shaded patio with a beautiful view of the harbour. He looked over the railing and saw the place where Gemelda had stood while staring at him. He turned and there she stood, shyly saying, "My father will be with you in a minute. Please come sit."

As he sat in the comfortable wicker chair her hand brushed his shoulder. He could smell the sent of Jasmine on her. It was as if he were being engulfed in an envelope of familiarity. The stroke of her hand over his shoulder left a tingling sensation and her body radiated comfortable warmth as she leaned over him scenting the air with her perfume.

They were interrupted by the squeal of Gemelda's two young sisters.

"Is this the man with blond hair?" shouted the youngest as she came bubbling onto the patio.

"Get out of here, Minerva, and you too, Ranji. Father is to meet with this man on business," scolded Gemelda.

Alvaraz looked around to see a man shooing out his daughters. He was dressed like an urbane Spaniard except on his head he wore a small red turban.

"Greetings master shipwright Alvaraz. Let me introduce myself. I am Timotemo Singh, the proprietor of the shipyard Campandaro. Usually I have meetings like this to attract a customer to allow me to build them a ship. I understand you on the other hand want not only to go into competition with me, but also take away my most valuable commodity, my trained ship builders What benefit would this be to me?"

"Please understand," Alvaraz explained, "I would not be in competition with you on the other side of the world. I am to build ships for New Spain, to be used to carry treasure home to Spain and bring workers from here to the unpopulated New world."

As he explained this, Gemelda brought plates of food and jugs of drink. It was hard for Alvaraz to concentrate as he felt her intoxicating influence. When she came near leaning over him, touching his arm as she poured fresh juice he lost his train of thought.

"Gemie, why are you serving? Where is Gelbinde?" asked Timotemo.

"She is in the kitchen cooking your eggs father," she answered boldly.

"You are obviously disturbing Master Alvaraz's thoughts. Please leave us now."

"Yes, Father," she answered ignoring his request while asking Alvaraz how he liked his eggs cooked.

"It seems—if I had some interest in your enterprise, I would be willing to help supply some men. Failing that, I can only tell you where to find the best stock of men for the trade. There is a village at the north end of the bay past my palm gardens. These people have been building watercraft for eternity. I've found them easy to train. If you talk to the chief and tell him you are my friend, I'm sure he will help you. How many men do you need?"

"I would like a hundred," answered Alvaraz.

"A hundred is a lot, but you shouldn't have any trouble."

"You will need a room to interview these people and keep records. I can help you with this. I have an empty room for rent on the street just above the quay."

Alvaraz hadn't thought of a space to keep records and administer the project. He readily agreed on the price, thanked Timotemo and left to find Rodrego. Gemelda, who wasn't far away escorted Alvaraz to the entrance and even followed him to the road. He turned back, after a few steps, waving and taking in her enchantment. She stood dressed in a peach colored sari loosely hanging over one shoulder, her angular facial bones enhanced the contrasting coloring of her eyebrows and full lips. He heard her father calling her, he stumbled, recovered and when he looked back she was gone.

Alvaraz ran into the ship's purser and some of the crew on his way to the dock. He was told Rodrego was aboard the Lydia. He wanted to have her hauled and had instructed the purser to look for supplies for the return trip.

"I have a key to a room I've rented on the shore to be used as an office for my recruitment project," Alvaraz told the purser showing him the key. "Let's go there now and inspect it. I will need someone to keep records, with the Captain's permission, would you like to use the office for stores and help me with the records?"

They examined the office and found it was more than an office. It had two floors, the second having a large deck overlooking the quay.

"This will do nicely," said the purser. "I'll use this desk down stairs and you can do your interviewing up stairs."

"I'm going to find Rodrego and tell him about this. I also want him to use Timotemo's yard for the hall out, because he has been so kind to us."

Rodrego was pleased with the office and suggested they bring in hammocks to stay in the upstairs room while the ship was being hauled. He found the office of Campandaro and made the arrangements to have the

Lydia hauled. The manager told Rodrego the Lydia would be the largest ship they had ever hauled. Just as he was leaving the office he met Timotemo walking towards the office of the Lydia. They entered the office together. Alvaraz dashed down the stairs when he saw them and introduced them.

"Allow me to introduce Captain Rodrego to you, Timotemo." Alvaraz said happily, "He has just been to your office to arrange for the hauling of the Lydia."

"My pleasure, I'm sure," answered Timotemo, with a flourish. "I've just come to see that everything is satisfactory, and glad I did, for now I have met the famous Captain Rodrego."

The two men entered into a discussion on trade with New Spain. Timotemo understood New Spain was filled with bullion and treasure where as the land of King Phillip had spices and fine hardwoods to build ships. The future for trade seemed limitless.

After Timotemo had gone the three men sat down and made up a timetable. If they were to be back in New Spain by November they would only have a month in Manila to recruit and provision the ship. The purser already had a list of men Alvaraz could interview the next day. Alvaraz decided to go to the next village, in the afternoon, to see the chief about recruiting some of his people. The purser would organize a detail to work with the carpenter to increase the cargo and accommodations needed to carry the extra compliment of men to New Spain.

After a brief lunch in a tavern near the office they all went their ways. It was only a short boat ride to the next village, but Alvaraz, liking the firm ground under his feet decided, after asking directions, to walk the two miles to the village on the sandy beach. There was a nice breeze blowing, he needed the exercise and he wanted some time alone.

He walked out of the town towards the beach stopping occasionally to talk to interested people. He bought a new hat and stuffed his hair into its crown so the wind could cool his face. The street seemed gay, filled with people wearing bright clothing, going about their business. Alvaraz notice a familiar figure of a woman wearing a cotton dress, in the style of the natives, but he couldn't see her face because she held a parasol blocking his view. When he found the beach at the end of the road, he happened to turn and there she was again. This time he could see it was Gemelda. He walked up the burm of the beach and hid behind a bush wondering if she by chance was taking a walk on the beach. She walked for a while on the beach, then stopped beside where he hid, looking around. He realized she was looking for him. He playfully stepped out from behind the bush startling her.

"Gemelda, you're looking particularly charming today. Do you often walk alone on the beach?" asked Alvaraz.

She stood, her lower lip quivering, as if she were embarrassed to be found out. "I saw you walking on the beach and wondered if I could help you find anything?" she said hopefully.

"I'm charmed," he said smiling. This was the first time he had spoken directly to her; "I'm on my way to the village on the beach to see if I can recruit some workers. Does your father let you out unescorted?"

"I do what I want. My father is always too busy; I have no mother so I'm allowed to go as I please. May I walk with you? I speak some Tagalong, and maybe I could be of assistance to you. "

"What happened to your mother?"

"She died with the birth of my youngest sister Ranji almost four years ago. She bled to death," she said brutally, "My father has never gotten over it. He puts all his time in his businesses and none with his daughters. When you came over, he changed. He paid some attention to me. You are a good influence."

Gemelda pointed out the two farms on the beach. Her father owned the first. They grew fruit and coconuts. I spend most of my time here helping out. I like the work and the people." Alvaraz looked at her slim arms noticing the well-defined muscles she'd developed from her work. She introduced Alvaraz to a native lady they encountered as they walked down the beach. Gemelda spoke Tagalong with her and explained to Alvaraz the woman was her father's employee and lived in the village they would visit. Gemelda wanted to show Alvaraz the farm, but he excused her invitation saying there wasn't time if he was to get to the village. Gemelda asked Alvaraz many questions about his family, did he have a pretty novia waiting for him, where did he live in Spain. Questions that Alvaraz enthusiastically answered as if he were talking to a close sister. His instincts told him he could trust her and with every word he felt closer to her.

Antonio, Timotemo's neighbor, owned the next farm. She told him the house he lives in was newly decorated. All the Saavadra's assets were abandoned for a decade until Antonio came. "My father was about to buy them when my mother died. It's as if my father's spirit left him. He gave up on everything. They are good neighbors and often invite us over. He has big plans for his spices. I think they will do well."

They could smell food cooking and as they entered the village. Gemelda seemed to know everyone and was constantly introducing Alvaraz to the villagers. The chief welcomed Alvaraz in Spanish and insisted they have a private meeting without Gemelda. The chief offered Alvaraz food and a palm wine. The chief said there were many in his village that would welcome the chance of a new life in an empty land. The only employment they had, was from the nearby farms and the ship yard. Many of his men were idle. He would send some men to him in the morning to be interviewed.

The sky was turning red as the sun set when Alvaraz left the Chief. Gemelda was waiting with some food.

"I have already eaten with the chief," he explained.

"I've already eaten too."

Alvaraz thought she looked a little disappointed. "We should hurry back, it gets dark very quickly here," she said.

She grabbed his hand and led him back to the beach, leaning into him as she walked. He didn't mind, enjoying her closeness. They walked like this in the twilight. As the darkness came the moon rose full, spilling its enchantment over the beach. They stopped to look. When Alvaraz turned to look at Gemelda he found her upturned head staring at him in the moonlight. She took off his hat allowing his hair to cascade to his shoulders. He followed his instincts leaning over and clumsily kissed her. She reached up behind his head and passionately kissed him, opening her mouth, running her tongue between his lips. He held her body close, feeling the shape of her slender body pressing against him, her breasts almost touching his chest separated only by a cotton dress and his shirt.

"I know a place where we will be alone," she said breathlessly, leading him up the beach, through the palms into a small house built of thatch." The lady I introduced you to, lives here. She has gone to visit her sister in Manila and won't come back until tomorrow."

"Your father will have me beheaded if he finds you alone with me."

"Don't be silly, he won't know. I told our maid I was visiting a friend and won't be home until late," she said as she lit a lamp, sat him on a wicker couch and kissed him.

She matched his passion, as she led his hands to her breasts. They were warm and soft centered by her erect nipples. She unbuttoned his shirt, and feverishly removed his trousers. Soon she was naked to the waist. Her legs spread over his abdomen. He realized his erection had found its way through the buttons of his underwear. She mounted him and rubbed his penis between her legs on her now wet silk panties. He could feel his member sliding in the groove made by her labia through the silk. Her movements increased as she put more pressure on him. She was gasping, and making sounds from the depth of her throat. She shrieked clinging to him. He could feel his seed pumping out of him. He seemed to spin through a current of white light, a mad pleasure taking him from the reality of the world around him. He came back to his senses to find her gently rocking on his still erect member sliding in the smooth mucus lubricating them. She clung to him in her passion rocking more strongly; gasped reaching her climax, then fell silent. Alvaraz didn't want to move and they stayed like that for a long time until she rose, looking at him with a deep love in her eyes.

"I was worried about you. Your eyes turned up into your head and you made some strange sounds," she said.

She rose found some water removed her panties washed them then used them to clean as best she could the jism clinging to Alvaraz's underpants.

"My mother took four days to die. I stayed with her for the whole time. She told me I would meet a man with blond hair and blue eyes. I would fall in love with him. We would marry and live together until we died. I'd forgotten about it until I saw you. She also told me about men, how you want to be inside me and I shouldn't allow it until a Mullah blessed our marriage."

He was in deep thought. His mind was in turmoil. He felt so close to her, so confident in her that he spoke his thoughts.

"I can't marry you Gemelda. I am a Christian, you are a Muslim, and I am betrothed to a girl waiting for me in Spain. She will be eighteen when I return. I don't know what to do. Please forgive me."

She looked at him defiantly and said, "We will marry, Alvaraz. It's the only thing that can be."

Chapter 15

He hardly noticed the moon lighting their path as she led him across the sand back to Manila. His mind kept regressing to the picture of his father smiling, as he descended the plank to the ship on the quay in Cadiz. He trusted me; he could hear his father's words in his mind.

"Our future will be secure when you're married to Maria. The families will be united. I can retire from shipbuilding and be secure in the blessing of the two families," he had said.

The thought of how his mother had died came to him, in a wave, as they walked hand in hand down the beach. Her death left a deep wound when he was fourteen that changed his life. His carefree childhood ended on that day and he was never the same again. It was a deep secret he held deep in his heart. He hadn't seen her. He was told to stay away. His mind reeled. He remembered her screams coming down the stairway shaft as he huddled alone staring at the passers-by on the road. The screams diminished and finally he had to cock his head to hear the last plaintive cry. It wasn't long before his father came down the stairs, his face a mask of despair, barely able to talk. Your mother—died trying to give life to your brother." His voice broke and he openly cried, punctuating his agony with gasps for air.

With these thoughts Alvaraz found himself openly weeping as he was led across the sand. He fell on his knees and cried, expressing his innermost secrets to Gemelda.

"I never said good bye," he looked into Gemelda's eyes in the moonlight. "My mother died trying to bear a son," he blubbered. "What secrets of this life could she have told me?" He sobbed.

She knelt with him and cried, the sorrow of her own mother's death coming clearly to her mind. She held him and proclaimed, with tears running down her cheeks, "I love you, Alvaraz. I will always be with you."

They held each other as he wept, his mind being purged of the sorrow he'd felt every day since the day of his mother's death. Gemelda grabbed him around the waist and said, "Let me lift you to where your mother would like you to be," She wiped the tears from her eyes and lifted him from his sorrow. He hugged her in the moonlight sucking up his tears. He was home and secure in her arms. It was as if his carefree childhood could begin again with her.

They kissed through their tears and she said," Your mother would want you to have me. I know she would, Alvaraz."

At that moment Alvaraz knew he'd found the one he could trust, someone he could tell his innermost secrets to.

They found their way to the end of the beach and up the stones to the road.

"You will need a person who can speak Tagalong to interview the men you want. Can I work for you? It would be a good way for me to be with you with my fathers blessing.

Alvaraz heard her voice. He also heard a voice in his head say; 'She won't be satisfied until you are her husband, Alvaraz.' A spear of anxiety shafted through him as he thought of her always there, clinging to him, reminding him of his sorrows. God always punishing him for his sin of lust, the devil so close, always tempting him, wrenching him through a life where he never finds salvation or peace, always torn between good and evil. He looked at her. She was holding his waist, comforting him. The expression on her sweet face was of caring and love. He knew her gentle kindness, her sympathy and the deep sorrows she had overcome. She is surely not a devil. He breathed in her scent, and was rewarded with the smell of an angel. Then he thought, she's right. I do need an interpreter.

"I can only take single men. Do you think this will be a problem for them?"

Gemelda stopped him on the road and said, "The reason I was suggesting you use me as an interpreter, is because I can find the ones with wives that are interested in moving. None of these men are going to move to the new land without women," she said incredulously.

"But, how do you know this," he asked.

"I talked to the people in the village, mostly the women, but the men I talked to were all planning a large family when they get to the new land. These people live for their families. The only way you can take them without their women, is to enslave them and I think your Pope forbids that."

The breeze stopped as the air-cooled. Alvaraz could smell the dampness of dew settling around him and see it glitter as the drops formed on leaves in the white moonlight. The reality of where he was came to him, with a clarity he couldn't remember before. The warmth and smell of Gemelda holding him close, the silhouette of the church spire in the glow cast by the moon in the air before the far off hills. He knew this was right; Gemelda was his peace; Gemelda was his salvation.

"Would you like me to ask your father for an interpreter," asked Alvaraz. "If you can convince him to give you permission, then yes, I would like you to work with me. I will come to your house in the morning and ask him. If you are there when I ask him you can convince him."

She looked at him with the innocent, joyous smile. She disengaged herself from him and skipped backwards before him, and said, "I'm so happy, Alvaraz." She stopped, grabbed him and kissed him in the moonlight.

Alvaraz found Rodrego sitting on the patio of the office overlooking the harbor in the moonlight. He was sipping brandy and offered Alvaraz some.

"I trust you had a profitable evening?" Rodrego asked.

Alvaraz was tempted to confide in Rodrego, to spill his guts about his love for Grmelda. But instead, held his council and commented.

"It seems we have some problems I didn't foresee. There are hundreds of capable young men that would fit perfectly into a shipbuilding yard. The problem is they won't leave without their women. Is there any way we can fit two hundred bodies on the Lydia?"

Rodrego turned to him in stunned silence. His brow creased, his glass of brandy held before him as he digested what Alvaraz had said. "You want to put a hundred women on the ship. It only takes one woman to sink a ship. What would a hundred do?" He slumped back in his chair, taking a gulp of brandy. "Are you sure about this?"

"The only way we will get single men is by enslaving them. This is what I have been told, but as yet I haven't interviewed a single man. The chief is sending me some men tomorrow and the purser has a list. I am going to ask Timotemo to supply an interpreter. With an interpreter I can find out the truth of this matter."

Sleep didn't come easily to Alvaraz. His mind struggled with the last images of his father sending him off to the new world. He remembered with clarity, the last screams of his mother, how they slowly lost intensity, and how he squirmed almost wetting his pants when he was told she was dead. The hopelessness, the uncontrollable tears from his father as they huddled together looking for comfort. He remembered his father, becoming distant for months after her death and the sallow face of the old nanny who incessantly scolded him. After that he spent most of his time at the shipyard, working to forget his deep sorrow. It all came back with Gemelda, and finally when sleep came he dreamed of Gemelda lifting him into heaven. His mother was there, she was stroking his hair, as she looked down. He followed her gaze to see Gemelda's sweet innocent smile. His mother didn't speak, but he could feel her thoughts, 'this is the only thing that can be'. Her image faded, but the tingling on his scalp where she stroked him remained as the early morning light brought him from his comfortable slumber, suspended in his hammock. He could hear Rodrego shouting from the patio, to the proprietor of the shop down the road, asking if he had breakfast ready.

Chapter 16

They found a crowd of men standing in the road as they made their way to the restaurant.

The leader of the group spoke in almost incomprehensible Spanish, which Alvaraz interpreted as, "We have come from the village to be interviewed."

"Thank you for coming," said Alvaraz, then not knowing what to do, said, "Could I ask you to come back at noon?" With hand signals and simple Spanish, Alvaraz got the message across. The leader pointed to the sun, and then moved his arm to directly above him, then pointed to the ground. Alvaraz agree enthusiastically.

Alvaraz was a bit apprehensive as he walked up the hill to the Singh household. Before he saw it he heard the familiar clacking of Antonio's carriage coming down the road. They exchanged greetings and Alvaraz explained he was on his way to the house of Timotemo to talk business.

"You should hurry, I saw his carriage being readied. He looked like he was going somewhere."

Timotemo's carriage was just leaving the driveway when Alvaraz arrived. As chance would have it Gemelda was in the carriage with him.

"What do owe the honor of this visit, Alvaraz?" I am just on my way to your office to talk to you. Gemelda has suggested you employ her as interpreter. She speaks good Tagalong and Hindi, and I know she would be an asset to you."

Alvaraz, with relief, smiled at the two of them, then said, "I was going to ask your assistance on that very matter. I talked to the chief of the tribe you recommended, but with great difficulty and was hoping you would know of a good interpreter."

"Please, ride with us. Gemi, sit with me. Give senor Consollese some room," he said while motioning Gemelda to sit beside him. "We can talk of it on the way to the office. I have written a letter to the governor proposing an alliance where I will finance the shipyard in New Spain for a sixty percent interest in the enterprise. I can also provide you with some trained workers and their wives."

"You mentioned their wives, are you proposing we take women with us to the new world?" asked Alvaraz innocently.

"I don't think they'll go if you don't take their women, but you can ask them." He responded.

The minute they arrived at the office Gemelda took charge. Alvaraz was shocked to hear her speaking in Hindi with her father. Alvaraz looked at her and she changed to Spanish.

"I'm sorry, we should speak Spanish when we are with these men, Father." She ordered new furniture, paper, a ledger, pens and ink. When she went up stairs she commented, "Men are such pigs, you've only been here a day and the place is a mess."

She straightened up folding blankets and piled loose cloths on an old trunk.

"Father, we should have some armoires brought up for their cloths."

Timotemo wandered up the stairs his hands behind his back and said, "Gemelda, their housekeeping is none of your affair." He then addressed Rodrego, "Please forgive her, she has no mother and has taken on the role of head of the house for the last four years."

"Its nice to have a woman around, my wife fusses like that when I'm home and I don't mind it."

"Do you want to hire her?" asked Timotemo.

"Do you approve Alvaraz?" asked Rodrego.

Alvaraz didn't reply right away, instead he looked at her and asked with a serious look on his face. "Only if Gemelda promises to obey us and not do anything unless we first approve."

A scowl passed Gemelda's face and Alvaraz quickly added, "Yes, of course, we will take her."

Always the businessman Timotemo interjected "Her wages will be a gold doubloon per month, with Saturdays off, to be paid in advance. What time should she start in the mornings?"

"This is very expensive for a single interpreter," said Rodrego.

"I'm giving you a good price for the rent of the office, now I'm giving you a reasonable price for an interpreter. I'm sure you'll get value for your money."

Alvaraz looked at Rodrego and quickly responded, "I think it's an excellent offer."

Gemelda with a businesslike expression looked at her father, who responded to her look with, "Then I guess it's all settled."

Gemelda immediately showed her organizational skills by organizing the office to take interviews while at the same time made a space for the purser's desk. At noon the crowd of men arrived. Gemelda assigned them all a number and made an appointment for the following day. She booked twenty interviews a day, giving each man a page in the ledger and a number so the men could be interviewed in sequence and all they needed to remember is who they were to follow. While she was handing out the appointments she lectured the men on the seriousness of their commitment. Some declined; but most accepted with enthusiasm.

Rodrego went to the shipyard to look over the facilities to haul the Lydia then later supervised the ship's carpenter, asking if he could possibly build enough storage to hold food and water for two hundred people. The carpenter gave him a blank stare.

"I've already cleared the forward hold, installed bars for hanging hammocks and built storage into the bilges. If we store grains or rice in the bilges we won't need to put the ballast in after we re-launch her. It's up to you how many you think we can squeeze in there. Just remember you can't use the foc'sle; that's for the men."

By the end of the day the ledger book had two hundred pages each with a name and number to identify the perspective workers. Alvaraz couldn't be happier. More furniture had arrived, a desk and chair for the purser and two armoires for the Captain and Alvaraz's clothes.

Alvaraz sat by Gemelda breathing in her scent while they talked about the requirements for the workers.

"I need three dozen strong men for the saw pits, they must be well muscled in their shoulders. We should record the width of the shoulders and take the ones with the broadest shoulders. Also ask the men about their fathers and grandfathers. Find out if they are still alive. If they have old parents and grandparents then they will probably be healthy and live to old age too. Make a note of their experience with boat building and if they have any experience with ocean passages. We must try to find young men without wives. The less people we have on the ship, the better. It's a very long trip and I don't want to consume all the food and water then die. Rodrego says we must sail a long way north into a cold climate in order to catch the west winds to get back to the Californias. This could mean we won't see land for three months. The men will need warm clothes. So maybe ask them if they have warm clothes."

As he talked Gemelda made a form to record all the criteria they would need to make their selection. She stopped when he mentioned warm clothes and said,

"Don't be ridiculous, these people hardly have clothes, let alone warm clothes." With a flash of inspiration she said, "We must find blankets made of wool and have the women fashion warm clothes to be worn in the northern ocean. I think I know where to find material for this, but it will cost some money. There is an Indiamen anchored in the harbor. The purser was trying to store some cargo and asked father to store it in his warehouse. I saw roles of wool. Do you want me to see if the ships purser will sell some?"

"We need it, but I should get our purser to see about the purchase," said Alvaraz.

"You know my father wants to finance your shipbuilding enterprise for the profits, if we tell him we need the material he will probably buy it for a song."

"Gema, I like the idea," Alvaraz said while absentmindedly leaving out the middle syllables of her name.

"You called me Gema, I like that. My father calls me Gemie, but you can call me Gema if you like."

"I like the name Gema, I hadn't realized I'd shortened it."

Gema looked at Alvaraz and excitedly said, "I've never been so excited in my life." She grabbed him and kissed him playfully on the lips then became more intense.

Alvaraz pulled away, "Gema, please, if we are caught I know they will keep us apart. Lets enjoy the time we have together."

"Would you meet me on the beach?" I'll tell father I am visiting Juanita. She is my friend who lives down the street. I've already told her about you and I and I know I can trust her."

Alvaraz with a smile of surrender said, "I'll wait for you by the rocks where the beach begins, now let's get back to business. "

That evening, before the moon rose, Gema came to the beach in the darkness and was swept up in the arms of Alvaraz.

"I've been waiting for what seems like an eternity," said Alvaraz, "God! you feel good in my arms."

They walked down the beach towards what they knew of as a hollow in the sand overgrown by green sea grass. Gema spread her blanket.

The sound of the waves breaking on the beach filled the air with a slow rhythm complimenting the faster rhythm of her heart he thought he could feel pulsing in her lips as he gently kissed her. He groped for her breasts finding she had already unbuttoned her dress to make the way easy for him. He struggled with his lust, trying to push her away, but to no avail. He gave up and allowed himself to be swallowed up in their shared ecstasy. As they kissed she undressed him. He took her erect nipple into his mouth and she massaged his engorged member with her long fingers. He felt himself releasing as she stroked him. He weakly reached up and kissed her as she directed his ejaculation into the sand. He held her tense body. She stared at him with unseeing eyes. He realized she was now rubbing herself between her legs. With her free hand she directed him towards her breast. He could feel her stiffen; her thin body arch and release with a short cry. He looked down at her bush instinctively wanting to kiss her between the legs. She began again to rub herself and this time let out short sounds coming from deep in her throat then stiffened and let out a loud moaning sound that resonated down the beach. They fell together, holding each other, naked in the moonlight, their passion spent but Alvaraz realized a closeness that he could only describe as love.

"Tell me about the girl you are to marry," requested Gema.

Alvaraz told her of his young life and of his life working for his father and how he'd been enticed to go to New Spain to start a shipbuilding yard. He told of his father's wish for him to marry the daughter of wealthy merchant. "Her name is Maria and I don't even remember what she looks like. She was only thirteen when I saw her last."

When he described his trip from Spain she was spellbound. She continually asked him for more details about the new land he had transited to get to the west coast. Alvaraz described the land, the rivers with their enchanting waterfalls and the feeling he got when he arrived at the sea riding proudly on his own horse. He told her how he found undisturbed places he could only describe as the Garden of Eden.

Gema told of her young life in Spain, then described her family's voyage to the Islands of King Philip on an Indiaman ship they had sailed down the coast of Africa to the Indies then to the Spice Islands. They almost talked the night through without making any plans for their future.

In the early hours of the morning Alvaraz escorted Gema to the house of her friend. He touched her lips with his, wishing her a good night. He snuck into his hammock at the office hoping he wouldn't disturb Rodrego. His brief sleep before dawn came, blessed again by visions of his mother. This time she was washing him when he was a small boy. He had an enormous erection and his mother told him proudly, that someday he would make some woman happy. Through the haze of his sleep he could hear Gemelda shouting his name up the stairs.

He woke with a start, "I'll be right down," he said fumbling into his clothes.

"Captain Rodrego says you came home late," she said forming their conspiracy as she entering with a tray of sweet buns and watered wine for the two men's breakfast.

"When did you return?" Rodrego asked seemingly adding to Gemelda's conspiracy?

"I wasn't that late. I drank some grog with a man I met on the street. I don't know what time I came home," Alvaraz said with a bit of annoyance in his voice, then continued, "What time should we expect out first interview?"

"There's two waiting for us now. The man, Tongan, who is always joking, is first. Then we have Bolo the older fellow who says he's built many ships."

They measured the obviously young and strong Tongan and asked him how old he was. He didn't know his birth date but thought he was probably about a hundred years old. When asked if he would go without his wife, he first answered yes. Then when Gemelda told him he would never see her again he changed his mind and said, No, he wouldn't go without his wife. He only had three children by this wife, but boasted he had many more by other wives. When asked what would happen to his children, he looked serious, and said, "I would like them to stay here with their grandmother and my brothers and sisters. They will be safe here."

"Does your wife want to go to the new land," asked Gemelda.

"Yes, of course, she wants to go."

The next man to be interviewed had a similar story. It became apparent none of them had any idea of their birth date or age. However Alvaraz found their physical characteristics worth noting. On the fifth interview he decided to assign the men specific jobs. The ones he found well developed in the upper body, he assigned to the sawpits. Even though he didn't speak Tagalong he was able to find the ones who were organized and meticulous in their manner; these he assigned to various jobs like maintaining the tool crib, firing the tar pots and melting the pitch, keeping the hammers well soaked and maintaining the sharpness of the tools. Then he had to find men who could work the augers, drilling long straight holes through hard woods. He made a list of the specialists needed to build a ship, assigning the name and number of the candidate to the specific tasks. He slowly filled up his lists while Gemelda listed physical characteristics and family ties.

On the third day Gemelda asked to change the schedule. "We should start the interviews at noon. The men go off about their business in the morning leaving the women alone in the village. I would like to interview the women in the morning and the men in the afternoon. That way I can get more information about the whole family, finding out which of them will work out the best."

On Friday afternoon a note arrived inviting Alvaraz, Rodrego and the officers of the Lydia to a dinner at the Governors estate for Saturday evening. Alvaraz didn't want to go because he didn't have any proper clothes to wear and didn't know where in Manila to find them. But when Gemelda told him she would be accompanying her father, he decided to find some clothes and go. On Friday morning Antonio and Antoinette mysteriously dropped by and Antonio offered to lend Rodrego and Alvaraz some suitable clothes and take them to the dinner in their carriage.

Alvaraz felt like Royalty. He was dressed in tailored trousers with proper hose, made from a checkered dark rose and black colored cloth and a matching blouse with frilled gold colored epaulets on his shoulders. He felt completely out of place with the aristocracy attending the dinner. He was formally introduced to the Governor and his wife then moved into the reception area, where they were served drinks and hors d'oeuvres.

Captain Rodrego was engaged with various merchants enquiring about shipping goods to Spain through New Spain. The distances were about the same and if there was a safe sea route it could be a better way than shipping goods through the pirate infested waters around the horn of Africa. With Rodrego engaged with the merchants, Alvaraz felt conspicuously alone.

When he saw Gema looking completely at ease dressed in a patterned gold sari, her bejeweled hair pilled on her head looking like a queen, he realized how far away from her class he was. When she approached him he had difficulty speaking with her, he was so in awe of her beauty.

"Gema," he whispered, while he held his glass of Madeira tightly in his hand, "I don't think I've ever seen such a beautiful maiden."

She slightly blushed and gave him an inviting smile of intense passion that could only be interpreted as submission to her love for him. He turned trying to distract her gaze; intoxicated with the gentle scent of jasmine and sandalwood she was wearing. Her presence always had the same effect on him. He changed from a worried boy to a man confident in what he was doing. The governor approached, he gave a slight bow and engaged in conversation. Alvaraz, in normal circumstances, would have shied away after stuttering a few brief words, but with Gema beside him he smoothly talked of the shipbuilding trade and how pleased he was with the men he was recruiting to be employed in his enterprise in New Spain. Alvaraz introduced Gema who the governor knew well, and said, "Gemalda holds the key to finding the best men. She knows the women behind the men and finds out all their secrets before I even see them."

Before long a small crowd had gathered around him finding entertainment in his descriptions of the native workers who stated they were a hundred years old and had dozens of children by other women.

The governor held his glass up and proposed a toast, "To the success of Alvaraz and Gemelda."

Gema, not having a glass to hold up, smiled lovingly at Alvaraz as if she were his bride. In the corner of her eye she saw her father looking at her. He had a look she remembered from her childhood. With a start she realized it was the look of jealousy. When she last saw that look she was ten years old. Shortly after, her father had killed a man in a duel. The man he killed was innocently cavorting with her mother.

She waved her hand, leaving the group, and immediately went to her father's side sliding her arm through his and gave it a squeeze.

He looked at her and said, "Do you like that young man Alvaraz?"

She didn't know what to say; if she lied to him he would know and things would get worse so she decided to try to be a frivolous young girl and enthusiastically responded with, "Oh father—I love him," she rolled her eyes giving him a silly little girl look, "You know I love all the boys I meet, especially that one."

"I warn you, Gemelda, if you want to work for that man, you can't get involved with him. Remember he's a Christian, His people won't let him marry you, and I as a Moslem won't let you marry him." He paused and looked at her, "Perhaps I should return your wages and end the contract."

"Do what you wish father," she bravely said, "But remember I won't be happy if you do."

He held her shoulders and looked at her face-to-face, "Gemelda, I trust you and I know what's best for you. Believe me I know what is going on in that man's head and it can only lead to trouble."

She raised her eyebrows and coyly said, "I know you trust me father."

For the rest of the evening she ignored Alvaraz in favor of the older guests. At the dining table she was seated at the opposite end from Alvaraz, beside her father. Alvaraz watched her entertaining the Governor's wife. The distance of a dining table separating them sent a cascade of feelings of separation and despair. What would his life be like when he sailed away, forever without her? By the end of the evening she felt she had defused her father's anxiety. Alvaraz played the game of ignoring her for the rest of the evening and when she said good night to him, he barely acknowledged her, sending her heart into a spin of despair. That night, lying sleeplessly in her bed, waves of doubt passed over her. In the end she silently cried herself to sleep wondering how she could appease the two men in her life she loved. She wished her mother were here to guide her and fill the huge hole she knew was in her father's heart.

The interviews went well; Gemelda's morning visits gave her more than just information about the women who would be going to New Spain. On one morning she sat with the chief's wife and some elder-women. She wanted Alvaraz to know what she found out so at the completion of the interviews that afternoon she told him.

"Today I talked to the chief's wife and some elder-woman. They told me their people came from the west settling on the island to the north a long time ago, longer than anyone can remember. Their tribe grew and soon there were too many people. Like their ancestors they built large canoes and sailed to new places on the Island. The chief's wife proudly told me, you could find her people all over the island. She also told me there are devil people who live on some of the islands and these people will eat you. Their tribe moved to Manila to get away from the devil people. Then she told me many of the tribes have sent out canoes, filled with people, on the ocean sailing to the east to find new lands. They sometimes get news from these people who now live to the south and east, but many they never hear from again. The chief's wife wants to know if her people can send word of their new life and will they encounter her people who have sailed to the east."

"Tell the chief's wife, that yes we will send word. There is much interest in trade between Manila and New Spain. I'm positive she will hear of their safe passage and some may even return."

By the end of the second week the interviews were complete. Of the two hundred interviewed Alvaraz had a list of seventy he approved of with a further thirty who could do the jobs, but probably not as well as the others. Some of the best candidates were eliminated after Gemelda found the wives couldn't be separated from their families and especially their children. There were six experienced men from the yard at Campandaro who wanted to come. The yard wasn't busy enough to keep them working and as soon as they found they could bring their women they decided they wanted to go.

In the mornings while Gemelda went to the village to interview the women Alvaraz often went to the boat yard where the Lydia was hauled out. Rodrego wanted him to check the work being done. He, Rodrego and the ship's carpenter made a thorough inspection of the entire ship making lists of jobs for the workers to complete. The purser found bales of rice and grains to use as ballast and also has a food source. Because the food would be consumed the trio inspecting the ship decided they still needed ballast so decided to put in half the usual amount of sand in the bilge. On the third week the Lydia was re-launched, the sand ballast was put in the bilge in sacks and the provisioning commenced.

Alvaraz repeatedly told Gemelda, they could never marry, and after the dinner party, they stopped going to the beach in the evening. In the mornings they both eagerly came together, never touching, but always talking of their yearning for each other. Then Gemelda would go to the village and Alvaraz would find something to do on the Lydia.

He often wandered around, looking at the equipment and finding the woods used in the shipbuilding industry in Manila. He had help from an old man who had worked for Timotemo for more than twenty years. He showed Alvaraz the different types of wood used in various parts of the ship. There were no ships being built at the moment. The old man told Alvaraz, "The governor won't let contracts to Timotemo's yard unless there is no alternative because he's not a Christian."

"This is the wood we use for planking." He showed Alvaraz a thin plank of a rose colored wood. Alvaraz took it and bent it on his knee.

"It's at least as strong as pine and far more beautiful. How does it hold up to rot and worms?" asked Alvaraz.

"It's not bad," said the old man. "It's a type of mahogany." He showed Alvaraz some brown colored wood. "This is the best wood for planking, it's not as flexible as other woods, but it's the most resistant to rot and worms. We call this wood teak. The people call all the wood here teak. So be careful if you are asking one of the natives for teak. You might get anything. It's also very toxic to the workers. The man in the bottom of the sawpit must wear a hood and mask made of tight cloth or they will die of a lung disease. It also dulls the saws very quickly."

He explained, "There is no wood as good as white oak for frames, but we use this wood for keels." He held up a piece of ironwood. "It's not at all flexible, it's very heavy, it's very hard to find and I've never worked with wood this difficult to carve. It can dull a Toledo steel chisel with a single stroke."

In the back of Alvaraz's mind he was wondering how hard it would be to import some of these woods to New Spain. He was very impressed by their qualities.

Chapter 17

It was Wednesday of the third week. The interviews were complete and the two of them planned to stay at the office in the morning to complete the plans for the villagers' final boarding of the ship. Rodrego and the purser left leaving the two lovers alone. They worked; making lists of things the villagers would need on the voyage and making a final list of who would be coming. If all went well ninety-three men and seventy-nine women would be on the ship for the return trip. Alvaraz could feel Gemelda's leg pressing on his as he sat on the bench behind the desk.

"We shouldn't sit so close together Gema," he said looking down at his work.

"There isn't anyone here, my love. Surely we can enjoy our love a little more," she whispered in his ear.

Alvaraz was instantly aroused. Before he could turn his head towards her, she had her arm around him offering her soft lips to him. They kissed and he grouped.

"I'll lock the door," said Alvaraz, breathlessly, getting up from the desk. He cautiously looked out the window after he locked the door.

"Lets go up-stairs," Gemelda said waiting for him on the bottom step. Alvaraz had his arm around her as they walked up to stairs. He realized she had nothing on under her dress. In the back of his mind he thought she must have planned this. Gemelda had put a beautiful thick Persian carpet on the upstairs floor. Alvaraz thought the carpet was too rich for two simple sailors, but realized perhaps Gemelda planned that too, because as soon as they came into the room she knelt down on it, pulling Alvaraz down to her. He felt his passion rising as they kissed. They lay together facing one another.. He found her breasts and fondled her firm nipples. Soon they were lying together facing one another. She had her legs around his, pulling him to her. She stopped kissing his lips and moved over him, her dress falling around her waist, her firm breasts capped with extended nipples fully exposed. She started undressing him, opening his shirt and removing his trousers. He lay before her, in total submission, his erect member desperate for her touch. She kissed him on the lips, swung round putting her lips around his desire. He gasped at her touch, at the same time she straddling him exposing her naked bottom to him. He put his arms around her buttocks and pulled her down kissing he naked vulva. She pulsed back and forth, pelvic rocking on him. He could feel her fragile body tense as she rocked with increasing intensity. He could feel his release as she disengaged from him, her hand massaging him, directing his discharge between her breasts; at the same time she moaned then shouted her pleasure as her orgasm came. They lay completely still for a moment then she began rubbing his enthusiastic tong, very quickly gasping letting out a sharp moaning sound as she came to her completion

As he lay with her he wondered what he should say at his confession. For the last two Sundays he had made his confession to one of the priest at the newly built church in the town. He confessed to fornication with an unwed woman. His penance had always been lenient; six Hail Marys and prayers for forgiveness. He didn't know if what he had done was a sin, let alone what to call his sin. They hadn't actually copulated and therefore was this little more than an innocent kiss? Alvaraz felt a mixture of intense pleasure and repugnance at what he had done. Again the question of whether this was the work of the Devil or God. He wanted to ask Gema as they washed and cleaned each other if what she was doing was a sin. However something in him made him keep his council. He would be far away from her soon and could return to his saintly ways. The thought of being away from her sent a shaft of trepidation through him. He turned, watching her put her dress on. It was as if she were part of him. The thought of abandoning the ship passed through his mind, then he resolved himself to follow his duty. He could see no other way.

They went down the stairs in silence both obviously thinking of the future.

"I'll miss you terribly, Gema," Alvaraz said. He could hear his voice falter with his honesty. Gemelda on the other hand, didn't seem to be at all worried. She seemed calm and businesslike. They still had a week and a half before departure.

They decided to go to the Lydia together that afternoon to inspect the accommodations with the idea of allowing the natives to go aboard the next day so they could arrange things. Gemelda was very excited to see the Lydia. She carried with her a case filled with writing materials. She insisted on Alvaraz introducing her to everyone they encountered. It seemed Alvaraz gained a new level of respect with the men having Gemelda around. They all seemed spellbound at her beauty, bowing and stuttering their pleasure at meeting her. Alvaraz was positive the oarsmen pulled harder at their oars as they made their way to the ship.

"We'll be going up to port, there's a barge to starboard loading supplies, Sir," said the Cox cheerfully.

"What's being loaded?" asked Alvaraz.

"There's grains and rice and also a shipment of spices from Timotemo's farm. He's trying the new route to Spain. If it works, there will be lots of shipping back and forth."

Gemelda after hearing this, said, "I didn't know father was sending spices. Is there going to be enough room for us? For all of your workers and their families?" she corrected.

"Most of the shipment will be going in as ballast, simply to keep the ship stable. We won't even see it."

There was a floating dock with a stairway going to deck level on the starboard side. Gemelda was the first off the ship's boat.

She stood on the dock, excitedly, "She is larger than I thought," she said as she gazed up at the forecastle and aft deck.

Alvaraz followed, after speaking to the coxswain, explaining why Gemelda was there. "Stay where you are, Gemelda," commanded Alvaraz as he disembarked, "I must get permission from the Captain before you can come aboard."

"Permission granted," roared Rodrego who was now standing on the aft deck, "Come aboard, Gemelda. What do we owe the honor of your visit?"

"We've come to inspect the quarters for the natives." she answered as she walked up the steps placing her hand in Rodrego's, who assisted her, as she mounted the main deck.

Alvaraz could smell the new tar and smell of humanity that always came from ships. He hoping it didn't offend her; instead she got right down to business. "Could you show me the rigging, I would love to climb to the top of the mast."

With a look of despair at Rodrego, Alvaraz said, "I'm sorry, Gema. There is no way we will let you into the rigging. I'll take you below to inspect the quarters for the workers and maybe show you the stores and the other features of the ship, but not the rigging."

Rodrego and Ismel both laughed at Alvaraz's unease. Then Rodrego said, "As far as I'm concerned you may have the run of the ship, me lady, but I won't allow you into the rigging."

Gemelda took out her papers and started to draw a large diagram of the deck. As they walked around she asked about every aspect of life aboard. Her only experience with ships was sailing on a Dutch Indiamen, when she was a girl, and she was never allowed to run free on the deck. They started at the bowsprit. Gemelda wanted to walk out on the footropes to the very end but Alvaraz stopped her on the last grating. She astonished Alvaraz with her total lack of fear of heights. Her confidence in her balance was evident as she stood on the last narrow grating using her finest carbon to draw the details of the blocks running out to the point of the bowsprit. It took an hour for her to roughly draw the detail of the deck including a wonderful rendition of the capstan winch on three pieces of paper. She was most curious about the latrines on the aft deck and was amused at the thought of the feces dropping into the water below.

"I always wanted to know where the contents of our chamber pot went when we were on the Indiamen. We should work out a system for the workers to use chamber pots and a detail of men to carry them here and empty them. The women won't be allowed back here, so they will have to use chamber pots."

Alvaraz was impressed and pleased with her planning. He hadn't thought of how the women would look after their toilet.

She insisted on looking at the officers' quarters under the aft deck and told Alvaraz his cabin was more like a broom closet than a cabin. When he told her he shared it with the navigator, she was dismayed.

"Do you not have any privacy at all?" as she noticed the additional berth.

"The navigator's name is Philippe. He's seldom here. He spends most of his time in the Captain's cabin with his charts. Look here, I had the ship's carpenter change the lee boards on my birth. I had them canted out to give me more room. I no longer sleep in a box. He told me not to complain when I fall out when the ship rolls."

"Why doesn't the navigator have his berth in the Captain's cabin?" she asked.

"He does sleep in there a great deal, but the Capitan of a ship has a private cabin. You ask so many questions, Gema. I'm impressed with your thoroughness."

The cleared hold for the workers gave Gemelda the most trouble. She immediately paced it off and calculated the space per person.

"This is inadequate, Alvaraz, There isn't any privacy for the workers, and if you calculate the space per person for hammocks there is barely sixteen inches per person."

The space had little light; it was some twenty five by forty feet, with ten feet of headroom. There were vertical supports every ten feet. The carpenter had put railings along the bulkheads and between the vertical supports to tie hammocks to. Gemelda walked back and forth in the space. "Alvaraz, there is enough height to put two layers of hammocks in here. To get into the upper one you would need a ladder up the side. If you put more bars on every second vertical support as ladders to access the top hammock you could hang blankets on them for privacy. This would double the space for sleeping. I know these people; they don't mind small spaces, but they want to share them with their family. It wouldn't be that much trouble to put the additional supports in, but it would make a huge difference to the people. The other problem is the lack of light. Is there any way we could put opening hatches in the deck. More air and light is what this space needs."

Alvaraz hearing Gemelda say the space was inadequate felt annoyed then a bit apprehensive. But as she discussed the changes he started to see there was a solution to making the space livable. He decided to find the carpenter and see if he could make the changes over the next week. "Stay here, I'll try to find the carpenter," he said.

Alvaraz couldn't find the ship's carpenter, but did find Rodrego who followed him down into the hold. Rodrego didn't seem to mind the changes. He said, "I'll get the carpenter to put in three opening hatches for air and light and putting more bars on the supports shouldn't be any problem. It's a good idea and will double up our capacity."

"Captain Rodrego, I would like to show some of the people the boat and get them ready. They are very curious, and I know if they saw it, they would be more confident. They also want to see the space so they can plan what to bring. Do you think I could bring some of them tomorrow?" asked Gemelda.

"Yes, of course. I'll be here tomorrow, bring them out in the longboat. How many do you want to bring?"

"Probably a dozen."

"OK, tomorrow then. I should have the carpenter working on the changes by then."

Gemelda diagramed out the entire main deck making suggestions to changes in the galley and asked if a small room next to the stove could be used as a meeting room for the people.

When they were leaving the ship Gemelda suggested Alvaraz accompany her to the village the next day to supervise the sewing of the wool costumes the people would wear in the cold north Pacific. "The women are having trouble with the men. They won't stay still while they try to measure them. If you come, first you can see if the suits will be adequate and secondly perhaps you could show the men its OK to be measured."

Chapter 18

It was difficult for Alvaraz to measure his feelings for Gemelda. First she was so passionate with their lovemaking; she was so bright, organized and officious while dealing with the village people. He reflected he wouldn't have made any of the changes without her. Her father was right when he said they would get good value for their money. On the other hand she seemed happy to see Alvaraz sail away. Could she be so cold, was this just a fling, meaning little more than an infatuation? He felt so close to her, even thinking of desertion to be with her and yet she seemed so aloof to any thoughts of being with him for the rest of his life. His heart was almost broken all ready. He knew he would suffer for the rest of his life without her. The thought almost strangled him as he tossed in his hammock that night.

When he walked down the beach towards the village the next morning, thoughts of the passion they shared on this very spot, gave him the courage to bring up the subject of his love for her. "Gema, I can't tell you how much I love you. My heart is in turmoil. On the one hand, I want to desert my ship to be with you, on the other I sometimes find you so cold to my heartbreak that it frightens me."

He heard a sob, and turned to her; tears were running down her cheeks. Against their agreement of no touching in public, she held him on the beach for a long time. The sun burning down in the damp air made it uncomfortable to hold her but they stayed like that for a time while she sobbed. "Don't worry, Alvaraz, I love you so much. I'll find a way to be with you, but not here. Perhaps I can find a ship to New Spain to be with you," she blubbered then looked up to him, her face a mask of hopelessness. They both felt relief with their confessed love for each other, but it didn't detract from the fact that they would be apart for a long time and probably forever.

The village was filled with the sound of laughter. One of the villagers named Tumbu was trying on a wool garment made by the women. He was laughing and squirming as his wife tried to pull up the pants. The garments were made of thick woven course wool. It was all natural, multi colored and very itchy. They stopped when they saw Alvaraz and Gemelda approach. Alvaraz examined the pants. They were made of two pieces of material sewn together along the edge. Alvaraz examined the pants with approval; the material was thick and appeared to be very clean. He was impressed with the material and workmanship, but decided they were inside out. When he pulled the legs through they looked much better. Alvaraz helped the man put on the pair of home made trousers. After the native had them on he danced around then wanted to take them off. Gemelda had some conversation with the women asking them to sew in some belt loops so the men could use a rope to tie their trousers. The women's outfits were designed by Gemelda and were simply large capes with a hood.

"They will be at sea for some time before they feel the cold. If we bring the material with us they can make them underway. Did your father buy this material?" asked Alvaraz.

"He didn't pay for it, he simply arranged for your purser to buy it for a good price," reported Gemelda.

While they were there Gemelda talked to some of the women, asking who of them wanted to come on a visit to the ship. They all wanted to come, but Gemelda chose twelve, telling them they would all get their turn. The groups of them walked to the longboat and were rowed out to the ship. Alvaraz was worried the incessant chatter from the women would anger the crew aboard, but the men took it in stride and the visit went well. The ship's carpenter and his helpers were working on the changes to the hold. The party of women didn't stay long but did find a few simple improvements the carpenters could easily accomplish.

It was a lazy afternoon, the village women had gone back to the village and Alvaraz and Gemelda back to the office. When they entered and found it deserted, they fell into each other's arms. They held each other, kissing, at the foot of the stairs when the door opened. They disengaged their kisses and turned simultaneously to find Timotemo standing in the door staring at them, his jaw dropped with an expression of disbelief.

A wave of nausea passed over Alvaraz as he quickly disengaged his arms form Gemelda. His fear pulsing through him he bravely said, "Good afternoon, Sir."

Timotmo stuttered, and then said in a steely voice, "How dare you!" his eyes aflame, he repeated, "How dare you!" in an even louder voice. "Get away from him, Gemelda," he shouted. He walked over, grabbed Gemelda, and pushed her behind him, then grabbed Alvaraz by the collar and with a hissing voice said, "You'll pay for this."

At first Alvaraz was shocked, his very soul shattered, he couldn't move, he was shamed and demoralized, but when Timotemo grabbed his lapel and tried to shake him while threatening him he realized what a frail person this man was. 'With one punch I could kill this man,' he thought, A rage rose in him and he grabbed Timotemo by his lapel. He heard his own voice say quietly as he held him off the floor, "Does this mean you don't approve of our relationship, Sir?" then he heard a tearing sound.

Gemelda was screaming, "Put him down, Alvaraz."

The tearing sound was the sound of the stitching tearing away on Timotemo's jacket as he fell to the floor. Alvaraz stood staring at the lapels of Timot's jacket in his hand, then watched as Timotemo picked himself up off the floor. He was visibly shaken, but had a crocked smile on his face. His looked a mess, his jacket in tatters, his face contorted in rage. He couldn't speak for a few seconds, then blurted out, "You will pay—you will pay!" as he dragged Gemelda down the steps of the office out of Alvaraz's life forever.

Alvaraz followed them out onto the street throwing the torn bits of cloth into the carriage before Timotemo had a chance to close the carriage door. There was no sense of remorse for the first few minutes as the adrenalin pulsed through Alvaraz' veins, then the implications of what he had done hit him. "What have I done? he thought as he moved around the office. I picked him up and tore his coat. Gemelda will hate me. Captain Rodrego will disown me, this whole trip will have been a waste because I've been such a fool and for the rest of my life I will think of Gema, 'I am ruined.' he thought. He paced back and forth listening to the clacking of his boots on the tile floor. He was so alone. "Is there nothing I can do?" he sobbed, hot tears of shame burning the back of his eyes.

The door to the office opened; it was Rodrego walking into the room. Alvaraz didn't know what to do. Should he prostrate himself and ask for forgiveness, should he beg to be left behind or should he just tell Rodrego the whole story.

"What's the matter, lad?" Rodrego seeing his distress came over to him with a look of concern on his face. "You look like you've just lost your mother. What news do you have, lad? Out with it," he said cheerily.

"Rodrego, please forgive me, I've just done something terrible. Gemelda kissed me; we thought we were alone in the office and Timotemo opened the door and caught us red handed." Alvaraz said with a tremor in his voice. "He threatened me; said I would pay for my indiscretion. He was right there breathing in my face. I don't know what came over me, but I picked him up by his jacket and held him. His jacket ripped and he fell to the floor. He's so angry, what should I do?"

Rodrego stood for a minute not answering, then said, "you picked him off the floor and held him." He made a pantomime of holding someone up and started to laugh. When his laughter ended he asked, "how high did you hold him? God I wish I were here. No one deserved it more; that man is a prig. Well done, lad."

"He may ask me for a duel and I may be killed, shouldn't I worry?" asked Alvaraz.

"He won't ask you for a duel. He'll keep this very quiet, mark my words. One thing I know for sure and this might hurt you more than anything, because I know how much she means to you, but I can guarantee you'll never see Gemelda again."

With these words Alvaraz's heart broke. He felt numb; he might just as well be killed in a duel with Timotemo.

"Don't worry, lad" said Rodrego like a father. I know this will hurt you, but believe me, you'll get over it, and it's for the best. I promised your father you I would return you to marry Maria. I can understand you having a fling once in a while, but would never give you my blessing if you wanted to marry Gemelda. She's a Moslem and always will be. I was worried about you. You didn't think I didn't know you were having an affair with her, did you, lad," he said with a wink, "this is a good way to end it. Consider yourself lucky to have such an experience and now put it behind you."

"Thanks, Rodrego, you are a true friend, a kind man and I know you are right. The problem is my heart doesn't. It will take some time, but as you say, I will get over it."

"I want you to see the priest, Alvaraz. Ask God's forgiveness and do your confession. It will help. I spoke with Father Antonio this afternoon about blessing the Lydia for our return to New Spain. He will be at the church now. Go there and be absolved."

The church was still under construction, the steeple wasn't completed, but the vestry and the vault were open when Alvaraz came by. Father Antonio was the priest he confessed to the last time he was there. When he left Rodrego he had felt strong, and now after the brief walk to the church he felt the agony of separation returning. He entered the vestry like an injured soldier finding a hospital.

"Father, I must confess," he said when he saw Father Antonio.

"You are in earnest, my son. Come I will take your confession in here."

They knelt before the alter and Father Antonio prayed for Alvaraz. He then took him to the confessional.

Alvaraz, knowing not what to confess to, confessed to fornication and lust, then confessed to the sin of battery going into some detail about what transpired not knowing what else to say. The priest prayed in his box for God to forgive him. He also prayed for the soul of the Moslems and asked God to deliver these godless people to salvation. Again Alvaraz was surprised by the easy penance he was delivered. Six Hail Marys and prayers to ask forgiveness. Again he walked away from the church feeling absolved, but within an hour the reality of being separated from Gemelda forever came back to haunt him.

Chapter 19

Over the next few days, he lost interest in his project and spent a lot of time walking the streets and the beach. It was on one of these walks he encountered the brother of Gugo. He wanted to talk to Alvaraz, so the two of them went to the village where they found a man who's Christian name was Guillermo, The chief had appointed him Alvaraz's new interpreter.

They spoke for a long time before Guillermo explained to Alvaraz saying; "This man wants you to know he is going to be the grandfather of your child."

He clapped Alvaraz on the back and insisted the three of them share some tubo to celebrate. For a moment Alvaraz was taken up by the lighthearted fun the two men were having. Suddenly he remembered the details of being with the women at the bathing pool. He could remember the lust, the intense pleasure, and his confusion after the event. He grappled with the implications of what he was told. He felt the devil was in his presence and these men were the angels of the devil taunting him. He said nothing as he took the coconut shell full of palm wine; he drank the wine down, thanked the men, turned and walked away. He was numb. As he walked he realized he was looking for Gemelda. He needed her to console him. He knew she would understand. She knew these people and knew how they worked. He couldn't sleep without constantly being interrupted with nightmares of loosing her. In one dream she was in a torrent of water looking at him. He had her hand but it slipped from his grasp, in another she was tied on a pyre; the flames getting higher and higher, she was looking at him with love in her eyes and he couldn't move to save her.

On the fourth day before he was to leave he found an envelope on the floor behind the door to the office. It was addressed simply "Alvaraz." He picked it up, examining it. He could smell her scent on the paper. As he opened it, the fragrance of frangipani and sandalwood filled his senses with a mixture of joy and anxiety. His emotions were in turmoil as he read her letter.

Alvaraz,

I yearn for you. The blue sky, the green hills, the song of the birds, they have all turned gray and their song blunted without you. We are meant to be together. My mother was right when she said I would fall in love with you. Just as no one can change the stars shining in the night or the moon rising in the twilight, no one can change the fact that you and I will be together forever. Don't worry, I will find a way.

The day father took me away he locked me in my room. That night he paced back and forth. I don't think he slept. I heard him ranting to himself and in the morning the maid told me she found him drunk, sleeping on the divan. They had a hard time getting him to his bed and then he didn't rise till late that evening. I'm not allowed out on pain of death to anyone who assists me. Father doesn't want anyone to ever know what happened at the office. I think he just wants you to sail away, so he can forget the whole thing. Please don't antagonize him.

Thank God I am allowed the companionship of my sisters. If this letter gets to you it is because of their work. I am to be sent to Spain on a Ship leaving tomorrow to live with my aunt in Seville. I am to attend a school for girls and marry a rich Moslem businessman, my father has picked out.

You will find a list of women and a list of men who will board your ship. You will find the lists in the second drawer beside your desk. I have already sent the lists to the governor. You must check the men and women off separately before they enter the ship. I know there are some who want to sneak on. Be very careful.

I know you want to follow your heart Alvaraz, but please do your duty. Following your heart will only cause both of us pain. I will end this letter with a kiss my love, the very thing getting us in this mess, but just you watch, that kiss is part of the plan to keep us together.

Be at peace my love, knowing all my love is locked in your heart and always will be.

Gemelda

He could feel the tears run down his face. He knew there was an Indiamen loaded with spices to depart on this very day. For the last few days barges, water lighters, and boats filled with people surrounded it. He ran to the patio and was just in time to see it set its sails at the outer edge of the harbor. The longboats that towed her out were already returning. He felt his breath shorten as he gulped, trying to find a solution to seeing her for a last time. It was no good, she had gone and he was alone.

The sun was intense; its burning heat melting his resolve. Like her, he thought, this land he found so enchanting, now appeared to him to be a hellhole. He could smell the sewage, and the palm trees, no longer representing the carefree elegance of this place; they looked like doomed soldiers, bent over, clinging to life, barely able to stand the heat while they clung to the parched sand. He fingered the letter; he could feel hot tears building up in the back of his eyes. He tried to stop crying, it was out of his hands. Timotemo had won and now he would pay—pay with sleepless nights and a lifetime of wondering and dreaming about her. He lovingly folded the letter, slipped it into the envelope and placed it in his breast packet next to his heart.

Chapter 20

He worked hard for the next four days. He inspected the ship several times; the image of Gemelda fleeting on the deck. He wondered where she'd put the diagrams of the ship. He couldn't find them anywhere in the office. He found he could dull his anguish by focusing on his work. Three times he went to the village with his new interpreter, Guillermo, a cousin of the chief. He would be the peoples' new chief when they arrived in the new land. He was a good man, but Alvaraz would never have selected him as he was fat and unhealthy looking.

With Gemelda's list in his hand, Alvaraz inspected the possessions each couple would bring: two hammocks, three changes of cloths, brushes, soap, washing cloths for their ablutions and an assortment of small brushes they used to clean their teeth and each with a new pair of boots, reluctantly requisitioned by the purser at Gemelda's insistence. Guillermo explained why the women each had a large box. "The boxes contain seeds for the garden they will plant. They all have palm nuts, an assortment of flowering shrubs, various vegetables, and fruit trees like mango and papaya. This is the tradition of our ancestors. They won't go without their 'seed boxes'."

Each box weighed fifty to sixty pounds. It seemed there was no end to the weight required to transport these men. First it's the women and now they all need seed boxes. He looked at the boxes and decided, they could be put in the bilges as ballast or perhaps used as furniture. They would have to be secured if used as furniture. He was the only one there who understood the potential violence of the sea. Those boxes could be lethal in a bad sea, finally he spoke, "They may bring them, but they will be stored in the bilges."

On the morning of departure four carts were hired to bring the villagers' belongings to the quay to be barged out to the ship. The passengers along with the whole village came and assembled in the square by the quay. The chief gave a speech in Tagalong interpreted for Alvaraz by Guillermo. "He talks of the courage of their ancestors sailing from the west, to this land, and the duty the new travelers have when they arrive in their new lands. The priest will be mad, but now he's blessing the people, asking the God of the Sea for a safe passage."

The chief's speech was followed by a catholic service asking for God's blessing and eternal love to go with these, his children, to the new land. A mass followed and all the new Christians took communion. After a long period of saying final goodbyes, where children cried and women wailed, the passengers were separated from the villagers. They lined up as instructed, by number, each following the one they knew was before them. Alvaraz, standing at the bottom of the ramp, inquired the name of each one, checked them off on his list, then sent them to the waiting longboat to be transported to the ship. He felt sad when the women came down the ramp one by one, some of them could barely speak they were so distraught. Many of them came as pairs supporting each other. As one pair of women went to the boat his senses brightened, as he smelled a familiar scent. Just as he was about to turn to take another look, a woman on the ramp fell and let out a scream. In the back of his mind he thought, 'how can this all work? What's it going to be like at sea?'

The coxswain of the ship's boat carried his gear to the waiting launch, and enquired, "Will there be anything else, Sir? You're the last to board, take a good look, Sir. This may be the last time you'll see dry land for a long time."

"That will be all. The tide will be ebbing in an hour. Take me to the ship. God knows how long it's going to take to get these people settled." responded Alvaraz as he boarded the boat and stood in the stern sheets.

Chapter 21

As he was rowed out to the ship, Alvaraz felt free. He wanted to be away, on the sea and somewhere deep in his subconscious he felt the key to his happiness could be found on the sea, far away from the troubles he found on the shore. He expected to see the decks filled with the village people, but as they approached all he saw were the faces of the crew looking down at him. As he mounted the ladder Rodrego bellowed, "Welcome aboard Senior Consollese." He then shouted across the deck to Ismel, bellowing, "secure the tow, and raise the anchor if you please and have the topsails set to port."

The windlass creaked as the men strained at the capstan and the oarsmen in the boats began the long tow to the wind. Within the hour the Lydia was safely out of the bay with all sails set, heading north around the far off point of land.

Alvaraz immediately went below to find out what happened to the villagers. All the deck hatches were open and he could hear excited chatter from below. Could it be the crew locked them in the hold? The door to the companionway was open and when he walked into the hold the people were working hanging blankets and arranging their living quarters.

Alvaraz found Guillermo and asked, "Why aren't the people on deck, I would have thought they would all be watching the land recede behind them."

"The Captain asked us to go below and make ourselves as comfortable as possible." answered Guillermo. "The people are quite happy to be here."

Alvaraz was amazed. There was a small passageway aft to the galley curtained off on both sides. Three women were being instructed by the cook who looked very happy as he showed them where to find the pots to cook in, where the food was and how to light a fire.

"I was worried," the cook said as Alvaraz approached, "I could never cook for this lot, but I may just be out of a job. I'm sure these women will do all the cooking," he said brightly.

With that Alvaraz took his gear and put it in his cabin. As he opened his cabin door he caught the scent of Gemelda. Everywhere he turned, he thought, I can smell her. He shrugged it off, carefully stored his belongings in the locker under his bed and lay in his berth. Minutes later, Philippe opened the door to their cabin and stood talking to Rodrego. When he saw Alvaraz lying in his berth, he said his goodbyes and addressed Alvaraz, "Welcome back, Alvaraz. I can't say I haven't enjoyed my solitude without you, but I welcome your cheery company. I'll probably be spending all my time in the Captain's anti-chamber when we're at sea. So you'll have all this space to yourself," he said as he crammed himself into the tiny cabin. He got what he was looking for, then left with the wish, "Have a good nap."

When he rose, Alvaraz could feel the ship rolling in the swell. He was feeling a little nauseated and knew the only cure was to stand on deck and watch the horizon. On his way he decided to have the people that feel sick stand on the deck with him. As he approached the companionway he could already smell the sent of human beings crammed together and the smell of vomit.

He found Guillermo and explained how the people who felt sick should go on deck and watch the horizon.

Guillermo answered, "The people expect this sickness, they will be better in time. Don't worry."

Alvaraz stood at the rail watching the sun go down in the rolling sea when a group of women came and stood beside him. They didn't seem sick. He thought they were talking about him; they smiled at him, their small bodies holding tightly to the rail swaying with the roll of the ship. He liked these people, they were clean and gentle, a happy people, and with their gleaming white teeth and smooth olive complexions they were very attractive. Guillermo came up later and explained, "The women were waiting for you to go on deck. With you here, they feel safe." he said. Before long a group of men came on deck and stood with the women. They all chattered excitedly while Guillermo translated for Alvaraz. "Only one person is sick, she's staying below. The women are looking after her. The people like the sea, they think of it as their mother. Now their mother wants them to be quiet, she's rocking them like a baby in a crib."

The sun's light was just a smudge on the horizon when Alvaraz returned to his cabin. He had no appetite for his dinner, so he retired to his bed, feeling ill and lonely.

For the next two days he ate and drank little. He helped the crew store some loose baggage and organized the villagers, so they could go on deck in shifts. Rodrego asked him to do this, because one day a whale was sighted and the whole group came out of the hold and stood on lee rail. With the press of the wind and the weight of almost two hundred people the Lydia suddenly heeled. Rodrego felt the list and immediately thought the ballast had shifted. He rushed out of his cabin and started shouting orders, "Bring the ship to windward, man the pumps, and Ismel get a detail together to take a look at the ballast."

Ismel stopped the Captain and pointed to the lee rail crowded with people. Rodrego's heart slowed down and he shouted, "cancel those orders—where's Alvaraz—we can't have those people moving around as a group."

On the third night they encountered a group of Islands. With two lookouts in the crow's nest in daylight Rodrego allowed the ship to sail through the islands, but as darkness fell he would anchor the Lydia in the lee of one of the Islands. Almost every night canoes would approach the Lydia. Rodrego would prepare the ship to repel boarders then try to talk to the islanders. None of the Manila natives knew their tongue. One evening Nino came forward and spoke some words to the visiting natives. The Manila natives had always accepted him as one of the crew. He spoke Spanish, not Tagalong, and worked as a crewmember: suddenly he became one of the man-eating people who lived in the islands.

"Nino, thank you for coming forward," said Rodrego gently." What do these people want?"

"I don't know all their words." These people are Milanese, they are my people, they are excited to see you. They want to trade and invite you to a feast on their island."

"We can trade metals and glass beads for fresh fruit, live pigs, and fresh water. Tell them no one is allowed on the ship on pain of death. We will shoot them if they try. Thank them for the invitation to the feast, but decline. We will lower a boat with trade goods."

Rodrego had an idea, "Nino, ask if there is anyone who knows these waters and can pilot us through to the ocean."

Nino became the center of attention that night as he translated for everyone. All night canoe after canoe came to the Lydia, with burning torches to light their way. In the morning four squealing pigs, a stack of fruit, a complete outrigger canoe with woven sail, a very old native man and his grandson stood on the deck. The ship's carpenter and his mates were busily building cages to hold the pigs, while the women and men from the hold prepared some of the fruit to eat and stored the rest. By midday the deck was cleared.

"The chief assigned his best navigator to take you to the ocean. He will guide us through some islands, then across a sea to a chain of Islands and show us a pass into the endless sea." translated Nino. Philippe, Rodrego, the old man and Nino stayed in the Captain's anti-chamber for hours. The old man came out and pointed to a high mountain, instructing Rodrego to steer straight to it. Philippe and the old man sat and drew a chart of the land and water. The old man, with unfailing accuracy, guided the ship between the islands into an inland sea then pointed to what looked like a solid face of islands, but as they approached they could see a pass between the mountains. They anchored the last night in the middle of the pass. They could feel the swell of the ocean gently roll the ship as they lay through the night. At first light a breeze came up from the islands powering them through the final pass. When they were safely at sea Rodrego gave the order to heave-to.

"You have been a good pilot." Rodrego said putting his hand gently on the old man's shoulder. "Thank you and your chief for this help. It would have taken us a month to find our way through this maze of islands." Nino translated and as he did the old man took Rodrego's hand in both his and gave a short bow. They lowered the out-rigger canoe, loaded the old man, his grandson, a generous portion of food and water, a gift of four knives of the finest Toledo steel and a dozen strings of beads, then sent them off. Their light craft skimmed across the swell like a gull skimming over the tops of the waves.

Guillermo stood at the rail with Alvaraz saying, "These people have always been our enemies. When I was a child we were attacked, they killed some of our people and burned most of our village. They take the bodies of the ones they kill and eat them. My family was spared by hiding in a cave high up in the mountains above our village. After that we moved our village to Manilla. They don't attack there because of the Spanish guns."

Chapter 22

Alvaraz was pleased to find he only felt a little nauseated with the new motion of the ship. He ate and drank and by the end of the day he was feeling well. They sailed northeast as close as the ship would point and keep speed. Alvaraz heard Captain Rodrego give the order to the helmsman, "Sail her by the wind, lads. We want to go as far east as we can." Some of the helmsmen, especially at night, were better than others at watching the flags flying from the masthead and steering to get the most speed out of the sails without collapsing them. When they went too close to the wind the sails would flutter, then they would correct the course allowing the sails to fill with a booming sound, waking the whole ship. It was a slow uphill process, but Rodrego and the navigator knew that sooner or later they would find the cold north pacific and the winds would turn around and push them east.

Nino became a close companion to Philippe. They learned from each other about navigation. Often Nino would tell Philippe there was an island in the vicinity, and sure enough, in a day or sometimes two they would sail by an island. Philippe stood on the rail for hours watching the pattern of waves with Nino. He always felt more comfortable at night if Nino said there was no land near by.

A routine was established; Before the fishing commenced and long before the sun rose, a dozen barrels used as chamber pots, were heaved up and emptied through the stern deck then, the fishermen would set up their lines on spools from the aft deck next to the heads. It was a rare day they didn't catch enough fish to feed the entire compliment of the ship. Later in the morning other men from the hold would come on deck to take over the fishing while the first shift would take buckets of seawater and wash the decks. The women kept busy preparing the wool capes and pants, helping the cook and cleaning their quarters. Father Emilio gave lessons everyday for first communion two hours before lunch. Captain Rodrego and Philippe could be found in the Capitan's antechamber adding details to existing charts and copying others. Capitan Rodrego took great pains to accurately record the voyage, because he expected to receive a good income from its publishing when he returned to Spain. Alvaraz kept busy taking his watches with the other officers and carving models of the hull he wanted to build when he arrived at his shipyard. At first the easy chatter of the natives and their seemingly continuous laughter irritated Alvaraz, but as time went by, he grew to like it, to the point where when he didn't hear it he grew uneasy.

Everyday Alvaraz found his cabin cleaned. He never saw anyone there and when he asked the other officers if their cabins were cleaned while on watch, they gave him a funny look and asked him why he asked. He confessed to finding his cabin cleaned and often a new sheet on his bed. "You must be a favored one, mate," they said, "we never get our cabins cleaned."

He came off watch early one morning and saw a woman leaving his cabin. She blew out her lamp, turned with her bucket and brush and hurried down the hall. Alvaraz just caught a glimpse of her in the new morning light, as he came down the companionway stairs. There was something very familiar about her. He missed the last two steps of the companionway ladder in his haste to catch up to her, almost upturning the scuttlebutt. She hesitated in the narrow passageway, and then turned towards him.

Alvaraz stopped; he couldn't believe his eyes. His mind reeled, its only explanation, a fantazma. Could he be so connected to this woman that he sees her everywhere. He often knew she was in his presence. There was a scent in the air, a whiff of her presence. With a crash, the logic came together. Somehow his soul knew she was aboard, she was here amongst the women, hidden in their multitude. As he walked toward her, he wondered if it were possible. How could it be; she's on a ship headed for Spain and her aunt in Seville. With a last gasp his mind settled and a new logic came to him. You are in a dream, Alvaraz; wake up! He stood staring at her, he was in full control of himself. He looked around in the creamy light from the new dawn. She stood still, her eyes glistening as she saw him. It was the tear that finally convinced him. She was crying and reaching for him. They fell together sobbing. Alvaraz couldn't bring himself to speak. He held her there, as if she were a dream he didn't want to release. Finally she spoke, in the voice of one close to loosing control of her emotions, "Darling—I told you I would find a way." Then she turned her head up and said with a tremor of laughter, "You checked me off as I descended the ramp to the quay."

He remembered clearly now, she had her head down and was being helped down the ramp by another women. He was distracted and never checked if it were truly she.

"I'm not a stowaway Alvaraz, my name is on the list."

"What name do you have?" he asked peering into her eyes with the look of compassion.

My new Christian name is Imelda, when I marry I will take on the name of my husband. I was baptized with the other women on the day before we left.

A wave of passion swept over Alvaraz, He cried freely, holding her in his arms sobbing. His love for her surpassing anything he had ever known.

No one came to investigate his sobbing. The noise must have been absorbed by the constant creaking of the hull as they rolled through the Pacific swell. He took her to his cabin. He closed the door and pulled her onto his bunk. They lay against the hull together as she told him her story.

Her father lectured her endlessly about who she was and the terrible shame she had brought to their family. While he spoke she dreamed of Alvaraz. She dreamed of his strength, his blue eyes and long golden hair. In those days before she was to be sent to Spain she found peace with her mother. She knew her mother was with her in spirit as she sat on her bed listening to her father. She could feel her strength and knew the calm she felt while her father ranted, was her mother's spirit helping her through this time of trial. Her father kept her in her room until the day of departure. In the morning he took her to the quay in his carriage, escorting her to the Indiamen. He waved saying he would see her in Seville the following year. He'd given her letters to his aunt and a man who he trusted to transport her from Cadiz to Seville. She thought there was no escape, but on the hour of departure, a native canoe from the village, came by. The women made a lot of noise about selling some last minute fruit for the passengers Gemelda recognized her friend Gabriela's voice. Gemelda saw her chance. She was hidden by the girth of the bowsprit and when she saw the native canoe come along the side she removed her, dress put it under her arm and slipped over the side. She swam undetected along the hull then hid behind the canoe. The people in the canoe knew all that was going on and had come especially for her. They paddled slowly away with her clinging to the outrigger. She hid in the village until the time came for them to go.

"I was so nervous you would find me, or the Indiaman would turn back. I left a note for the Captain of the Indianan saying Gemelda would be going on the next packet to Spain. Please deliver her belongings to the address of the man she was to contact in Cadiz. Signed Timotemo Singh. I even attended communion with the others at the service before we left. Father Emilio baptized me, as Imelda. I have been to two services with him on the ship since we left, and he's teaching me to have my first communion. He's never known me as Gemelda," she paused for a few minutes, listening to the sounds of the ship.

"It was easy to hide on the Lydia, I know her so well. I studied the diagrams when I was locked in my room. I did get terribly sick on the first day out. I was told you came to warn the other people about seasickness and to go on deck. The problem is I know the crew and Captain Rodrego so well and they know me as Gemelda. If I did go on deck I would be found out and sent back, but oh how I wanted to see you there. I sent some of my friends up to report to me how you were." She paused studying the tiny cabin sole,

"Alvaraz, I need to change my appearance."

"Why?" asked Alvaraz. "There's nothing anyone can do now and I'm sure Rodrego won't mind." As he said this he remembered the talk he had with Rodrego after the incident with Timotemo. He promised my father he would return me to Cadiz to be married to Maria. "Well maybe you should stay hidden for a while longer. We can think of something."

"I hear you're a father Alvaraz."

Gema's words sat for a minute in Alvaraz's mind, He was feeling so relaxed and contented, the two of them together at last, as they should be. Her words stirred his peace and soon a storm raged in his mind. He turned to her and she said, "I heard all about it, Alvaraz, every detail. The women are very curious about you," she said, smiling, her lips turned with that mischievous smile he knew so well. "I think they exaggerate about you, but, I'm proud and happy you're mine," she said looking at him with her expression of uncluttered love. She leaned over and kissed him gently on the cheek. He responded with a kiss on her full lips. They rolled up onto his berth. There was just enough room to lie side by side. A wave of urgent passion erased their connection to reality. Their bodies touched in their joint need to satisfy the other without having sexual intercourse. Alvaraz found himself holding her naked bottom to his lips, her body became rigid as his seed pulsed. This time she didn't disengage, as he swirled through his pleasure, stars bursting around him. He felt her pelvis rocking and eagerly massaged her erect nub with his tongue. Her legs were clamped so tight to his ears he didn't hear her loud gasp and moan of pleasure

They stayed like that for a few minutes. Alvaraz expected to see eyes watching, but found the cabin door still shut in the light from the deck prism. They didn't speak; instead they gently held each other communicating their love with their eyes. In the ocean swell the ship made creaking noises, thumping noises and the sound of the wind singing through the rigging. It seemed they were part of a symphony, the ship moving through the waves, the harmony of their love part of the rhythm of life. Only one thing took away from the feeling of harmony and that was the threat of discovery.

"I could cut my hair and become a young boy."

Alvaraz heard her, but the notion seemed so preposterous that he let it go.

"You could discover me and keep me in your cabin."

Alvaraz burst out in quiet laughter at the thought.

"I have very small breasts, no one would know I wasn't a boy," she said looking seriously at Alvaraz.

Alvaraz was silent for a few minutes as he thought of the ludicrous thing Gemelda was saying. He was so happy she was there; it was as if his mind and body were relaxing for the first time since he last saw her. This was so amazing seeing her, he couldn't think of the future. Instead he hugged her and said, "Can't you just hide with the native woman for a while and I'll feel out Captain Rodrego. If we both told the truth, we would expose ourselves as frauds," as he said the words he realized telling the truth would be as bad as living a secret life. "I'm sure Captain Rodrego and Father Emilio would understand."

She looked deep into his eyes and said, "I don't know Rodrego, would your God understand?"

"I'm sure my God would understand, it's the people representing him I worry about." He took Gemelda's hand in his and asked, "when will I see you again? My watch starts again at midnight, I'm off at dawn. Is there any reason why we can't meet again in the morning? I have a lot to think about?"

"I'll be here," she said.

Alvaraz opened the door to his cabin; "Ismel was standing at the scuttlebutt with Nino. He was speaking very slowly in Spanish so Nino could understand. "I want to teach you the ropes Nino. We should start today," When Ismel saw Alvaraz emerging from his cabin, he said loudly in the confined space, "Alvaraz, I need you to help me teach Nino the ropes. I need more men in the rigging; if the weather blows up I want to be able to get those sails down in a hurry. Could you give up some of your carving time to help me train Nino?"

"I've just come off watch and need a bit of sleep, but later I'd be glad to," Alvaraz said nervously as he walked over to the butt and took a dipper of water.

"Oh, and here I am keeping you awake," Ismel said sarcastically, "I've got some time at three bells, so I'll meet you on the foredeck at three bells if that'll suit," he said.

"It's good with me," said Alvaraz as he drank the water. He turned to go back to his cabin; only three paces away, hoping Ismel and Nino would disappear so he could get Gema out of his cabin. They slowly went up the companionway stairs making small talk in slow Spanish. Alvaraz, now nervous as a cat on a hot tin roof, quickly opened the door to his cabin and let Gemelda out. "See you tomorrow," he said briefly kissing her and nervously watching her walk the short distance to the cargo hold. He breathed a sigh of relief, entered his cabin and flopped down reeling at the new complication in his life.

All that day he thought about how he could resolve the dilemma about Gema. He could just let everything stay the way it was. All the other possibilities seemed ridiculous. If things stayed the same Gema would be below decks for months. He racked his brains. Maybe she could alter her appearance as a woman enough so the crew wouldn't recognize her. She had a new name after all. How long would it be before they realized and then he couldn't be with her any more? Why is my life so complicated he thought.

Three times that day he went into the cargo hold with lame excuses to talk to Guillermo, or ask the cook if he had a spare biscuit telling him he was hungry, even after the enormous lunch he'd eaten. He thought he heard Gemelda's laughter coming from the other side of the hold, but never saw her. His frustration and anxiety grew as he grappled with these new problems.

He half-heartedly helped Ismel with Nino's training. Each line on the ship had a specific purpose, but before a sailor learned, to identify, and how to use each rope he had to know the working of a block and tackle and a capstan winch. Ismel didn't seem to be in any hurry as he and Alvaraz gave Nino a pile of line and some blocks and requested he rig them and pull one of the cannons from its pit. If Nino were wearing a shirt he thought he wouldn't look that much different from Gemelda with her hair shorn, then he snorted and thought about the scandal when they were found out; which they surely would.

The sky was filling with more than the usual trade wind scud. "I think we'll see the weather get up with that lot coming at us," said Ismel while showing Nino the proper knot to tie around the bale of the block.

Just as Nino was to heave the cannon with his newly assembled block the Lydia healed sharply. "I'll be going to see Rodrego," Ismel said, "Carry on, Alvaraz. I'll be back."

He left and Nino said, "I should look at the water."

The warm breeze became very humid as they walked to the rail. Nino studied the waves for a minute then pointed, explaining to Alvaraz the significance of the high long swell lifting the ship. It was almost unnoticeable, but on the top of these waves there were a set of opposing waves growing at an alarming rate. Alvaraz noticed Nino take a deep breath before he explained. "These are the waves of a big wind to the south. Soon the wind will reach us. Sometimes these waves become as tall as your masts."

Alvaraz shouted at Ismel who came and looked at the sea. Soon Rodrego and Philippe joined them. After hearing what Nino had to say, they discussed a plan to save the ship if a storm of this magnitude should strike. In the mean time the wind had changed directions and was now driving them northeast.

"If we stay on this course at this speed we will be at latitude thirty, in five days," said Philippe.

"I'll double the watch and keep some men aloft to quickly furl the sails if need be," said Ismel.

The ship hurtled along all evening as the sea built, but the wind remained the same. At midnight Alvaraz started his watch. He made up his mind; after he talked to her in the morning he would talk to Rodrego privately; he would come clean and ask Rodrego to simply transport Gemelda to New Spain. He only needed to be near her and know she was safe to be happy. She could stay with the women and he could visit her occasionally. They didn't need to live in carnal sin for the entire trip like she was suggesting.

Chapter 23

The ship was rolling heavily when he went off watch. Waves would break over the bow sending a cascade of water down the deck. The two forward deck hatches were closed tight and if the water started flooding the hold through the aft hatch it would be closed as well making the passengers very uncomfortable. Alvaraz expected to find Gemelda in his cabin that morning but all he found was a mess. The bedding of both berths was strewn on the tiny cabin sole. He cleaned it up leaving his cabin door swinging. When she didn't come he closed the door and lay on his berth. He awoke with a knocking on his door. He had slept till past noon. He emerged from his cabin to find the air was cool and the ship was riding on a gentle swell. He idly thought they must have missed the predicted storm as he saw Philippe standing at his door.

He yawned as Philippe said; "Rodrego wants to see you in his cabin. In the night a stowaway was discovered hiding in the firewood bin. It's a young lad who swam away from the Indiamen. He tells us he wants to be a shipbuilder."

Alvaraz blanched; the feeling of calm, having slept on a settling sea in the cool air, instantly disappeared and was replaced by a knot in his bowels indicating he needed to use the head. "I'll be right there, mate, first I must use the head."

On his way to the head, he thought, what shall I do? Could it be this stowaway was genuine? God, please don't let it be Gemelda. Oh please, God, he prayed as he sat oh the head. He finally stood with the thought; I must face up to this. Why doesn't she obey me? Damnation.

The door to the Captain's cabin was open and when Alvaraz walked into the Anti-chamber, he saw a sulking young boy, his hair short and unkempt, his face smudged with charcoal. He looked skinny and unhealthy, dressed in torn trousers, and a dirty loose shirt. Alvaraz was relieved; this was a legitimate stowaway. He walked over to take a closer look, and when he did he could smell her. His heart stopped with the recognition of her scent. He barely maintained his composure as his mind tried desperately to find a solution. He wanted to say why; why can't you just obey? Instead he heard himself ask, "What's your name, boy, and where did you grow up"

"Alfonso," she replied, "and I grew up in Granada."

Alvaraz found himself smiling.

Rodrego interrupted, "I know you're off watch Alvaraz, but we have a problem. I understand Philippe filled you in on the details of our stowaway. He wants to be a shipbuilder; in the mean time we need him for the rigging. There's no room for him in the foc'sle. We could have him sleeping on the deck, looking after the pigs, but Philippe kindly gave up his berth in your cabin if you'll have him. You can teach him the art of shipbuilding and maybe he can help you with your models. What do you say?" Rodrego asked.

Alvaraz scowled at the young boy. He didn't want to seem too happy with the idea and at first said, his anger at Gemelda's disobedience clear on his face for her to see, "Why doesn't he stay in the wood bin, where you found him?"

"Can't; that's next to the women in the hold." Rodrego quickly responded.

"Does he have any other clothes?"

"No, we were hoping you could help him out with that," said Rodrego.

With a sigh Alvaraz agreed to take the young stowaway into his care. Ismel said, "We'll be training him the ropes with Nino. Have him up on deck at three bells today."

This is insane Alvaraz thought with a mixture of excitement and annoyance as he led her to his cabin. How the hell did she pull this off? I just don't believe it.

Three of the crew were standing around the scuttlebutt at the foot of the companionway stairs. When they saw the stowaway one of them jeered and said, "We'll be putting him through his paces eh, lads.

Alvaraz in an attempt to act normal grabbed the sailor's shoulder playfully with his large hand and said, "I'll be watching, mark my words. You'll be looking after this one, he's in my care and I don't want any rough stuff. Now let me introduce you to the new member of the ship. This here being Alfonso a runaway from Granada." He led the boy to his cabin and when he opened the door, bellowed, "What a mess. Get up on deck and get a bucket of water and a brush to clean this place up."

She came back with the water and started cleaning, the men left the scuttlebutt and Gemelda quickly closed the door to the cabin.

"I knew I could do it" she said. "Oh Alvaraz, I'm so happy."

He couldn't believe it, and said, "What are you going to do now, Gema? They're going to send you up in the rigging in the middle of pitch-black nights. I can't let this happen."

It's OK my darling. I know I'll love it, don't worry about me. This is so incredibly exciting. You know, I've always wanted to do this." She grabbed him excitedly then said, "Alvaraz, we're going to be together. I'm strong and can do the rest. She undressed and he could see she was wearing a tight cloth binding her breasts. She saw him looking and said, "if they see this, I'll tell them I broke a rib and use this to bind it."

She washed herself and without hesitation dug into his cloths locker. "These are all too big, go to the hold; ask for Gabriela, she will have a bundle of clothes for me."

When Alvaraz returned with the bundle of clothes Gemelda had a clean boyish looking face and with the clothes she fit the part perfectly. Alvaraz resigned himself, he had no control over her so he might just as well play the game and suffer the consequences when they arrived.

At noon she went through the same exercise Nino had the day before, rigging the block and tackle and using it to single-handedly pull the canon out of its pit. In the afternoon she and Nino rigged a safety rope and climbed the mast. Nino stopped at the first set of cross trees, but, Alfonso, a name Alvaraz concentrated on using, climbed to the crows nest and then beyond to the very top of the mast.

Ismel stood on the deck with Alvaraz gazing up at Alfonso. He was holding on with one arm, using the other to shade his view as he peered around the horizon, the long red pennant at the top of the mast fluttering just above his head.

While Ismel announced proudly, "Looks like we've got ourselves a sailor," Alvaraz, his heart in his mouth, was having trouble breathing, his fear for her so great, tightening his chest. Ismel hollered for her to come down. She stopped her self from apologizing to Alvaraz when he scolded her for going so high, instead she said with confidence in an attempted low voice, "I've been higher on the Indiaman."

The next exercise was one Alvaraz learned soon after leaving Spain. Every member of the crew must know how to hand the sails. He climbed up with Gemelda and Nino to the first set of booms and walked out on the footropes tied below the boom. "These are called footropes," he told them. "When the order comes to reduce sail, you and three others come up here and furl the sail as the loose-footed boom is raised."

Ismel gave the order to raise the boom, "release the sheets on the forward main, hall the clew lines and bunt lines. Look sharp there, sailor," he yelled at the men at the blocks, "We've got trainees up there; show em how it's done now. Pull the yard arms tight," he yelled.

The bottom boom came smartly up to the yardarm with a thunk. Alvaraz looked across the yardarm to make sure his students were supporting themselves by holding the upper part of the yardarm, and then instructed, "never hold the yardarm from beneath or you'll be hanging here till the next set of the sail."

The deflated sail flapped in the wind ahead of them, while the three of them slowly gathered the sail tying it with every fold. They were very slow, but Alvaraz told them they would be able to do this in their sleep with lots of practice. "This job must be done very quickly if a squall is coming. Usually the Captain will start with the topsails and work his way down as the wind increases. Some times the boat rolls so bad you almost get dipped in the water even though you are way up here on the yard arms."

He watched Gemelda and realized she was struggling to pull the heavy sail material. Her arms were well developed but she needed to develop muscles to do this work. He remembered her hands and the calluses he found there from working on her fathers farm and decided not to interfere. As he helped her he was reassured when he saw the look of determination in her eyes as she struggled. Alvaraz helped them hand the heavy sail material, tying the gaskets to finish the job. Ismel came up to check the knots after they furled the sail. When he was satisfied it was properly done, he had them untie the gaskets then yelled at the man at the ropes. "Release the clew lines, and bunt lines and haul the sheets to port." They released the ties as the boom fell. The sail made a mighty crack as the wind filled it, pulling the yard arm around and almost spilling the students clinging to the yard arm into the sea." Well done, lads," said Ismel, "get down and have your grog and slops. We'll continue this tomorrow."

"I'll train Alfonso for the topsails, he doesn't have the strength for the big sails, but I like his spirit. He'll do fine," Ismel said, reassuring Alvaraz.

Every day the new sailors climbed the ratlines into the rigging, furling and unfurling the sails, pulling and releasing sheets and servicing, by lubricating and replacing lines through the blocks at the end of booms. This work needed to be done. The experienced sailors supervised the work and appreciated the brave young sailor who didn't seem to mind climbing out to the end of a boom holding on with one hand while using the other hand to inject seal oil into the shaft of the block. Gemelda had no trouble with the sailors, who saw in her, a person who had the courage to do the most dangerous tasks in the high rigging.

As the days passed the wind came more from the south, then slowly died. The sea became calm and glassy with a long swell beneath to roll the ship. For three days the ship rolled, the crew became restless and irritated by the constant racket of the sails booming and banging above. On Sunday Alfonso disappeared.

Gemelda with a sparkle in her eye said, "For a few hours I am changing to Imelda. I want to take communion with Father Emilio and give my confession to God, with the other women from the hold." She put on a dress pulling a thick scarf over her head, kissed Alvaraz, asked him to check the companionway. When he reported it was clear, she was gone. The ship rolled, almost pitching Alvaraz into the scuttlebutt. He climbed the companionway stairs, walked across the deck and steadied himself on the port rail. He had settled into a routine with Alfonso. When she closed the door to his cabin she changed from a skinny, serious young boy into a sensuous woman. Alvaraz had given up worrying about her. She found tasks few were eager to do, and saved the other sailors the burden of their fear. Alfonso was respected and, to all appearances, very obedient to his master. He worked with his master carving ship models, training to be a good sailor by learning the ropes and rarely ventured out of his shared cabin on his leave.

Alvaraz liked the arrangement. Gemelda was truly a fearless women, constantly bringing Alvaraz to the brink of a breakdown, then somehow slipping through the tangled web of lies and deceit they shared coming out the other side unscathed. His fear of discovery was diminishing and often he watched calmly as she played whatever role she needed to play to make the ruse seem plausible.

The wonderful part of their life was the intimacy he shared with her. The cabin was small and almost impossible to move around without touching the other. Gemelda would sleep in the upper bunk, but to get to it she would sometimes rub against Alvaraz's arm hanging from his berth. She would gently pick up his arm place it on his cot and lean over to give him a kiss. In his sleep he would reach up and pull her to him. They never had sexual intercourse. There was a powerful urge to couple, and many times they came close, but always managed to satisfy each other's sexual needs without the actual act.

Alvaraz turned to watch the women disgorge from the companionway led by Father Arturo dressed in his finest robes. They unsteadily assembled on the main deck. Alvaraz joined the other sailors who were on their off watch to attend the service. Prayers were made asking for a safe passage. The priest then gave a sermon relating their voyage to the new Christians following Jesus to the Sea of Galilee to bring the greater glory of God to a new land. The priest gave a communion then stood by the steps to the upper deck giving out the host and blessing each person in his care. Alvaraz was close enough to Gemelda to hear Father Arturo say, "May the Lord bless you and keep you, Imelda." Hearing the name Imelda sent a spasm of fear through Alvaraz's bowels, and he had an urgent need to use the head. He took his communion then hurried aft.

Chapter 24

Upon returning he heard Rodrego make an announcement. Today they would slaughter two of the pigs and open a keg of beer to brighten up the mood of the ship. The crew cheered while the natives looked around. Guillermo stood and explained to the people what the Captain had said and they all brightened up and looked at the pigpen. There was a short discussion the conclusion being, the natives knew how to slaughter a pig best and so they were given the job. Within minutes people were changing out of their church cloths into their light working cloths. A large pan was brought from the galley and a group made up of sailors and native men wrestled the biggest of the pigs from its cage. The men held the squealing pig still, while a man with a machete made a quick cut to its throat. The blood was collected in the pan and taken away to be coddled. The pig was eviscerated, the good eating parts of the innards collected and the offal placed in a pan.

A young native man took the unwanted guts and tossed them over the side. Alvaraz watched this as he held onto the rail of the rolling ship. For a minute the strips of bowels just sat in the water, then a few fish came to investigate. Soon the water was alive with fish biting and tearing at the waste. Alvaraz saw a fin slicing through the clear water from quite a distance off. The fish fled as the huge predator approached. With one bite the entire chunk of intestines was in the power of the shark. Out of both sides of the shark's mouth, pieces of bowel streamed behind, slowly being consumed as the shark jerked the food down. How long would a helpless man last if he fell into this sea, Alvaraz thought as he turned to find the pigs completely butchered into cook-able pieces. Many hands make light work he said to himself as he watched the cook take the pieces of meat down into the galley to be prepared for the feast.

Even though the ship was rolling and the sails rattling and banging the party began with much good cheer. Some of the sailors brought out musical instruments and some of the natives used blocks of wood as percussion instruments while others played a type of reed pipe. The beer flowed and the party heated up. Gemelda still in her Sunday dress danced with Alvaraz and then the two of them took a plate of food to the base of the bowsprit. They sat there watching the sunset cast an eerie orange glow on the sails.

"Do you know what I want to do when we get to the new land?" she asked Alvaraz, her mouth half full of food. He couldn't see her eyes for the scarf that hid her lack of hair.

"No, Gema, tell me."

"I want you to build me a house, with a veranda overlooking the sea. In that house I want to have many children. Do you think we can have this Alvaraz?" She asked dreamily.

"Your dream is my dream," he said as he cleaned his plate. "I too want to have a big house with many children and a wife I can love without any doubts for the rest of my life."

He bent over to kiss her then held back, turning to see all the partiers very close at hand. As he turned back to her, he felt it; it was a breath of wind, He could see the jib rising and filling. In the last glow of sunset he could see way off in the distance a black shroud of clouds covering the sky to the south. "You should get back to the cabin and change into Alfonso, don't you think," he asked.

"Will you come with me?" she asked sensuously.

"I'll follow in a few minutes, first I'll return these things to the galley."

As he walked across the deck towards his cabin, Rodrego, who was on the aft deck with Philippe, Ismel, and the sergeant at arms stopped him. "Alvaraz, we have some weather coming in," He leaned towards him over the counter rail, "see if you can find Nino, we want to ask him his opinion."

Alvaraz found Nino in the galley carrying buckets of water for the wash up. He said his hellos to the cook asking if he could borrow Nino. On the way up the stairs Nino blankly stated, "there is a storm not far away, I thought the Captain knew, and that was why he was having a last party."

Alvaraz stopped him on the stairs, "Will it be a big storm Nino?"

"When the waves grow from the south, the wind can blow over palm trees, it is so strong."

They rushed up the stairs to the waiting group of leaders. When Rodrego heard the news, he visibly paled, pulled himself together, and ordered all hands on deck to double lash anything movable on deck, then turned to Ismel and said, "Get some men aloft I want the sails furled and storm sails set."

The wind was building at an alarming rate and the swell was causing the Lydia to gyrate unmercifully. Alfonso came across the deck giving Alvaraz a stab of remorse. He wanted to run to Gema and hold her, instead he listened to Ismel assign the tasks for reducing sail. He was to go aloft and hand the main while Alfonso and two others were to go to the topsails. Alfonso seemed to fly up the ratlines ascending to the very top of the main mast. He was the first to move out on the yardarms. When Ismel saw Alfonso in the last light of sunset scamper out on the foot ropes he ordered the men on deck to release the sheets and haul the topsail yard up with the clew lines and bunt lines. Within minutes the two forward masts were furled and storm sails rigged at deck level between the masts. The crew on the forward mizzenmast was having trouble getting the huge lateen sail down. Usually these sails came down simply by releasing the block at the top of the mast allowing the jaws to close. Unfortunately the block was jammed. There was no way the men could get to the block so it remained fully open causing the stern of the ship to yaw wildly with the waves.

A huge wave caught the ship on her starboard quarter and washed the deck clean of any left over party paraphernalia. When Rodrego saw the wave he was thankful the villagers were all below decks but realized the deck hatches were still open. He shouted to some sailors, holding onto the main mast, to close the hatches, but his words were carried away by the wind. Ismel stood beside him and shouted the order in a much louder voice heard by the men and they immediately closed the hatches and pounded in the wedges to secure them.

A crowd of sailors accumulated on the aft deck beside the mast with the fully deployed lateen sail. The Lydia almost rolled on her beam-ends, her hull shrieking with the agony of the press of sail in the increasing wind. Rodrego inquired where the carpenter was; thinking the only way to save the ship was to saw the mast off. Without asking he saw the carpenter lumber awkwardly in the impossible motion of the ship up the steps to the aft deck.

"We have a bad leek in the port bilge sir, you should have the boys man the pumps," he shouted in Rodrego's ear.

Ismel overhearing this assigned the gunnery officer the job of recruiting some men to man the pumps. In the mean time the carpenter asked Alvaraz to assist him in the bilges to see if he could think of a way to staunch the leak. It took twice as long as usual for the pair to get below decks, go through the galley and down into the bilges because they were continually being thrown around by the violent motion. The rising fear Alvaraz felt as he descended the ladder into the bilges was justified as he saw in the lamplight a horizontal sheet of water spraying through the planking of the ship.

"This frame is cracked, must have cracked when we hit the reef and no-one detected it. When the ship rolls she twists; opening up these seams and blowing out her caulking. We've been trying to drive more calking in but it just blows out when she rolls," said the carpenter.

Alvaraz; his fear gone, as he analyzed the problem, saw the two foot by two foot oak frame and wondering how it could possibly crack. He examined it closely and detected a flaw in the wood. It was a black line running through the grain. It caused a weakness and when it was tested with the reef it was weakened and now with the force of this incredible storm it had broken. To do a proper job he would have the carpenters remove a foot of the frame five feet on each side of the break then replace it with new oak fastening it every three inches. Water cascaded over him as the ship rolled opening the planks.

"We can make a temporary patch by nailing lath over canvas to the surrounding planks. Get some men down here," said Alvaraz calmly. The carpenter sent his assistant up and before long a patch was nailed securely to the hull. Water still leaked through the hull but it was a mere trickle easily handled by the pumps.

When Alvaraz was satisfied he left the men to finish the job and ascended the stairs to the aft deck. The weather had deteriorated to the point that it was difficult to move on deck and impossible to see through the mist even with the multitude of storm lanterns burning. Rodrego was leaning back on the rail looking up at the top of the mizzen with the flailing lanteen sail. Alvaraz pulled himself across the deck holding on as a wave washed over him. He found the railing to the aft deck and scrambled up before the next wave came intending to give Rodrego a report on the leak. Instead Rodrego leaned over and said, "Alfonso has shinnied up the mast with an ax to cut away the jammed block."

Alvaraz visibly jumped forward, in an involuntary move to stop her. The wind caught him throwing him to the deck. He recovered himself and gazed aloft. With a dozen lanterns flickering he could just make out the image of his Gemelda just about at the top of the mast, an ax dangling from a rope tied around her waist. He could hear his heart pounding in his ears above the roar of the storm as he leaned back, paralyzed with a confused fear. He watched helplessly as she straddled the top of the mast clamping her legs, using her feet to lock her legs so she could grip the slippery mast. She found the ax and made some clumsy attempts, flailing at the rope attached to the top of the mast. On her fourth attempt the ax bit into the line. It didn't sever it but strands of line could be seen blowing in the wind unraveled from its parent. When the ax bit for the second time the top boom jumped but didn't come down. Alvaraz could hear Ismel telling the men to clear the down wind part of the aft deck, when suddenly the rope broke with a crack and the boom came down with a violence Alvaraz hadn't experienced before. The ship turned off the wind swinging the mast in an unimaginable motion. Alvaraz; his eyes glued to the top of the mast watched helplessly as the body of his Gemelda was thrown into the sea on the port side of the ship.

He knew what he had to; with an unexpected calm, he watched the trajectory of her body. She fell into the sea just aft of the main mast to port. He scanned the aft deck in the flickering lamp light with the flailing sail billowing out aft trapped by the second mizzen. He saw a coil of rope on the rail. It was a sounding line. He ran towards it, in his haste almost crashed into Rodrego who was trying to regain his balance. He heard his voice cry out in a very clear loud voice, "Gemelda is in the water to port; I'm going in." He found the line tied it to the rail the other end around his waist, kicked off his boots, climbed over the rail. He stopped. It was as if he were watching someone else. This other person was calm beyond understanding; he was organized in this turmoil with a single-minded determination to find her. A wave washed through the main deck and with steely concentration Alvaraz searched the boiling sea in the lee of the Lydia. She was nowhere to be seen. The wind and spray screamed around him as he searched, The green of the phosphorescence grew as the water from the deck poured into the sea to the lee. Could it be; he saw a silhouette of a body blocking the green glow. Without hesitation he dove as if he were diving for coins of the quay in Grenada when he was a boy. The water enveloped him in its cool glove and the sound of the raging storm ceased for a minute, then he was sputtering, trying to get a breath in the foamy top layer of the sea. He swam high, breathing and orienting himself. He swam to the spot he remembered last seeing her from the rail. She was nowhere to be found. Again he swam along side the ship and turned searching and there she was. He could feel his frenzied strokes were strong and just as his out stretched hand touched her body the rope around his waist came taut. He untied the knot freeing himself in a panic, then swam towards her lifeless body. He grabbed her up. She seemed so small in his arms. He could feel the binding around her chest and a surge of emotion flowed through him, followed by an adrenalin surge of fear as he looked around for the Lydia. She was moving away, there was no way he could catch her, then he felt something sawing at his neck. It was the rope he'd tied to the rail. As he grabbed hold wrapping it around his wrist he heard her coughing, then the line tightened and his arm was almost pulled from its socket. He looked up to see two sailors grab the line and pull while another ran the free line to the waist of the ship. It all happened so quickly. When the ship rolled down they grabbed her from him, then two others grabbed him under the armpits and dropped him on the deck.

    He regained his footing and was helped up the stairs to the aft deck. Gemelda was bent over coughing and sputtering; she had blood running down the side of her head. Rodrego was leaning over her and when he saw Alvaraz he congratulated him by slapping him on the back. "Well done Alvaraz," he yelled.

    Alvaraz could feel he was getting the shakes after the adrenalin rush, but he held his composure and said with out thinking, "I'll get her below, Sir."

    Rodrego gave him a quizzical look as he gave his consent.

    Alvaraz carried her, on his shoulder, to the steps leading down to the main deck waiting for a wave to spill from the deck then carried her down the steps with one hand holding her, the other holding the rail. He jumped the combing to the companionway, slid back the hatch, mounted the stairs, then quickly closed the hatch behind him. There was a strong smell of vomit and human waste in the crowded companionway. Men and women were bracing themselves against the walls. There was no water left in the scuttlebutt to spill and run down the cabin sole. Alvaraz opened his cabin door, gently laying Gemelda on his berth when Gabriela grabbed his arm. She said in poor Spanish," Leave her with me."

Alvaraz wanted desperately to check the patch the men had put on the inside of the hull, he also wanted to stay, "I'll be back," he said as he closed the door leaving the two women in the cabin alone.

The lantern light showed water above the lower walkways. A sign the pumps weren't keeping up with the leaks. The carpenter and his assistances were madly hammering on thicker laths and binding in more canvas in an attempt to slow the flow of water.

"The patch holds for a minute then it opens up just like the planking under it. It seems when the bow raises with a wave the seam opens, letting in the whole ocean, tearing the patch in half, then when she settles with the bow down she seals up like new. For the last few minutes she's been fine with the stern rising she doesn't leak a bit and we've put a patch in just the same."

"The reason she was pitching so, a few minutes ago, was the first mizzen lateen sail couldn't be lowered because the upper block was jammed. Alfonso shinnied up the mast with an ax and set it free so the Lydia could turn her tail to the wind. She should be fine now, I reckon." Alvaraz said the words with such pride and emotion. He thought of his Gemelda lying in his berth, her head bleeding. No one would notice that the tears of pride running down his face weren't the water that occasionally squirted through the planking. He had trouble controlling his voice as he said, "I'll report to the Captain." As he ascended the ladder he noticed the water level was already below the walkway. The pumps were working.

He went straight to his cabin to find Gabriella had redressed Gemelda in fresh cloths to make her look like Alfonso. The bandage around her head gave even more credence to her identity as Alfonso. When she saw Alvaraz she held him without a word. Gabriella quickly closed the door as Gemelda bawled her thanks to Alvaraz.

"I didn't mind climbing the mast as it whipped around. I think the end of the yardarm hit me as it fell; It hurt me Alvaraz." She made a weak smile reaching for him, "I did like waking up in your arms. Thank you for saving me," she blubbered.

"I must go, Rodrego is expecting me to give him a report, I'll tell you all about it when I return. Mark my words, I think the entire compliment of the ship will thank you when the storm abates." He kissed her and was gone.

"The wind has shifted from the north west to the west, I think we're through the worst of it." It was Philippe; he looked dry as he shouted, above the roar of the storm, the report to Alvaraz who was dripping on the wet cabin sole as he entered the Captain's cabin. "If we can survive this for six more hours we'll be in the clear."

Minutes earlier Alvaraz crawled across the deck, clinging to what ever he could find, as the Lydia pitched and rolled to impossible angles. The sea, once flat had become mountains of ghostly green foam cascading with tremendous noise around and on the ship. He could see the glow of the last lit lantern illuminating the faces of three sailors straining at the wheel. Before he made it to the Captain's cabin the moon made a brief appearance through a hole in the clouds. When Alvaraz turned from the spray-laden wind to take a breath, he no longer saw most of the Lydia. She had become part of the sea. He noticed absently the topmast was broken and hanging at a crazy angle, gyrating behind the bowsprit that suddenly came out of the water like a breaching whale, then the moon's light was gone and the world returned to a ghostly green in the violent shrieking wind.

Rodrego came out of his cabin, "Alvaraz, It's like seeing the dead, I can tell you I thought you were on your way to purgatory, I'm sure it was the hand of God lifting you back onto the ship. What news do you bring?"

"Now the ship's running with the wind, the patch is holding. How are the men managing the pumps, I couldn't even see the deck when I came up?"

"Ismel's with them, they brought up the big pump and mounted it in the hold. Father Emilio took the passengers to the forward part of the hold to give the boys some room to work the pump. Last I saw he was on his knees praying with your natives. They're a brave lot, Alvaraz, they don't complain." Rodrego grabbed Alvaraz by the shoulders as if to steady himself and asked with a knowing look on his face, "and how is our Alfonso?"

Alvaraz didn't say anything for a minute as he paused for thought. "Alfonso is well. He has a nasty bruise on his head where the yardarm struck him. It'll take some time but I think he will recover," he said carefully.

"We should talk of this when the storm abates," responded Rodrego with a fatherly grin on his face. "Now, you say the patch is working because we are running with the wind. We have three men at the wheel. We should follow the wind as it turns to keep the stern to the wind. How was the water in the bilge when you left?

"It had been above the bottom walk way, but when I left it seemed to be below it. There isn't much water coming in anymore. When I left, the carpenter was expanding the patch. I expect it to hold."

With a relieved look on his face Rodrego released Alvaraz and grabbed the table Philippe had jammed himself next to. "It's just after four bells, we should see the sun in three hours. I think the storm is abating. Check the bilges for me again and if the water level is going down, you should try to get a little respite. When the sea settles I want to make you and Philippe officers of the deck while Ismel and I get some rest."

Alvaraz made his way to his cabin. When he entered he found Gabriella sitting on a trunk, she was dozing with her head wedged into the v where the bulkhead joined the companionway wall. Gemelda was sleeping in her berth wedged in with pillows and rolled up blankets against the hull. Alvaraz noticed the air was cooler than usual as he blew out the lantern and climbed into his bunk. He pulled the mattress out before he got in and lay on the bare slats with the mattress pushing him up against the hull.

Chapter 25

The light through the deck prism flickered across his eyes waking him. His first sight was the stained horsehair mattress in his face. He felt cold, thinking it would be nice to have a blanket. He lifted his head to find the cabin empty. He must have fallen into an exhausted sleep. He climbed out of the bunk realizing he needed to relieve himself. The ship was still rolling, but it was the motion of a ship underway in a heavy sea. He found a woman in the hall on her knees with a bucket and brush. Thing were returning to normal.

He heard Ismel bellow as he left the companionway, "Alvaraz, you're alive, Thank God in heaven." Ismel was standing by Alfonso, a huge grin on his face," I hear we have the two of you to thank for our lives."

Alvaraz looked at him in stunned silence—after a minute of thought said, "Thank everyone on this ship. The ship made it through the storm because of a strong crew." He then hurried off to the head.

A wave of anxiety swept over Alvaraz as he sat on the head. He remembered shouting to Rodrego, "Gemelda's in the water." He must have heard me, for when I told him I was going to take her below referring to Alfonso; he had that knowing look in his eye. What is he thinking?

The wind settled, blowing from the west. Rodrego kept his council all that first day after the storm, while he and Philippe set a course a little north of east. Rodrego put in some time filling out his log then retired. It was a relief when he disappeared into his inner cabin and he and Philippe were left to supervise the deck.

"I'm glad we ate the pigs before the storm hit," said Philippe, "We should have eaten them all."

The other two were washed overboard along with their pigpen. Alvaraz imagined the shark feasting on the still living pigs. "I saw a shark feasting on the entrails of the pig we harvested, I'm sure the flesh will be appreciated by the sharks out there, but you're right we should have eaten the lot of them, the ones we ate were so good."

The air was cool in the sunshine. Alvaraz noticed many of the natives were wearing the wool pants and tops made by the women. Alfonso came to him with some food. He noticed he had a large bruise on the right side of his face with a black eye to match. They talked like two sailors. Alfonso trying to sound like a young man with a low voice. Whenever Gemelda was around him, in the form of Alfonso, his anxiety returned. Shortly after they finished eating he ordered Alfonso to his cabin to rest.

The seas calmed, all that remained was a long low swell. Over the next few days a thorough inspection revealed the extent of the damage. The most obvious, the topmast was broken just above the second set of shrouds. It was now lying on the deck. The carpenter and his assistants were shortening it and didn't see any problem in re-attaching it to the upper stump of the main mast. Almost half of the bales of rice were on deck drying after being immersed in the bilges. Some of them were already split open as the rice inside expanded. The women were trying to re-dry the rice on the deck, but there was insufficient room and the sailors were getting annoyed.

It was on this day Rodrego revealed his understanding of Alvaraz's relationship to Alfonso. "What do you think of women working in the rigging?" he casually said to Alvaraz while they both leaned on the aft rail looking at the calm sea sliding by under them.

"You know, don't you," was all Alvaraz could say.

"I want you to tell me everything, I am filled with curiosity. This is a story I will tell for the rest of my life and I want to hear it accurately. Tell me how did you get her aboard?"

"The truth is I did nothing and I knew nothing," said Alvaraz. "I want to show you something. He removed the letter from his breast pocket. This is a letter I received after I thought she had left. I want you to read this as if you were my father."

Rodrego took the letter and read it.

Alvaraz told him everything with the exception of his intimacy with Gemelda.

Rodrego after hearing the story took some time to reply. He seemed uncomfortable, as he stood at the rail staring at the horizon, then he finally said, "It's a remarkable story, Alvaraz. You know, if I know something about this, I must do something about it." He then paused again, "I choose to know nothing about it. As far as I know you are sharing your cabin with Alfonso, a person who is interested in shipbuilding. I do not condone you sharing that cabin with Gemelda. I don't know anything about it." He turned from the rail and looked at Alvaraz and asked, "Do you agree? You never told me this story."

Alvaraz was stricken with grief, He felt ill and even a little faint as he waited for Rodrego to make his judgment. When he heard Rodrego ask him to lie he was struck by the irony of it. "Is it not a sin?" he asked.

"Alvaraz, I've been around long enough to know, I don't know what's right and what's wrong. I leave that to God. Your love for Gemelda has given me great pleasure and I will not destroy that. I knew from the start you were falling in love with her. I could have stopped it then, but now it's too late. From what I've seen of Gemelda you are a lucky man. She will look after you more than you will look after her. Believe me, Alvaraz, you will have some trials with her, but I think you are a lucky man to have her. When I get back to Spain I will tell your father you married a girl from a rich family. You say Gemelda is a Christian now; No one will contest you joining her in marriage."

In some ways Alvaraz was disappointed. He thought Gemelda would be taken away to live with the native women leaving him free of the fear of exposure and her safety, but he knew he would pine for her. He liked the idea of the informal blessing of Rodrego. He also liked the idea of Gemelda being free on the ship. He was also deathly afraid something would happen to her if she played the part of Alfonso. He would talk to her and ask Rodrego and Ismel to keep her away from the dangerous jobs on the ship, since after all, Alfonso had saved the ship and almost died doing it.

Chapter 26

As the days past the ship was put back together. The main topmast was re-attached; some of the stored rice began to rot and was thrown overboard; the cracked frame was repaired, by fastening three long pieces of wood around its girth. The ship was becalmed for a day, then a cold mist came, soaking the entire ship with its dampness. The only dry place on the ship was beside the cook's stove. Many of the natives put on their wool garments, and hovered as close to the stove as they could get. None of them had ever experienced anything like this. With the mist came a strong west wind. The Lydia made excellent progress through the waves back to North America and New Spain.

Every week a new storm would pass, the wind increasing, the waves growing to enormous size then it would pass, the wind would decrease slowing the Lydia to a snail's pace then gradually increase with the approach of the next system. The seawater became cold, and the fish the native men caught changed. They still caught tuna but one day they managed to land more than a dozen silver fish identified by Rodrego as salmon. The cook had no trouble cooking them, as they were his favorite food when he lived on the west coast of northern Spain. On the seventh week out of Manila a gale blew through. Then the wind clocked around first from the west-northwest then from nor-northwest and in the end almost directly from the north. The north wind increased hour by hour, the clouds disappeared from the sky, the air became bitterly cold and the sea formed mountains capped with charging white crowns so deafening as to drown out normal conversation. They could no longer keep the ship on a westward course. The hatches were closed and wedged down as the seas spilled over the deck. The routine of the ship ended as the sails were reduced to two lower storm trysails.

Rodrego and Philippe, anticipating this wind from the records of previous voyages, sailed the ship to almost forty-five degrees latitude. The Lydia was sailing almost due south, her bows being driven into the waves then rearing up on the next wave. The carpenter's assistant came on deck with word; the ship is making water again through the repair on the forward port bilge. This time when the carpenter and Alvaraz went to inspect they found the plank that always shed its caulking had sprung. The water was pouring in at an alarming rate. They worked in the freezing water for hours applying a patch of canvas as best they could, but the water persisted in its inundation of the hull. At the present rate the ship would sink in a matter of hours. All three pumps; the two deck pumps manned by freezing sailors who were constantly being dipped into the ice cold water as waves swept the decks and the one in the hold, by frantic sailors assisted by the native men. And still the water level rose.

With an exhausted look on his face Alvaraz reported to Rodrego, "We may be able to save her if we can get a line around the hull, then pull a sail over the leak from the out side. Within minutes six sailors including Alfonso organized to get a line under the hull. "Throw the damn fist, man," shouted Ismel. No matter how hard they tried they couldn't get the line below the martingale because the dolphin striker always snagged it. I need a man to go down the martingale to pull the line over the dolphin striker," boomed Ismel. Alfonso was standing next to him on the last grating on the bowsprit. He looked by him, not wanting to jeopardize this young man's life.

Alfonso shouted in his ear, "I'll do it, Sir."

No one else came forward so Ismel shouted," get a rope around Alfonso and make it tight now."

Alfonso thought it was a piece of cake, as he scurried down the footropes to the tip of the bowsprit with the messenger line in his hand. He waited for the bow sprit to start rising on a wave, swung down on the martingale to the dolphin strider, forced the line to the other side, then started making his way back up the chain towards the footropes on the bowsprit. He was wearing heavy oilskins, boots, a sweater and a heavy linen shirt. Suddenly the sea came up to him, completely immersing him. He was torn from the chain; the rope that was tied around his waist underneath his clothes came taut, pulling him, hips and legs first through the water. A second later all the clothing on his upper body was washed off by the force of the water moving by the ship. The sailors on the deck quickly pulled him in and were astonished to see he had the full ripe breasts of a woman. They got her on deck, some of the sailors gasping with the sight, while others looked on, some smiling, with uncomprehending looks on their faces.

Ismel came up, saw Gemelda's bare chest and stared uncomprehending for a minute, then shouted, "get on with it, lads. I need six cables under the ship, and you, Paulo, attach the stoutest sail we've got to those cables, your life depends on it."

Gemelda held her arms over her chest as she ran, before the next wave could wash over the deck. She was shivering violently as she ran down the companionway ladder strait into Alvaraz who was returning from the bilges. Her face contorted with the agony of her situation, her body suffering with the shock of exposure, her hands torn and bloody after being wrenched from the martingale chain, she fell into Alvaraz' arms and the tears fell like rain. He held her tightly as he moved her into his cabin. His brave Gemelda; now a frightened tiny girl in his arms, wouldn't let him go.

Alvaraz's mind was boiling with anger, "Who did this to you," he asked, his anger pushing his fear of the ship sinking, and his need to do his duty aside. "I'll find Gabriella," he said as he pulled the blankets of his bunk and wrapped them around her.

"Don't leave me," she said in a weak voice

"You must pull yourself together Gema, I love you so. I won't let anything happen to you." His embrace almost crushing her, then he tenderly picked her up and put her on his berth. "I'll be right back."

He found Gabriela and took her to his cabin. He could feel the ship wallowing with the added weight of seawater in her bilges. He had no choice; he had to leave her to do his duty to save the ship.

"Alvaraz; no one tore my clothes from me, I fell into the sea and the waves pulled them off. Go now, save the ship," she commanded.

With a smile he realized Gemelda was back. She found her vigor and now passed it on to Alvaraz, who, with renewed strength left the two women, threw open the companionway hatch and bounded up the stairs.

Not one of the crew had any experience with putting a sail under the hull of a leaking ship. Ismel organized them into four groups each with a coil of rope. The sail maker provided a stout piece of square canvas used for an awning over the aft deck. They had six ropes under the hull by the time Alvaraz came on deck. Four of the lines were attached to the corners of the canvas. The men were trying to pull it around the hull, but the sea conditions were horrendous. Not a man had a dry spot on his body. Alvaraz peered over the side of the hull between waves, measuring in his mind the ship and where the leak was. They were putting the patch far too far forward.

Alvaraz cupped his hands around his mouth and shouted almost directly into Ismel's ear, "It must go further back, the leak is just aft of the main mast."

The men ran the ropes around the shrouds and heaved it back. It was hard to tell if it was coming. It seemed to be stuck on something. When it was in place Alvaraz ran below to see if it was helping slow the leek. He found the carpenters with water to mid thigh, frantically hammering in canvas and blocks of wood under a frame they had built on the ship's ribs.

"Belay that," shouted Alvaraz realizing they would push the hull out further and maybe spring more planks.

"But it's working, the water has slowed," said the carpenter's assistant in the relative quiet of the bilges.

"We've just put a sail on the out side of the hull to slow the leak. It's the sail slowing the water, Alvaraz said with a look of triumph. "Stuff your patch as best you can, but don't force out the hull. I'm worried we may spring more planks, then we'd go down like a rock," explained Alvaraz.

The carpenter looked at the mess of boards and canvas and said, "You're right Alvaraz." We'll try to box in the leak, that won't put any more pressure on the hull. It'll be like a second shin, but will take a day to do."

"Do your best, lads, I've got to report this to the Captain."

Ismel had the deck hands working on another piece of canvas when Alvaraz came on deck. "The water's slowed, I think it's working."

"We are trying another sail, said Ismel. "We'll lash the canvas down then string ropes to hold it tight to the hull."

Alvaraz noticed the wind was calming a bit. He could hear Ismel plainly and the spray in the air seemed less. "I better report to the Captain, do you know where he is?"

"He was in his cabin. He and Philippe are looking at their charts, trying to find a place to beach the Lydia."

Rodrego was with the men at the helm when Alvaraz spoke to him.

"We've managed to slow the leak, Captain. We've got a sail hauled around the outside of the hull, Ismel's working on another."

Rodrego looked at him like he was a saint from heaven, "Do you think we can get her pumped out? Philippe says we are on the same latitude of a fine protected bay, reported by the English sailor, Drake. There is a chance it's not far to the east. We must get the ship turned to the east, but with all the water in her bottom, I'm afraid she'll capsize."

"The men at the pumps are exhausted, I'll ask Guillermo if he can get his men to help man the pumps and we'll keep working on the patch."

Alvaraz maneuvered himself across the deck without being hit by a single wave. The weather was moderating he decided. Guillermo didn't need to be asked to provide manpower to man the pumps. The pump in the hold was fully manned by a double compliment of natives. When he asked for help on deck he was overwhelmed by volunteers. Soon all the pumps were manned. As the water dropped in the bilges and the ship became noticeably more stable the exhausted sailors concentrated on getting sail aloft and the ship on a course towards the east. A low scud obscured the sun as it fell below the horizon. The patch was holding and Philippe was patiently waiting to measure the angle of the pole star so he could establish, with accuracy, their latitude. The sun was long gone before the pole star peaked out behind a cloud. After several tries with his astrolabe, Philippe had Captain Rodrego adjusted the course just a little south.

Chapter 27

Alvaraz hadn't slept for forty eight hours and upon returning that evening to his cabin he found Gemelda, her hands bandaged, wearing a cotton dress sitting beside Gabriela who was sewing him some new shirts, he didn't know what to think. He fell into his berth without a word. Gemelda was contented with this, because before he fell asleep he smiled approvingly at her. The two women put blankets on him and continued their sewing.

They sailed through the night, the pumps just keeping the water level down but never fully pumping out the ship. When the morning light came they could see nothing to indicate land to the east. Nino was consulted and reported there was a point of land to the north bending the waves. They were either sailing behind an island, into a huge bay or they would find land shortly to the east. He then left them and went back to his favorite place beside the galley stove and his favorite chore of keeping up the fire in that stove. He was never warm even dressed in everything he could find.

Alvaraz woke late in the day, he felt like an old man when he tried to rise. His joints were tight from the previous day's exertions and exposure to the cold. He sat on the edge of his berth and listened. There were some sailors talking outside his cabin door undoubtedly standing by the scuttlebutt discussing the news. "I knew he was a woman. Did yah see the shape of her ass in those trousers?" "I'm glad I didn't know, or I would have had her in the foc'sle before you could tie a bowline. The man to watch is that Alvaraz, It's a tidy piece he's been keeping in his cabin. What's she see in him anyway?" An old man's voice said, "I've never seen a better sailor." The other voices agreed. Then there was silence.

How could he face these men, he thought, as he hurried to the head. No one said a thing to him that afternoon as the ship moved through the rolling sea to the east. The sun disappeared in a thick fog and the wind died to a whisper. It was in the afternoon when a man reported hearing the barking sound of a sea lion. Rodrego had the men launch the long boats and sound the sea ahead as they towed the Lydia through the still air on long hawsers. Soon they found the source of the sound. It was a sea lion colony on the end of a point of land. It became dark, but they persisted in sounding and pulling the Lydia, her sails furled, anchor at the ready around that point. They were assisted by a current and soon found themselves in a protected bay with a sand bottom. Rodrego gave the order to drop the anchor and they waited for morning their pumps working through the night. By morning a wind had come up blowing away the fog and they had their first look at the bay they had sailed into during the foggy, dark night.

Gabriela stood on the deck with the other women, their excitement dulled, as they peered at the barren rocky land with hardly a green tree in sight. It was nothing like the green expanse of paradise they were expecting. They could hear Ismel giving orders to the men to man the boats so they could find a suitable place to beach the Lydia. Gemelda explained to the women what was to happen, and wondered if they could stay aboard while the repairs to the hull took place. If not they would set up camp on the beach near the ship.

Within the hour the long boats returned with good news. The best place was in the northwestern corner. The beach rose at just the right rate to beach the Lydia, She would be canted towards the shore exposing the loose planks on the port side. The passengers were to be transported the short distance to the beach where they would set up camp while the repairs were being made.

The tide receded that evening. At last the pumps could stop as the Lydia gently touched the sandy bottom exposing her undersides as the tide carried the water away. It was difficult to see the full extent of the damage in the lamplight, but after the removal of the sail, the sprung plank could be seen sticking out of the hull forming a scoop to draw in the water. Alvaraz was perplexed. It wasn't as he suspected, the fasteners fastening the plank to the frame hadn't failed. The plank itself had a ragged end as if were cracked. The wood around the leak showed deep scoring.

"I believe this is the place we damaged when we hit the coral pinnacle just after leaving the reef we sailed through," said Rodrego. "All this time it was slowly working till finally it broke. We should all thank God, we survived this time of trial."

They decided to replace the entire plank. The carpenter thought they could find enough wood to replace the two damaged planks beside it. At the same time Rodrego would have the men careen the hull and Rudder. The new pintles and gudgeons installed in Navidad on the rudder still looked new.

After inspecting the hull, Ismel commented, "She's like a fresh apple with a tiny bruise that could have caused the whole thing to rot. God was with us, praise God in heaven."

No one said a thing to Alvaraz. He expected Rodrego to have a talk with him and perhaps punish him in some way. He also expected jeers and constant ribbing from the crew, but not a word. In some ways his fellow crew treated him with more respect. It was as if everyone accepted the situation. Alfonso was now gone, no one could expect his heroics, no one expected the extra willing crew. It was obvious the entire ship knew the entire story.

Philippe commented one day, "I hear you have a private cabin now, I may come back," as if to say no more hanky panky in there.

Alvaraz stayed on the ship. His berth was canted in to the hull, which made it quite a nice spot to sleep in. Aside from the pain of separation and the anxiety he felt everyday, life went on as usual. He knew Gemelda was safe, on the beach, having the company of her many native friends. He was contented busying himself with the repairs to the ship. With each passing tide the Lydia was floating higher on the beach. The repairs were complete four days after she was beached and now the problem of re-floating her became a major concern. Before the ship was beached the anchor was set in deep water. Everyone expected the ship to re-float on the first tide, but as hard as they tried she would not budge. On the second try triple blocks were rigged on the anchor hawser. The ship moved a few inches on the highest tide. The problem was the anchor seemed to moved a few feet as it was dragged against the incredible pull of the anchor capstan and the three heavy sets of block and tackles, their line stretched to singing tight.

"The full moon is coming up in three days, I don't expect the tides to be any higher for at least a week after that night." Rodrego appeared very tired as he said these words to Alvaraz and Ismel while they sat on an improvised bench built on the upper deck. There was no need for a sunshade. Any and all warmth from the evening sun was welcomed. "If the weather turns to the south, this bay could become a boiling caldron. We should set another anchor as far out as possible to stop the waves from pushing her further up the beach. I didn't want to have to do this but I fear I must. The ballast and cargo must be unloaded to lighten the ship. I fear this is the only way we will re-float her."

"It's what we thought," said Ismel, "we'll start at first light tomorrow morning. I'll have the cook give the lads a good meal and I'll have'em in their hammocks early. The camp on the beach is going well. They've made some nice shelters with the old sails we gave them and they found a small fresh-let of water on the rocky side of the bay. They have a dozen barrels of water filled. If yah have no objections, I'll ask Guillermo if he can send some of the Manila men to help us."

Chapter 28

Alvaraz went to the beach for the first time the next day. His obsession to repair the ship had kept him aboard. His only distractions were his thoughts of Gemelda. Somehow his work fulfilled a need deep inside to protect her. The strain he felt constantly worrying about Alfonso's safety was lifted when she lived with the Manila women and he knew she was safe on the shore helping build the shelters and working with the people. The repair unearthed the full extent of the damage to the hull. He was positive God steered them to this sanctuary before the ship sank. If the weather had remained bad the ship would have gone down, there was nothing they could have done. He found three more planks in the same area with the same cracks caused by the collision with the coral pinnacle on their journey to Manila. A thread of brittle wood held the planks together. When removed, he managed to break the planks with his bare hands. Fear cursed through him as he stared at the plank he broke laying on the deck. It was a miracle they'd survived.

He had the men row him around the Lydia, before he went to the beach, to take a look at her lying on her side waiting for the water to rise. She looked strong with her hull newly careened, her masts and spars neatly held in place by their shrouds.

The beach sloped up slowly where they landed. Sand was blown into heaps, by the wind, capped with patches of coarse grass and thistle. The hills were red and barren. He remembered the patches of dry land around Navidad, but nothing remotely as arid as this. "It must be heartbreaking for the people from Manila to see this barren land for the first time," said Alvaraz to the ship's carpenter who was going with him for the first time to the beach.

"I've never seen people so cold as these poor devils. I'll bet they all wish they hadn't come," responded the ship's carpenter. "No one could live here. You couldn't even raise cattle on those thorn bushes up there. The few trees growing in the ravines are stunted and barely alive. I wonder if there is gold or silver in the mountains beyond?"

The camp built by the Manila people was substantial. Two rows of tents made from sails surrounded a courtyard where a dozen water casks stood ready to be reloaded along with tons of supplies and cargo unloaded to lighten the ship. Two long benches were set up; on one the women were washing the wool garments worn by the people on the trip across the sea. On the other men were filleting fish while some women and the cook prepared a large kettle of fish stew. Most of the rice was gone, having rotted in the hold after being immersed in seawater. They were boiling the rice which was wetted but not rotted then spreading it on canvas to dry. All the women's seed boxes were opened with the seeds spread on a canvas sheet in an attempt to save them. The cook had had a ready supply of spices, some dried fruit and the remainder of the rice and grains, stored high enough in the aft hold where the water hadn't got to it, to make a fabulous chowder.

"I don't believe the taste, this is wonderful soup," commented Alvaraz to the cook.

"Eat up, lad, yah won't be eating like this for long, when we get back to sea we'll be rationed for sure. I can only find a single bale of untouched rice, and six sacks of grain. All the bread's gone and we have no fruit. Let's pray to God it's not far back to Acapulco. If we ration, we'll only have enough for two weeks with this compliment."

While Alvaraz ate his food, Gabriela came up behind him and touched him on the shoulder. Startled he turned, "Gabriela, you look well, where can I find Gemelda?"

"She's collecting water. She worries so much about you, Alvaraz," Gabriella said in her clumsy Spanish. "We should go see her. We heard you were working to fix the ship and couldn't come to the beach camp, but Gemelda, she worried you don't love her," she said quietly.

"We will go to her now. She should never worry about my love for her." Alvaraz said with conviction. Then he said with a resigned tone to his voice, "The whole ship knows about us, but no one will talk to me about it."

He saw her in the distance. She was with two Manila men maneuvering a wooden cask into a groove below a wooden trough discharging a weak stream of water from the bank behind the barrel. She looked thin and frail, wearing a cotton dress to her ankles, her cropped hair under a scarf to hide her boyish look. His heart surged when he saw her and his pace quickened.

'What had she done to herself, and why was she working so hard,' he thought. When she saw him she was in the middle of aligning the wooden trough over the hole in the barrel. She dropped it and the water poured over the outside of the barrel. He ran to her and held her with out regard to what he was doing. One of the Manila natives took over from her; he smiled approvingly and started talking loudly to his friend. Gemelda, hearing what he said blushed. "We should go somewhere," she said, then disengaged. He held her at a distance with his hands on her shoulders looking at her, and she sputtered, "Thank you for coming," He could see a tear in her eye and knew they should go somewhere quiet and talk.

"Would you like to walk with me? There's a beach on the other side of this hill." she offered.

Gabriella helped the men fill the tanks while they wandered up the hillside. "Those men are so rude. They said we should go somewhere private to make babies. We must do something, everyone knows about us."

Just as she was saying these words they heard a man's voice calling from the beach below. It was Father Emilio asking them to stop. Father Emilio was hiking up the hill towards them his brown full length robe billowing out behind in a gust of wind. He came up breathlessly and said, "I must talk to you, my children. Please come, let's sit on these stones."

Alvaraz sat with Gemelda, ready to confess his sins and his love for Gemelda. The cool wind carried the scent of the sea and the sun gently warmed them. A sense of peace came over Alvaraz as he tried to make himself comfortable beside Gemelda on some stones that were too high and sharp to make a comfortable seat.

"I've watched you, I prayed to God for an answer. I've prayed for your soul and know you are not under the influence of the devil. Soon Imelda will take her first communion. Then I want you to marry. I've talked to Captain Rodrego and we both agree you must marry. But fist Imelda must become a Catholic. In the mean time you must live apart."

Father Amilio said these words between gasps for air. It was obvious he had rehearsed them many times and wanted to get them out.

"Father Amilio, I agree with all you've said. I only have two more lessons to complete before my confirmation. Could we speed up the lessons so we can marry sooner? I think you know it's an agony for me to be away from Alvaraz," she said with a look of despair on her face.

"My child, we can. If you study hard we can complete the lessons before next Sunday," he said with obvious relief. "That gives us four days. We should start this afternoon. If all goes well you will be married on Monday."

"Do you want to marry me, Alvaraz?" she asked.

"I do," he hesitated as he thought what name he should call her, then decided to call her by her baptized name, "Imelda—I should be asking you the question." He got off the stone he was sitting on, knelt on one knee and asked, "Will you marry me—Imelda?"

"Yes, before God, I will answer Yes! I will marry you, Alvaraz." As she said these words Alvaraz could see tears filling her eyes. They embraced before the priest. Father Emilio said to Alvaraz, "I will take her to her lessons now, don't worry, son, I will look after her for you."

He could hear Father Emilio, "You were baptized, you have taken the Eucharist and now you must finish the Catechism and be confirmed. Then, my dear, you will be a true soldier of God. By marrying Alvaraz—" the wind blew his words away. She was so skinny and frail, her dress blowing against her in the wind, he wanted to go to her and protect her, but this way they would be together and nothing could separate them. He smiled and looked up the hill, then started walking to the top. He wanted to see the beach his Gema had seen. He would call her Gema he decided.

The vista from the top of the hill was quite beautiful; from the rocky headland he stood on, he could see the land stretching to the north edged with a white beach as far as he could see. To the west the headland ended with the sea stretching beyond the horizon to the land he had sailed from. He climbed down the hill to the small beach bordered by rocky outcrops. He sat on the sand leaning against a log and soon took his shirt off exposing his skin to the soft rays of the sun. The contrast between the barren land and the sea filled with life gave him pause for thought. He could see whales working the shore, their water spouts louder than the waves breaking on the beach. The constant barking of sea lions from the colony at the end of the headland could be heard above a closer seal colony, where the plaintive cries of baby seals, almost human sounding, covered the chattering of the sea otters working the nearby kelp bed. The sea was full of fish as evidenced by the abundant catch of the Manila men. He drifted off into a well-earned sleep.

Chapter 29

He didn't know how long he slept, maybe it was only a few minutes, but the next time he opened his eyes he saw a flotilla of large boats coming towards his beach. He stood up and hastily made his way up the hill so he could warn Captain Rodrego. Normally they would move the ship to deep water, load the cannons with shot and meet with the natives, but this time they were so vulnerable. He quickly explained what he had seen to the ship's carpenter and found some sailors to man the boat to take them to Rodrego.

"I've seen at least a dozen large boats. They are huge, almost the size of a small ships, powered by a dozen men paddling on each side. They are coming from the north and I expect them to investigate this bay," said Alvaraz excitedly to Captain Rodrego.

Before he spoke Rodrego paused for a long time while he looked around the ship. Alvaraz could see the skin tighten around his jaw and the color leave his cheeks, with the strain of this added development. "We must prepare cannons with shot to cover the ship and put the two smaller cannons ashore to protect the camp and arm every man capable of bearing arms."

"Aye Captain," said Alvaraz, "I'll find Ismel."

It was impossible to arm the ship properly with cannon because of the slope of the deck, but the two small cannons were taken ashore with a gun crew and all the crew were armed.

The boats stopped by the point at the head of the bay for some time then proceeded to the opposite beach beside an estuary where they set up camp. They seemed civilized, their boats neatly lined up on the beach and several fires set. A watch was posted on the ship and in the Spanish camp and all was quiet through the night. At first light a single small canoe paddled over to the ship and observed as the men worked trying to drag the ship into deeper water.

These people were different from any of the islanders. Nino was summoned. He tried speaking to them. They immediately started speaking to him in an unknown tongue, some of the words sounded almost like they were spitting. The men in the canoe stood up holding up their hands in a sign of peace and soon the canoe and a long boat were beside each other. These people were almost comical in appearance. They had short legs supporting large chests, long powerful arms and healthy walnut colored skin. An old man in the canoe talked softly to Nino and through sign language indicated he wanted to talk to Nino's chief. Rodrego came to the rail. With a series of gestures they learned about each other. The American natives came from the north. They wanted to know what was to the south. The old man indicated it would take half a moon to travel back to their home. Rodrego indicated it would take a moon to travel the distance to Acapulco.

It was sketchy at best, but Rodrego thought they agreed they would trade then separate one group to the north, one to the south. Rodrego sent six armed men and Nino in a longboat; with beads some iron bar stock and some blades to their camp.

"The tide will be higher in the afternoon four days hence," Rodrego stated as he planned his escape. "If we can keep these people at bay until then we should be OK. Do you think that old man was the chief or just an elder?"

"I've never seen anything like it, they don't seem in any hurry, as if they are just waiting for the best opportunity to attack. I'd love to see their boats up close. How did they build them? They are small ships, I couldn't see any seams in their hull at all," said Alvaraz.

The day was coming to an end when the long boat returned filled with dried salmon, beautifully made cedar boxes filled with a type of sweet powder and some soft skins made from sea animals. The men described the people as friendly, but incorrigible tricksters. A jester came out wearing a wooden mask joking and throwing snot around. It was very funny. When they wanted to trade, the chief first filled their long boat with gifts as if he expected nothing. When the trade goods were brought out the Chief examined them passed them around, the only sound a gasp from one of the young women when she saw the contents of a bag of beads. She kept fingering them and pushing off the Chief who finally talked to one of his men who forcefully removed them from the young women and passed them on to the other elders. The Spaniards were allowed to return unhindered.

"Did you look at their boats?" asked Alvaraz, "How are the planks fastened?"

None of the men had taken much notice, however one did comment, "They look like they were carved from a single tree."

"That's impossible," said Alvaraz, "I must go over and look."

The next morning one of the native boats was launched and landed near the Spanish camp. There were perhaps forty men aboard and a dozen women who came ashore and set up a camp consisting of woven cedar bark squares assembled into a small lodge. The chief was amongst them.

Rodrego prepared a guard and was taken to the shore where he met the chief, his wife and the young woman who was obviously his daughter. The chief only spoke to the old man who spoke very clearly but quietly and used a series of recognizable hand signs to translate what the Chief was saying. Again the question of what was to the south came up. Was the land as dry and barren to the south as this land? Did it never rain here?

Nino took on the job of interpreter and followed the example of not allowing Rodrego to talk directly to the Chief. He explained they knew little of the coast to the south. After a lot of hand gestures Nino said, "They think you are a God or a spirit of some kind."

"Tell them we come from the other side of the great ocean. We are not Gods, but we do have a single God that we each carry within us, who protects us," instructed Rodrego.

Alvaraz and the ship's carpenter bravely approached the natives' boat. Soon they were surrounded with native men, who proudly showed off their boat. At first Alvaraz didn't believe what he saw. It was a huge open canoe over fifty feet long made from a single log. Its high bow and stern were decorated with intricately carved animal shapes. It had a beam of perhaps twelve feet with a shelter in the middle made of woven bark supported with stout timbers made of a red wood. Alvaraz was intrigued with the wood and indicated he would like to see a small piece up close. One of the natives found a thin piece of this type of wood and handed it to Alvaraz. I was dark red in color, very light, a bit too brittle to be used as planking, but did have a wonderful scent. Alvaraz identified the smell of cedar. Cedar was a beautiful wood and rare in Spain. He couldn't believe this entire canoe was made from one piece of cedar. He could see black scoring, on the inside of the hull, as if the hull had been burned from the inside. One of the Indians standing around him started talking and pointing at the hull. He leapt into the canoe struggling to get over the gunnels with his short legs. He dug into a box and brought out a stone adze. Its handle was made from a wood Alvaraz thought was ash. The stone was bound, in the crook, with a strong fiber resembling the fibers used in the Indian's clothing. The Indian man slapped the outside of the canoe then made a motion like he was stripping the bark from the tree. Alvaraz realized the baskets, the hats, and the binding for this adze all came from the bark of the same tree the giant canoe was fashioned from.

"Do you think this fellow would like an adze made from fine Toledo steel?" Alvaraz asked the carpenter.

"He'd need a good file to keep it sharp," responded the carpenter.

Things went smoothly with the natives that day. Nino and Rodrego understood they were invited to an Island far to the north, where these people lived. They were also invited to a feast at the Indian camp the next night. The Chief decided, because the summer season was coming to an end and the geese were flying from the north, it was time for them to return to their land. Many of the Indian men walked freely through the Manila camp seeming to not bother anyone.

"Sir," it was the Sergeant at Arms, the next morning, requesting to speak to Rodrego. They were standing on the improvised aft deck of the grounded Lydia, "It seems the Indians have been pilfering. Without us knowing they took several wash tubs, a whole set of spoons, two of our picks and we think three shovels."

Rodrego smiled, "I knew they were up to something. Post a guard around the camp and forbid any entrance. Do you have the men?"

"Should I reduce the night watch to two and double the daytime watch? The men are tired doing double duty as sailors and guards, Sir."

"I think we could use some of the Manila men, I'll ask Guillermo this evening and see if he can find a half dozen men who can bear arms."

The next morning three canoes showed up. At least a hundred Indians were met by six armed Manila men and four Spanish sailors all armed with blunderbuss. The Indians seemed contented to watch the goings on in the camp. One of the Manila women walked alone towards the water collection area. A large Indian man suddenly appeared beside her, grabbed her and started dragging her back towards the canoes. She let out a plaintive cry and Imelda immediately started running towards the two. Within minutes three of the Manila guards were in pursuit of the Indian and his captive. They intercepted them on the beach. Imelda ran to the Manila women and started hitting the Indian trying to get him to release the woman. At this time a dozen American native men appeared jeering and laughing at the Indian kidnapper. The guards stopped the man as he approached the canoe, but he wouldn't release the women holding her effortlessly. Imelda was almost knocked unconscious when the big Indian swung his fist catching Imelda in the jaw. The crowd of Indians around the scene, armed themselves with spears, chanted and encouraged the kidnapper. When the man started moving towards the canoe one of the Manila men pulled the trigger on his blunderbuss. The bullet ripped through the Indian's shoulder throwing him back. He fell heavily on Imelda, who was just starting to recover from the impact of the Indian's fist. The smoke and sound of the blunderbuss brought a stunned silence to the group and all that could be heard was Imelda, screaming to get the Indian off her. The freed woman ran off towards the camp. The Indian man rolled off Imelda and was helped to his feet by a single indian boy. The rest of the natives had moved down towards the water.

It was apparent Imelda was hurt. She couldn't stand. Somehow her knee had been dislocated when the Indian man had fallen on her. She was helped up by the two Spanish guards and hastily carried to the Manila camp. Alvaraz was summoned and came immediately to find Imelda pale as a ghost, sitting, holding her injured knee.

"Thank God you're OK. Oh please Gema, try to stay out of harm's way." Alvaraz said as he held her gently.

He examined her to find her knee swelling. Head bowed she said, "I'm sorry, my darling," she lifted her head and said with a look of defiance, "You would have done the same thing."

"Yes, you're right, my love, but I probably wouldn't have broken my knee."

They made a splint for her knee and bound it. She was able to hobble around. The three canoes departed with all the Indians leaving the camp. Rodrego came by with Ismel and the Sergeant at arms planning the defense of the camp if the natives chose to attack. The sky darkened with clouds the next morning obscuring the sun. Soon a brisk wind was blowing from the south.

"We have no more anchors," said Rodrego standing on the beach with Alvaraz and Ismel." The tide will be high this afternoon. We must put every effort to keep her from going further up the beach if this wind builds."

Ismel stood scratching his beard then said, "Sir, with the lightened ship, if we use the Manila men to man the capstans and pull the blocks, we could ballast the longboats and get them up to speed and jerk the ship out. I know we can."

Rodrego with a look of hope said, "Make it so, Ismel."

Chapter 30

There was fear on the faces of the people in the camp. Rodrego and Alvaraz stood on either side of Ismel while he explained the plan to save the ship to Guillermo, who translated the plan into Tagalong. The camp would be dismantled and made ready to load if they could get the ship re-floated. As Guillermo translated Ismel looked apprehensively towards the Indian camp. All the canoes were lined up on the beach with no apparent change to the camp. The Manila natives listened patiently then immediately started dismantling the camp the minute Guillermo finished speaking. Ismel decided to load the long boats with water barrels for ballast saving them the trouble of reloading them if they got the ship off the beach. The wind had increased and large waves were now breaking on the beach. Sixteen men fully armed, half of them gun crews for the two small cannons that stood loaded and ready to fire, surrounded the group of some seventy women who huddled behind the cargo and stores in the clearing. The tide was on the rise and Alvaraz, who had taken an oar amongst the sailors in the center longboat, was pleased to see the Lydia was floating on her starboard bilge. There was perhaps two hours before the tide was high and if all went well the Lydia would be standing on her keel before the tide met its zenith. Long lines coming from the bow of the ship were attached to the long boats.

The men pulled on the oars getting the long boats up to speed then felt the lines tighten as the weight of the long boat tugged at the ship. The lines going to the anchors were singing tight from the efforts of the Manila natives. The waves in the bay grew making the Lydia bob up and down on the largest of the waves. Rodrego watched, in dismay, as the same waves and wind slowed the long boats as they struggled out into the bay, the men rowing for their lives. An hour before the tide was up, when all three long boats happened to jerk simultaneously, the Lydia slowly rose up and fell on her other bilge. This was a positive move, but could also be devastating. If they didn't float her on this tide she would probably be flooded with the waves breaking over her if she settled on the windward bilge when the tide went out. Rodrego paced back and forth on the deck that was now canted towards the oncoming waves. For a minute he thought the ship had come free as the men were turning the capstan on the foredeck then he realized the main anchor was dragging. In a panic he signaled the men to belay turning the capstan and for the long boats to return to the ship. He calculated it would take an hour for the crew of the long boats to pick up the forward anchor and re-set it.

Just at this time, one of the largest of the canoes paddled over with the Chief. Nino went to talk to his speaker. By this time Nino knew a few words of the Indian language. He came back to Rodrego. "The Chief wants to give you more gifts," said Nino.

"Ask him to come back later if you can? We must get the ship floated or we'll loose her," said Rodrego.

The wind was increasing and now the bay was filled with whitecaps and it looked like it would start to rain. "What else can go wrong?" shouted Rodrego his normally neatly combed hair blowing recklessly in the increasing wind. He slammed his fists into the railing in frustration.

The forward anchor was hoisted up between two of the long boats using block and tackles supported by a huge beam set on the gunnels of the two long boats. The third long boat collected the chain and a long rope-hawser in its bilge. With the water barrels and the chain weighing down the boat, it looked like it was ready to sink in the increasing seas. With a huge amount of effort the long boats set out as far as they could get away from the ship until all the hawser line and chain was laid out in the bay, then the anchor was dropped. The men at the capstan were instructed to pull in the line, the long boats returned to take up their long cables to resume the tugging. After two mighty efforts by the long boats with all the anchors pulling as hard as possible the Lydia remained stubbornly unmoved.

Rodrego had little hope, he knew the tide was already going down, but one thing he hadn't noticed were the canoes from the Indian camp had all left the beach. Nino came to him and pointed. There on the sea moving comfortably with the waves stood a dozen canoes, their prows standing proudly against the gray windswept background.

The small canoe paddled up beside the Lydia with the old man. Nino conversed with the old man then came bounding up the stairs to Rodrego on the aft deck.

With a defeated exasperation in his voice Rodrego responded with, "What do they want now?"

"They want to pull Capitan. They want us to give them lines and they will help pull us off."

Ismel who was remounting the ship, his voice hoarse, after shouting orders from the long boat came up to Rodrego. "What are we going to do with that lot then?" he shouted in his gravely voice.

In a kind of dreamy voice Rodrego answered. "They want to help us free the Lydia. Find some long lines and give one to each canoe. Then I want you to take a halyard from the top of the main mast and see if you can heal her over by pulling with one of the long boats. This might lift the keel from the bottom."

As soon as Ismel gave the lines to the canoes they moved out tying each canoe powered by forty men to the next. In the end two lines of six canoes stretched out into the bay and waited for the two long boats to start pulling. Ismel stood on the bowsprit grating and shouted orders for the long boats to pull the ship over with the topmast halyard.

Rodrego couldn't believe it. The hawsers from the two lines of canoes almost pulled the cleats off the deck. The Lydia healed slightly, her bow turned into the waves and floated into deep water. Rodrego with a sigh of relief looked to the heavens and gave thanks to God.

The native canoes departed without a word not bothering to return the sizable amount of line Ismel had given them. Rodrego didn't care, he was so happy to get his ship back from the clutches of the beach.

The Lydia was securely anchored and as planned the water barrels in the long boats were hoisted on deck and the empty longboats returned to the beach to reload the cargo and supplies. There wasn't a man amongst them who wasn't sore and exhausted, but their spirits couldn't have been higher. Alvaraz and the ship's carpenter went below to find the repair job on the hull was holding nicely without a single leak.

"I was sure we were going to loose her," said Alvaraz to the ship's carpenter.

"God was with us," he responded, "What do you think about those Indians, We would never have gotten off if it weren't for them. When I saw them I thought they were going to attack. They had every opportunity."

"I've never seen anything like it. They have the strangest traditions. They want to give us gifts, and expect nothing in return. I wonder how the man who was shot is doing?"

Chapter 31

The first load of people and supplies was already loading when Alvaraz and the ship's carpenter came up on deck. Gema was amongst the women in the first long boat.

She managed to climb the ladder to the deck unassisted with her right leg hobbled in the splint. Alvaraz rushed over to help her up the last step. He didn't say anything just hoisted her up and publicly embraced her, then embarrassed held her at arms length and moved her back away from the ladder to let the other people ascend onto the ship.

"You look well and healthy, my darling," said Alvaraz.

"I am so happy, my love. I've finished my Catechism, Alvaraz—Father Emilio wants to have a service this evening to confirm me, then tomorrow we can be wed."

Alvaraz held her close and whispered, "At last, my darling, Things change so fast, only an hour ago I thought our ship would be destroyed and we would all be dead, killed by the Indians and now the ship is free and tomorrow I am to be wed to the most beautiful woman in the world."

"Alvaraz, Rodrego needs you," it was Ismel standing behind him with a smile on his face.

Alvaraz disengaged himself from Gemelda, kissed her lightly on the cheek and followed Ismel up the now level stairway to where Rodrego stood with Nino and the Chief's speaker. The small canoe was bobbing in the sea tied to the other side of the ship.

The chief wants us to come to a performance, he specifically wanted you. I suppose it's because of your blond hair. He also wants my speaker, myself and one other. I have chosen Philippe. I am leaving Ismel to supervise the reloading of the ship. I don't think I can refuse him as he saved us today. I want to bring him a gift. Do you have anything in mind?"

"But sir, Gemelda is to be confirmed at a service this evening, I can't miss the service," begged Alvaraz.

"I don't think this will last long, we should be back in time, he did specifically request you. Now what about a gift."

"I'll ask Gemelda, she'll know what kind of a gift to bring."

Alvaraz explained the situation to Gemelda. At first she was sad about him not being at her confirmation, but said, "You must go and if you don't get back on time I'll understand, but don't be late for your wedding tomorrow, my love."

She paused, thinking, then said, "Bring them spices, beads and printed cloth for their women. Bring the men knives, fish hooks and steel to make sharp points."

This gave Alvaraz an idea; he would give the builder of the canoe a steel adz a file and stone to keep it sharp.

When he told Rodrego what Gemelda had said he immediately ordered the gifts be put in a long boat. There was a delay while Rodrego gave Ismel orders, "If we don't return, by tomorrow, do not engage the Indians in hand to hand combat, they will overwhelm you. Shoot one round, with the cannon, into their camp, a half hour later shoot two rounds, after an hour shoot three. If they attack you, destroy their boats with the cannon. I can use this threat to negotiate our return."

"Understood, Captain," responded Ismel.

The sun came out from behind the clouds as they approached the beach. The brief wind from the south had ended and all that remained was a low swell. There was a strong smell about the place of fish oil and humanity. It was hard to believe the camp came from the canoes. There were organized shelters, racks with drying fish and clams, a huge lodge in the middle of a clearing, workbenches and tables and cedar mats everywhere. The old man stopped them at the entrance to the camp. They could hear a drum beat start and women's voices singing. The old man indicated they should enter. A row of young and old women danced waving their arms gently while they sang softly as if welcoming the sailors to their camp. The old man led them into the lodge and sat them on a log facing an open space with a crackling fire in the middle. Soon the chief, his wife and his daughter came and sat on the same log giving a slight bow to their guests as they entered. At first a man with a large moon shaped mask came out. He was obviously a clown. He mercilessly taunted the crowd, seemingly throwing snot at them. The "snot" was obviously a type of seaweed, which he pulled out of the nostrils of the mask. Time went very quickly and soon it was dark. Group after group of performers came out dressed in colorful garments and wearing intricately carved masks in the shape of mystical animals accompanied by singing, the beat of drums and the rhythm of drum sticks on hollow logs. One dance consisted of a man wearing a mask that changed as he sang giving the performance a mystical quality, another was a group of men wearing masks depicting ravens and eagles, their jaws opening and closing on hinges controlled by strings. Alvaraz was enchanted.

When the players took a break he thought it was over but found it was only beginning as they were led to a long table covered with different types of dried fish, clams, fish eggs, a type of leek, and fresh cooked fish held to a stick with woven cedar strips so it could be toasted over an open fire all mixed with the smell of almost rotten fish oil. The food was delicious, but Alvaraz couldn't eat the grease the men tried to entice him with. It smelled like badly rotted fish.

They ate their food in wooden bowls with the chief. Nino and the Chief's speaker talked together and made many hand signals. "I like the tradition of never having to speak directly with the chief. Nino does all my talking for me," said Rodrego after he instructed Nino to ask where these people lived.

"He says they live to the north in a place where it rains all the time. They are called Kauachins. They have many people and the land is good with much fish. They are looking for people to take home to do their work."

With out a hint of remorse Rodrego said to Alvaraz, "We are taking people home to do our work, are we not? Nino, find out what happened to the man we shot."

With a lot of signs and a few words, Nino responded with, "He is with his woman, I think he wanted another wife."

"How did these people know how to tow our ship off the beach?"

Again after a lot of discussion with the old man who was constantly interrupted by the chief, Nino replied, "I think they say, they tow barges all the time, so for them it is natural to tie the canoes together to make it easier to tow. When the weather is bad they can't do this."

Rodrego said, "Nino ask the chief if I can send Philippe to the long boat and have the men bring in the gifts?"

The gifts were brought in but the chief wouldn't accept them. They waited for the meal to end then they returned to the lodge where a ceremony was performed and the gifts were exchanged. Many masks and fine furs were put in the long boat as gifts then the Captain was allowed to have Nino present the gifts to the Chief who directed his men to give the gifts to his people. The chief looked at the adze and directed it be given to the man who Alvaraz recognized as the builder of the canoes. Later that evening he showed the man how to use the file and stone to keep the edge sharp.

After the gift giving, the old man gave a long speech. Nino knew nothing of what was said but Rodrego acknowledged the smiles and nods from the Chief. Another performance was given by different masked men then another break.

"Nino tell the Chief we must go," as an excuse Rodrego said, "tell him we must prepare to marry Alvaraz in the morning."

Nino using hand signals and all the words at his disposal tried to make their excuses. He pointed at Alvaraz and made a sign for a man and women being joined. The old man brightened as he explained what he thought would happen in the morning. The Chief and his party started talking excitedly and soon it was arranged. The wedding would be held on the beach by the Indian camp. After the wedding the two parties would go their separate ways.

Chapter 32

Not knowing what to think, Alvaraz left the Indian camp. He found Gemelda, late that night, with the Manila ladies and told her the wedding plan and how it had come about. At first she looked stunned, but Alvaraz could see her mind working and soon she and Gabriella shooed him out and told him to get some sleep. He didn't remember getting into his bunk; he was so exhausted from the day's ordeals. He was standing with his mother, who was kissing Gemelda on the forehead. His mind was struggling to fit the noise of persistent knocking into his dream, but instead he awoke to the reality of a new day. He could feel his body tingling in the comfort of his berth, then he felt the need to relieve himself and reluctantly rolled over and mumbled, "Yes."

It was Philippe at the door, "I've been sent to ask you to get up. If you don't hurry you'll miss your own wedding."

The thought of his wedding brought his mind to full awareness and suddenly he could hear and feel, all around him, the sounds of the ship gently moving in the low swell. He had a wonderful feeling as he leapt from his berth. "I'll be right there," he shouted as he found his cloths. As he moved to the head, Philippe filled him in on the plan. The men were to take him forward, clean him up, shave him, and dress him in his best clothes. He was forbidden to see Gemelda who was being dressed by the Manila ladies as they spoke. Father Emilio was on the beach with most of the crew and many of the Manila men who were setting up a suitable place to hold the wedding. As soon as he was ready Alvaraz would be taken to the beach, then Gemelda and the Manila ladies would follow in the boats.

As he sat on the head relieving himself an image of his father came to him. He could feel his heart beat faster as the implications of what he was doing came to him. His father would, at the least, be sad to find his son married to a women he didn't know, a woman of a different faith, a woman who would rob him of his place in Cadiz. He would send a message he decided. There was no turning back, and then the paralyzing thought of his return to Spain, with his new bride. Would she be reluctantly received, or would his father banish him from the family. Today he would change the path of his life, he could never turn back. The thought of never and the conflict with his family and his love for Gemelda swirled in his mind as he left the head.

His uncertainties soon left him when he was physically grabbed by his friends and fellow sailors, who seemed to think the only way they could clear up their own moral quandary was to get this young man married. Alvaraz was taken to the pump on the foredeck, he was stripped of his clothes and bathed in seawater the cook had warmed, then scrubbed with lye soap. The ship's barber who doubled as a sailor carefully shaved his beard and trimmed his full blond hair and finally he was allowed to dry off and dress in his best pantaloons, hose, the shirt and coat he had worn to the Governor's party in Manila, and a pair of high black boots. The entire exercise was accompanied by riotous laughter and several bottles of Madera wine. Ismel gave him a big hug explaining that he, the gunnery officer and four gun crews were to stay on the ship in case there was trouble. Alvaraz could see a huge group of people on the beach as his friends jovially rowed him to the shore in the smallest of the ship's boats. Father Emilio was working with the sailors to position the alter from the ship in front of a large stone. A line of armed sailors dressed in their marine uniforms guarded a cleared area where Alvaraz supposed the witnesses would stand and surrounding this there were several hundred Indians milling about.

He was led to the alter, then he and Father Emilio had a private conversation about the responsibilities he would carry for the rest of his life after he married Imelda. Alvaraz, upon hearing the name Imelda, confessed to Father Emilio, "Her real name is Gemelda, Father."

"My son, we must forget the past. The girl you will marry was baptized Imelda. In the eyes of God, she is Imelda. She is no longer a Moslem, she is a Christian and a soldier of God, " explained Father Emilio.

Alvaraz turned to see the Bride approaching in the long boat accompanied by the Manila ladies who occupied the two other long boats. When he saw her, even from the distance, he wondered how accurate Father

Emilio's words were. She was dressed in an orange and red sari with a matching veil checkered with gold. On the outside she resembled the princess of a Raj. As the boats unloaded Alvaraz noticed the Manila women were dressed in fine long dresses made of printed cotton with their hair uplifted, all carrying bright smiles marked by healthy white teeth. A beautiful young girl and Gabriela, dressed in light green silk saris, their hair adorned with gold, escorted Imelda, who limped to a place on the beach to wait. The Manila women who were joined by the Manila men, Capitan Rodrego, his officers and a group of sailors moved to the area in front of the alter.

The old Indian man came over to Nino and said, "the women want to dance before the ceremony and the shaman wants to bless the new couple after the ceremony." With some discussion between Father Emilio and Captain Rodrego the native Indians were given permission.

The sun was shining in the clear, cool air smelling of the sea when the American Indian women started to sing and dance. They made a gate with their arms swinging to the rhythm of their song and a gentle drum beat. It was a natural setting for the entourage of the two attendants followed by Imelda to enter through the line of dancers towards Father Emilio and the handsome groom standing proudly, a radiant smile on his face. Alvaraz could see his beautiful Gemelda through her veil, her mascara slightly smudged by the glistening tears that filled her eyes. The words were said, the promises were made to love with out question for as long as they both should live. Finally, father Emilio pronounced them to be joined by God and the service was over. At this time an Indian man dressed in a costume of feathers and bark, wearing a beautifully carved mask with a high crown filled with white, downy feathers, started to sing the song of an eagle. He blocked the passage of the newly weds. Soon another person dressed as an eagle with a high crown filled with feathers joined him, wearing a slightly different mask, the beak being slightly shorter, and sang with the voice of a woman. The two dancers moved gracefully around the couple, their beaks clacking and their heads bobbing to the rhythm of their song. Soon the motion of their dance caused the down feathers in their crowns to spill into the air and settle on the newly weds.

Alvaraz and Imelda stood, holding hands, transfixed by the enchanting music and rhythm of the dancers. In the background they could hear a woman's voice singing with haunting tones leading the welcoming dancers towards them. They surrounded the couple and led them up the hill to a bench set with a ceremonial feast. There were three fires burning, all surrounded with cooking-sticks with fish in the shape of butterflies supported by thin woven cedar strips sizzling in the heat radiating from the fires. The chief stood at the end of the bench while the old man said a few words, then the eagle dancers swooped and bobbed covering the chief and his family with eagle down. They stopped, then the women dancers singing and waving their arms welcoming Captain Rodrego, his officers and men, who all received a generous coating of eagle down as they passed the eagle dancers. Except for Gemelda's two attendants and a few of her close Manila lady friends the Manila people were too frightened to come to the feast; instead they were taken back to the ship.

The feast carried on for a few hours accompanied by dancers doing skits wearing different carved masks. After eating the tasty fish and other interesting foods Captain Rodrego went to the chief, and with his best dress uniform and gleaming sword, made a low bow of thanks then instructed Nino to thank the chief and tell him they were leaving.

Alvaraz and Imelda were on the last longboat rowed out to the waiting ship. They stood in the stern sheets watching as the people lining the shore, waved and grew less distinct. It was a sad moment; he had grown fond of these gracious, generous people and wondered if he would ever get an opportunity to visit them in their home to the north.

"I haven't had a chance to tell you how beautiful you are. Where did you get this beautiful gown, and how is your knee" asked Alvaraz.

"It was my mother's wedding gown," said Imelda holding Alvaraz and looking up invitingly, "and my knee is much better. The swelling has gone down and I have little pain."

A flashback of their night on the beach in Manila passed his mind complete with a memory of the emotions flooding through him, the sadness of a young girl waiting out her mother's death, and the agony he remembers of never seeing his mother again only hearing her last plaintive scream as she passed beyond life.

He put his arms around her, exposing his love for her to the sailors rowing the longboat, and said, "I will always love you, Imelda."

Chapter 33

The tide had passed its zenith and the ebb was pulling the Lydia away from the shore. Before they found their feet on the deck they could hear the sound of the capstan pulling up the chain while four sailors passed them, descending into the long boat to begin the tow out to deep water. Rodrego marched up, patted Alvaraz on the back, bowed to Imelda taking her hand and kissing it gently. "We're away and congratulations to you. I am granting you a day and a night's leave, I hope you will enjoy it."

The sailors on deck were busy at their tasks, but without exception they lifted their hats from their smiling faces giving the newly weds a strong sign of approval. Gabriela led them to Alvaraz's cabin and stood by the open door. His cabin had been transformed with soft pillows embroidered with gold thread. Colorful silks hung from the deck head. Gabriela explained, "When someone is married in our village their hut is filled with flowers, but we could find no flowers. I like the silks Gema brought just as well. May your love bring you many children."

She closed the door from the outside and left them alone, standing facing each other, a soft light penetrating the cabin from the deck prism. Alvaraz could feel the press of the wind on the sails and the influence of the ocean swells as the ship gently healed with the familiar sounds of the hull working in the long ocean swell. The air was fresh and clean and Imelda's cheek was cool to his touch as he kissed her. They stood there for a long time holding each other. Alvaraz could feel his passion rise as he held her, he could also feel her hands working on the buttons of his shirt. Soon she had his shirt and jacket off and he removed her veil and helped her with the clasp on her sari. She had a silk undergarment on under her sari revealing the shape of her breasts and the curve of her waist. He was relieved when Imelda managed to unbutton his trousers. She pulled them down with his under shorts. He stepped out of his trouser covered boots and stood naked before her.

He held her, feeling her slim body beneath the translucent silk. He unbuttoned her undergarment and it slipped to the cabin sole. Looking at her nakedness he found his love for her filled him with an intense need to protect her. He gently picked her up and laid her on his berth kissing her first on the lips then her neck, her breasts, under her breast and down the length of her body. He could hear her moaning; she began to rock her pelvis as he kissed her, then with a breathless passion she sat up on the berth and pulled him up spreading her legs directing him. The feeling of her hand on his ripe phallus intensified his need for release, but he held off feeling the soft slippery mucus around her labia. He felt a great resistance. He could go no further without hurting her. His mind swirled with intense pleasure. He could feel her frailness under him gyrating and gasping and finally she made a loving almost growl holding him tightly, her body stiffening. His mind swirled, stars burst with intense pleasure and he realized he had not yet penetrated her.

They lay together their passion spent for a long time. Imelda laying in her back ran her finger lovingly around Alvaraz's face, over his eyebrows down his nose then drew the shape of his lips as if she were learning his shape so she could later paint him. "You must push harder my love. My mother told me she had a very strong hymen and it took a long time for father to burst her maiden's head. You won't hurt me, I promise you."

With these words he could feel his passion rising, he could feel the ring of her hymen still constricting his half inserted penis. She started to move under him and he could feel his shaft penetrate a little further and the ring of her hymen slip around the head of his penis. She stopped suddenly then asked him to change places; she would be on top. When they tried to move he realized they were stuck together. He couldn't remove his penis. She managed to position herself above him and with a look of determination on her face she bent down and began to experiment by moving her pelvis up and down pulling at his penis. It wasn't comfortable for either of them, but she persisted, sweat glistening on her forehead. Her thrusts became more energetic and suddenly Alvaraz felt his stock slide into the glove of her vagina. He could still feel the ring of her hymen, but now it gently massaged the root of his stock. She was now slipping in her own sweat, her passion rising as she clung to him. He could hear her ragged breathing interrupted by moans of her passion. He held her tight, the bond of his love cursing through him. He could hear her sound, a piercing wail, as he found his mind filled with so many stars as to make a pure white envelope of passion. He could feel her joined to him in this liquid pleasure of their love. His body and hers were gyrating on their own; while he and she, their very essence joined in the purity of their love their bodies' far away.

When he opened his eyes there was no light penetrating the deck prism. It was late in the night. The ship rolled and the rigging creaked and he had his beautiful Gemelda. It would be hard to call her Imelda he thought as he felt her softness surrounding him. He thanked God for this love, for this spirit he could truly love and be with, trusting her and caring for her for the rest of his life. He felt truly blessed. She woke, first kissing him then disengaging. He lay there in unbelievable comfort his body tingling with pleasure.

Chapter 34

The next thing he remembered was opening his eyes to a soft light coming through the deck prism. The noise of the rigging banging with the rhythm of the swell told him there was no wind. He slipped out of his berth into the cold half-light wondering if his marriage to Gemelda was all a dream. There were no more silks hanging in his cabin, but when he looked around he found some of the special pillows embroidered with gold thread. He dressed, then stumbled on deck almost colliding with a pair of Manila men heaving up a barrel filled with sewage from the previous night. He emerged into a world of thick fog punctuated by the noise of banging rigging in the still air.

"You look like you've slept well," commented Philippe as Alvaraz mounted the steps to the aft deck.

Alvaraz smiled naughtily and responded with, "It wasn't bad," then proceeded to the head.

The wind had been good until the early hours of the morning when a thick fog bank rolled in obscuring the stars and now it was impossible to see across the dripping deck. They were still making way following a compass course with two sailors on the bow trying to find the bottom with their sounding lines.

"The last fix I got showed us to be at thirty seven degrees latitude. We must sail south now until the North Star is only eighteen degrees above the horizon. If all goes well it will only take us about ten days," answered Philippe to Alvaraz's questions.

Alvaraz went below looking for the cook and some breakfast, but instead found Imelda carrying a tray of cooked fish and biscuits made from the flour the Indians had given them. When she saw him she smiled warmly then said, "Darling, I have your breakfast." She was limping because of her sore knee, but she also seemed to be moving carefully with her legs slightly spread. When Alvaraz inquired about this, she put the tray down gave him a hug and said, "I still love you. I'm told this happens to all newly weds."

The fog persisted for three more days. It was agonizingly cold and damp except around the cook's stove. The food was simple with only a small amount of rice served with the predominantly fish diet. With the exception of the newly weds who seemed to enjoy the dimness, every person on the ship was hungry and getting more depressed in the gloomy fog. The men wanted to tow the ship but when a boat was launched they found they could barely keep up, let alone tow the ship. Rodrego upon hearing this news said, "When you have a clean hull it doesn't take much wind to drive the ship."

In the afternoon of the fourth day the sun could be seen through the shadow of vapor and just as it was setting the fog lifted, exposing the blue sky with low clouds on the southern horizon. A fresh wind came up from the west giving the Lydia a slight heel to port and a white bone in her teeth as she sped southward. Philippe found the pole star and reported they were almost two degrees further south and only had fourteen more degrees to go.

It was in the early hours of the next morning when the lead lines found bottom rising quickly up.. They could see no land, but Capitan Rodrego had the ship heave-to until morning as a precaution. Before the sun rose they could smell wood smoke in the wind blowing from the east. The dawn revealed land to their port and an explanation to the smoke smell. The hills were alive with smoke billowing across the land and now trailing to the south. They sailed on all that day watching the same wind carry the flames of the wild fire down the coast. As the sun disappeared to the west the orange color of a raging inferno could be seen to the east crawling up the hills acting as a beacon for the sailors to steer by in the moonless night.

The next day the wind blew harder and the waves built. The topsails were furled and only the big mainsail closest to the deck was used to drive the ship. The following morning they passed a point of land. On one side of the point the wind blew cold with a vengeance with huge square waves tossing the ship around. On the other side of the point the sea became smooth, the air blew hot from the land and at last the people could remove their wool suits and let the hot air caress their bodies.

The lookout reported seeing land to the west. Philippe who was drawing a chart of their passage thought the land to the west was an Island because he and Nino had studied the swell and found it refracted from two directions as if the waves had passed on either side of an island. Nino thought there were many islands to the west.

All that day they sailed through the shallow sea. At times they sailed through a dark substance that smelled like hot tar. In the night the wind died and they sat gently rolling in the low swell.

"Ahoy on deck," it was the lookout. "I see a cloud on the land that could be a dust storm," shouted the lookout.

It was the morning of the second day in the calm sea. The sailors had just changed watch, Alvaraz had gone below to rest and Rodrego was lazily coming out of the head yawning at the new day when he heard the news. The wind started as a light breeze from the land then rapidly built

"Ismel, get some men to the topsails and mainsails. Furl the lateen sails, put the ship to weather," shouted Rodrego.

Like a demon, the hot wind lifted the sea to the east, changing it from a cool green to a frothing white. The sails were half furled when the wind hit. The ship healed, almost putting the ends of the yardarms in the sea. One of the sailors lost his grip on the foot rope and was dangling over the sea holding onto the buntline in mid air. Slowly the ship turned to weather, loosing her heel, and the sailor found his grip on the footrope.

Alvaraz stood beside Gemelda taking in the morning air as he watched the spectacle. "You better get below, love," shouted Alvaraz in the increasing wind.

She looked at him in defiance and said, "I'll be staying on deck in case I can be of assistance."

Alvaraz noticed she had been wearing pantaloons under her dress lately, and without hesitation she dropped her skirt, throwing it down the companionway hatch then scampered up the ratlines to assist Nino who was struggling to furl the top sail. By now the wind was screaming and the waves were building. Alvaraz helped the sailors pull up the clew lines then, ran to the foredeck to see if Captain Rodrego had any other tasks for him.

The ship, without sails, was drifting rapidly out to sea towards an island. The wind was so strong it was almost impossible to sail in it, but they decided they had no choice; they would set the staysails and attempt to sail to the south. The Lydia rolled heavily in the increasing sea while she clawed to the south. Within the hour it was apparent she was drifting closer to the island.

The leadsmen found the bottom was far below the reach of the anchor and didn't seem to be coming up as they approached the island.

"Who's the sailor on the top yard arm?" asked Rodrego, peering up into the rigging watching the flags at the top of the mast cracking and streaming forward.

"Its Gemelda, I insisted she go below, but she defied me. She saw Nino struggling at furling the sail and ran up there to assist him. What can I do?" asked Alvaraz with a look of frustration on his face as he watched her come down the rigging to the deck.

Rodrego smiled and said, "You're going to have a lot of trouble with that one. Maybe you should let her run free, I have no objection, and she knows her business."

"We'll need more sail, Captain, if we want to get around this island, I thought it ended there, but you can see it goes on for a long way to the south," shouted Ismel his voice barely heard above the shrieking of the wind in the rigging.

"Try setting the aft topsail, the worst that can happen is it will blow out," screamed Rodrego. If we can get more way on we can try the small lateen sail aft as well."

The topsail didn't blow out and when the yardarms were pulled round to go to weather and the lateen sail was set the flags at the top of the mast blew towards the island as the Lydia crashed through the building waves to the south. The problem was they were making too much leeway to the west and it would be a near miss with the last point of the island. Rodrego had to decide if he should claw as close to the wind as possible and maybe clear the island, try the anchor or go about in the near hurricane force winds. He could feel his bowels loosen with fear and feel himself swallowing involuntarily as he thought of a hidden rock tearing out the bottom of the ship as they tried to round the island too close. "Ismel set the forward topsail and someone find Father Emilio."

With the second topsail set the Lydia moved faster and the leeways decreased, but everyone could see it would be a near miss.

"It's too deep to anchor and even if we did we would surely drag into the island; if we went about we would loose more offing and be in the same position we are now only in the opposite direction." Father Emilio interrupted Rodrego as he explained his decision to Alvaraz."

"Can I help you, Captain?" asked Father Emilio.

"We need God's help in getting around this island, would you pray for us?"

Father Emilio visibly paled when he heard the request. His gown was almost blowing off him in the screaming wind, his hair blew across his face as he looked at the nearing island, then he gasped and yelled, "I'll pray Captain."

They were heading straight for a rock evidenced by waves breaking white over it. Alvaraz pointed it out to Rodrego who screamed at Ismel, "Can we get her any higher in the wind?"

"No, that's all she's got," responded Ismel.

They were moving as fast as the Lydia could go, the seas were breaking over her hull, she rolled and pitched in the huge seas, straight into a rock at the end of a reef. There was nothing they could do. It was as if the entire crew was transfixed, holding on, staring at the impending disaster. They would not make it around the rock. Suddenly to make matters worse the wind shifted more to the south and the Lydia turned towards the island as if accepting her fate.

They all stood there, the wind washing the water over the deck in a deafening roar. The Lydia rose up, her keel grinding on the rocks below, her momentum carrying her higher. Then unexpectedly she fell causing most of the crew to loose their balance and fall to the deck. She sped on; she'd missed the rock by going inside of it. She was free. The crew recovered themselves not believing what they saw. They were speeding away from the disaster. Father Emilio stumbled up beside Rodrego and said, "God is great"

"I'm going below to check for damages, Captain,' said Alvaraz.

Alvaraz found the carpenter at the entrance to the companionway. Gemelda saw Alvaraz descending the stairs with the carpenter and followed. They found and lit lanterns in the galley then descended into the bilges. All they found was dry ballast, nothing seemed to be damaged, but Alvaraz could imagine a huge gash in the keel caused by the impact with the rock as the Lydia skipped over it, barely missing the rock visible on the surface. Gemelda found herself alone with Alvaraz after the carpenter went along to check the earlier repair job.

"Darling, I hope you aren't angry with me," She said, bending down her lantern, casting long shadows moving across the damp hull.

Alvaraz was trying to dig between the sacks of sand, "Here, give me a hand with this," he said heaving a sack up and piling it on the top of the other ballast. "I want to take a look at the fastenings where the frames meet the keel."

She struggled trying to move the heavy sacks of sand away from the hole he was making. She heard him mutter under his breath, as if he were talking to himself, "I don't know what I'm going to do with you Gema?"

Finally, after heaving up a couple of dozen sacks, he was able to see the keel. Aside from the usual ooze there was no apparent damage to the join where the hull met the huge piece of oak some 14 inches wide that extended down almost three feet from where he stood. A strange feeling of love for this ship came over him. She was strong and would take care of her passengers and sometimes she would change course of her own free will as she had done just before they hit the rock. He looked up to see the carpenter moving over the ballast behind Gemelda who was looking with concern at him standing up to his chest in ballast. When he saw her concerned face, shadowed in the light of her lamp, a similar feeling of love came over him and he accepted her disobedience.

"She's probably weakened, but I can't see any evidence of it here. Did you find anything?" asked Alvaraz.

"I can't find any damage," stated the carpenter.

The three of them replaced the ballast as well as they could. They left the bilges to report to Captain Rodrego. Gemelda held back and Alvaraz sensing her unease let the carpenter ascend the ladder out of the bilge then made an excuse to lag behind.

"Gemelda, I know you must do what you do, but please be careful! I couldn't live if anything happened to you."

She made a crocked smile, her eyes brimming with tears as she embraced him.

They held each other, the lamp light flickering, the air permeated with the damp wood smell of the bilge, the ship was no longer moving violently as it had been a few moments earlier from the giant waves generated by the vicious wind. They ascended the ladder to the hold, and then moved through the narrow corridor past the scuttlebutt, up the companionway stairs to the deck. The air was clear of dust, the sun brilliant, causing them to squint as they found their feet on the deck. The ship had found some shelter from the waves behind an island to the south. Gemelda hesitated at the bottom of the stairs to the upper aft deck, a place usually only occupied by the officers and the helmsmen. Alvaraz smiled at her, then ascended alone to the upper deck.

"I suppose the carpenter's told you the good news. We can't find any damage. I'll check again later, but I think we won't know until we can dry-dock her," said Alvaraz instantly concerned by the look of Captain Rodrego.

Chapter 35

"I keep thinking I'm living a dream. I was so sure we would find our end on those rocks," said Rodrego his voice almost giddy with excitement. "I think we are in the hands of God. I could feel him, as if he were above us, his hand lifting us, carrying us safely away from our deaths. I'm not surprised there is no damage. The hand of God is a gentle hand."

Alvaraz wondered if this man's strength was gone, broken by the strain of so many sleepless nights, punctuated by the horror of imminent death and the worry he suffered for the safety of his ship and her crew. He saw in him a caring man, who gave his heart and soul to his ship and the people residing on it; a man babbling, his hands clinging to the rail, his knuckles white, his body palpably shaking and his eyes, sunken in their sockets filled with mad excitement. It was obvious he needed a rest. Alvaraz looked for Ismel, but found Philippe standing beside the helmsmen. "We should talk to Ismel," Alvaraz said quietly to Philippe. "I think Rodrego is beyond reality. Perhaps we could take over some of his responsibilities allowing him to rest."

Alvaraz and Philippe found Ismel. "Earlier he told me he wants to relinquish his command to God," said Ismel, "I trust God, but know this is folly."

"We must find a way to give him some rest," said Philippe, "We should talk to him. I think we can convince him to give Ismel the responsibility of being Captain for a time. He's always complaining he doesn't have time to work on his journal. It's time we gave him that time."

The three of them stood around Captain Rodrego. When asked Rodrego readily gave Ismel command of the ship. He didn't seem to care one way or another. His hands seemed stuck to the rail. With total sympathy the three men gently pried his hands from the rail one finger at a time. Rodrego cried out in his madness as they carried him to his cabin and gently lay him on his berth. They released his mental paralysis with a healthy draft of brandy and he fell into an almost death like sleep. Gemelda and Gabriella agreed to bring him food and tend to his needs.

After settling Rodrego they asked Philippe, "What course do you propose we sail?" After a minute of thought Philippe answered, "I think we should steer south and east. I know nothing of these islands, how far they extend or what to expect. I've been trying to chart this coast, but find it impossible. We could be off the coast of the main land or simply sailing through a group of islands. My astrolabe tells me we must sail thirteen more degrees of latitude to the south. I'm sure Acapulco is to the east so we should try to make as much easting as possible."

The violent wind from the east blew for three days, its fury diminished by sailing in the lee of a series of islands. Slowly they washed the dust from the deck and scrubbing it up from every nook and cranny of the ship. Philippe and Ismel decided to set a course away from the land when the sunset and head towards the land four hours before the sun rose and further east if they didn't sight land. It was an uneventful journey, the winds shifted to the north remaining cool and the land they sighted was barren and scared with deep gullies stark in the crystal clear air.

Although the spirit aboard seemed high Alvaraz noticed he and some of the men had bleeding in their gums around their teeth. He also noticed how slim everyone was getting with their eyes sunken, on a diet of mostly fish and only a spoonful of rice each day. The men complained constantly and Alvaraz often heard them talking about the thought of eating cakes and bread as they congregated by the scuttlebutt. The fish the Manila men caught were rich in flavor and filled with oil, but there was something missing. It was obvious they couldn't go on without rice or flour for long.

Rodrego improved with rest and the care he was given by the two ladies. Shortly after his breakdown he would come out of his cabin at any time of the day or night and rave at the moon or shout at the waves in the sea. As the days passed he settled down coming out of his cabin only to quietly stare at his surroundings in a pensive way. On the fifth day he came out of his cabin and stood by Ismel. He watched what was happening on deck then surprised Ismel by saying in a lucid voice. "You're doing a good job, Ismel. I think you'll find I'm better now, but I want you to carry on. I like this and I can get on with my journal."

They sailed by large bays and rocky out crops and on the morning of the tenth day, after their near disaster, they passed a point of land where the rocks on the beach were worn away in such a way as to form a series of arches where one could clearly see through the stones to the other side. The land fell off at this point and Nino was consulted. He stared at the sea for a long time before he came to the group of officers with his report. "There is no land to the west and I can see no waves indicating any land to the east. This is the end of the land. Ahead there is only ocean."

Philippe knowing Acapulco was somewhere to the southeast, convinced the officers to sail southeast through the night. According to his calculations they were only four degrees north of the latitude of Acapulco, and he was desperate to find some landmark to confirm his idea of where he was.

As Nino had said there was no land and little wind. Unknowingly they were sailing in these waters in the middle of storm season, but their luck held and the one storm they were affected by, created large waves and a wind from the south. The only direction they could sail was east. It was this wind that brought them into a large bay.

The officers decide they could go on no further and they anchored in a quiet area on the north side of the bay. They found a village there but when they approached the shore the inhabitants ran away. The village was deserted except for a toothless old woman who babbled, went into her hut and came out with a bag of yellow powder, made a fire, then began mixing the contents of the bag with water. Alvaraz remembered seeing the little native man, Gregario, preparing the same food. His mouth watered at the thought. While the fire was warming up, the old women took Alvaraz's arm and led him to a covered area beside her hut. Alvaraz found some baskets filled with the yellow fruit he knew, called tomatl, in the Nahuatl language, baskets of squash, peppers, and beans. He picked a tomato up and ate it, and then he carried the basket out into the sun for the other men who were milling around. There was something in the fruit they craved and within minutes the basket was empty. The old women cooked tortillas and the men ate them. Alvaraz looked at the sailors around him and understood why the old woman was feeding them. Without exception they all looked starved.

He found more baskets of tomatoes and he and the sailors rowed them to the ship. On the way to the ship he could feel his body changing as if a wave of healthy energy was sweeping through him. There was a palpable taste to this land, a taste and a sense of returning home. His excitement was evident as he and the other sailors handed up the baskets of tomatoes.

Without any explanation he said to the crowd at the rail, "You must eat these tomatls, they are so good," The crew of the ship ate them ravenously, but the Manila people looked at them suspiciously having never seen them before. Imelda followed Alvaraz's example and ate one, then told the people in tagalong they were good.

The only word Alvaraz could think of to describe the change in the occupants of the ship was a miracle. Captain Rodrego was the best example of this. In the course of a single day he changed from an unsure, unkempt skeleton; his eyes buried in his head, his teeth red with the blood from his bleeding gums to a confident self-assured healthy looking gentlemen and the acknowledged captain of the ship

The villagers returned, from their hiding place, to their village shortly after. They prepared a kind of feast for the people on the ship. The old women must have told the villagers they had nothing to fear from these starved sailors. They only stayed for two days. There was little or no communications with this tribe of people. Before the sailors left, Rodrego rewarded the villager's kindness with some fine knives, steel gardening tools and glass beads.

Epilogue—1595

Alvaraz never returned to that place where he set foot, for the second time, on the land of New Spain. He sat mesmerized by the memory of the hot earth, the tangy flavor he got from that first bite of tomato and the strong feeling that this land was home. He could still remember the small group of villagers smiling and waving to them as they rowed back to the ship. They set sail the following morning catching the morning offshore breeze. A strong wind carried them down the barren coast in the night. Before the sun rose the next morning Philippe announced they were on the correct latitude to find Navidad. The sun rose over the land cutting through the morning mist and there, in front of them, was the curve of the beach and the familiar stones guarding the entrance to the familiar lagoon.

The Lydia didn't stay long after disembarking the passengers. Rodrego felt an urgency to report to the governor. Alvaraz never did get a chance to see the damage to the keel from the time the Lydia skipped over the rocks weeks earlier. The purser gave Alvaraz a copy of the list of the people disembarking and had him sign a bill of landing saying he had received said cargo. Alvaraz noted Imelda's name on the list, he also noted not a single casualty. Every one of the Manila people had arrived safely. Later that year he would be given payment for his work in bringing these people to New Spain. The three hundred and forty four gold doubloons the purser received were divided between Rodrego, his officers, crew and Alvaraz who received forty-seven. This wasn't bad for six months work.

Alejandro Jose and Juan, with the help of whomever they could recruit had been busy. A small herd of Oxen lazily chewed their cud under the shade of some trees. They would be used to tow the ships out of the water and move the heavy lumber around the yard. They'd built a dry-dock of stout timbers and a track to hold the rollers to move the dry-dock up the beach. There was already a stack of logs waiting to be sawn in the newly constructed saw pits and best of all there was a shed with a room to hold the models Alvaraz had carved on his ocean passage.

After all the luggage, trunks and seed box were transported to the beach, Imelda and the Manila ladies scrubbed from top to bottom the cabin she had shared with Alvaraz and the hold that had been home to the people from Manila. Alvaraz couldn't understand why they did this, it seemed clean enough to him, but thought Rodrego and his crew would never have a cleaner ship.

Gemelda bore her first child six months after they arrived. She wasn't alone; that year almost forty children were born. They were all conceived on the voyage from Manila. For the next ten years a steady supply of healthy babies were born in the village behind the shipyard. Alvaraz wondered idly, if the child from his first encounter with the woman in the land of King Philip was alive. He often wondered about his first-born child. He or she would be twenty-six now.

"Are you sleeping up there?" It was Gemelda running up the stairs. Alvaraz turned to see her, breathless, with the look of excitement on her face he hadn't seen for a long time, "I have a surprise for you and I need your help."

"I wasn't sleeping," Alvaraz said, justifying his idleness, "I was just remembering our trip from Manila."

She stopped, a smile came across her face, She was still a strikingly beautiful women, her hair cut short with a touch of gray. Her body hadn't changed much. She was still slim and aside from a few wrinkles on her face she was still the woman he loved. "That was such a long time ago, Alvaraz, and yet today it seems like only yesterday.

I loved that time of our lives," she said pensively, putting her arm around his shoulder. "Now I want to travel with you again and this time to Spain." She pulled her hand out from behind her back and in it she had a letter. "I hope this is good news, I think it's from your father. The messenger arrived from Acapulco; he's having lunch at Tina's and must leave in an hour. Sister Mini sent me another letter and enclosed was a letter from father. I think he has forgiven me Alvaraz. I want to write to them and tell them when we will be arriving. How long will it take to get there?"

He'd pondered the question of a journey back to Spain many times and had a ready answer for her. "If we leave right after Christmas, we should be in Vera Crux by the end of January, then a month to get to Puerto Rico, and two months to get to Spain. Tell them to expect us in Cadiz say late April or early May."

Alvaraz fingered the letter given to him by Gemelda. He had written many letters to his father but never received one. This letter was obviously written by a letter writer. The penmanship was too perfect to be his father's and if his memory served him correctly his father could barely write at the best of times.

Alvaraz,
Last month I had a visit from a young lady. She says she met you once a long time ago. Her name is Minerva; she is the younger sister of your wife, Gemelda. For years I have harbored an anger in my heart at you for your disobedience, but this young lady has brought me to my senses. She lives with her father, her aunt and her other sister. They never married and consequently there are no children in their lives. Although Minerva has never visited you she told me about your lives in New Spain through the letters she receives from Gemelda. The first time I talked to her she brought me to tears. I am so proud of you my son. She told me she was bringing her family to Cadiz for a holiday and invited me to meet them.
Yesterday we met. It was strange for me to have Muslims in my house, but they proved to be good people who respect my Christianity. I think we are now friends for Gemelda's father told stories of you as if he were a proud father. He told me a story I can't believe. He boasted about your strength. He told me for many years he hated you with a vengeance and never wanted to see you or Gemelda again, but time has softened him and

now he boasts about you. Is it true you picked him up by his lapels, dangling him in the air while you calmly asked him if there was a problem with you having a relationship with his daughter?

Thank you for your last letter. I am so happy you are returning to Cadiz. Why aren't you bringing your daughters with you? I can assure you we have room for them and for that mater I would love to see your sons if you can drag them away form their work. When will you be arriving?

I hope you can find it in your heart to forgive me for not responding to your letters. Capitan Rodrego visits me regularly; he is with me now as I write this letter. He extends his good wishes for a safe and easy passage. He wishes you God's speed and sends you his fond regards.
  Your loving father
  Arturo

It was signed with his father's hand. So many years had passed since he had seen him. Alvaraz sat in stunned silence until Gemelda woke him from his thoughts, "Is it from you father?"

"Yes, and I think he has forgiven me. He wants us to bring the girls. What do you think?"

"We should all go. It would be wonderful Alvaraz. Quickly write him and tell him we'll try to bring the whole family."